Out with the Tide

OUT WITH THE TIDE

Brian Cooper

Constable • London

Constable & Robinson Ltd
3 The Lanchesters
162 Fulham Palace Road
London W6 9ER
www.constablerobinson.com

First published in the UK by Constable,
an imprint of Constable & Robinson Ltd 2006

A copy of the British Library Cataloguing in
Publication Data is available from the British Library

ISBN 13: 978-1-84529-224-9
ISBN 10: 1-84529-224-3

Printed and bound in the EU

Author's Note

Those readers who search for Breckton and Sunningham on maps of Norfolk will fail to find them, for they do not exist. Like the people who pass in and out of these pages, they are mere figments of the author's imagination. But, not far from Holt, there does exist a tower which has, at various times, been a windmill, a prospect tower, a dwelling, and, during the Second World War, an observation post for the local Home Guard. After years of neglect, it has now, once again, been restored as a private residence. It is, however, inadvisable to approach it too closely, since its owners are naturally jealous of their privacy, and are not inclined to welcome casual visitors.

The case of Sourav Singh was suggested by an incident which occurred in Rangoon some three-quarters of a century ago. For its details, which, of necessity, differ somewhat from mine, I am indebted to Maurice Collis's book of memoirs, *Trials in Burma*.

To Tony
who did everything save write the book himself,
and to the rest of the family, all of whom,
in their different ways, helped me to finish it

Contents

'People can't die, along the coast,' said Mr Peggotty, 'except when the tide's pretty nigh out . . . He's a-going out with the tide.'
Charles Dickens: *David Copperfield*

Prologue

THE DINGHY

What the ebb brings, the tide will fetch away.
English proverb

His garden was covered in bacon rinds.

That at least was what he thought, till he looked a bit closer and saw that they were earthworms.

Thousands of earthworms, every one of them dead.

Earthworms, and a dinghy.

It lay toppled against the wall of his cottage, keel facing outwards, its black tarpaulin cover still lashed tightly into place, its name in black letters still clear on the boarding.

Spindrift.

And underneath, *Morston.*

He leaned on it with both hands and rolled it back on to an even keel, but, as he did so, something heavy rolled inside it.

Finding the end of a rope, he unwound it from the cleats and peeled back the tarpaulin.

That was when he saw the face.

A white face, as dead as the earthworms around it.

Circumstances alter cases.

The villages of Morston, Blakeney, Cley-next-the-Sea and Salthouse lie close together on a four-mile stretch of the north Norfolk coast, yet for ex-Detective Chief Inspector John Spencer Lubbock to find a dinghy washed up against the wall of his retirement cottage below the church at Cley was distinctly unusual, since the cottage was a mile and a half from the sea.

There had been a time when Cley-next-the-Sea had indeed been next the sea. The village had once been a considerable port. The River Glaven, in Lubbock's time no more than a stream, had then been a broad deep-water channel, and the Green in front of the cottage a long quayside where merchant ships had been moored to unload. Sailing ships they were, with biblical names

9

such as *Matthew, James, Gifte of God* and *Trinity*, and they came from far away, from the frozen north, from the old Hanseatic ports and the Mediterranean. They discharged their cargoes there on the quays: vegetable oil from Greece, spices from the Levant, fish from Iceland, coal from Newcastle, bricks from Flanders: all to be stored in warehouses down by the water, then loaded on to wagons to be taken inland.

For hundreds of years the village was a thriving centre of trade, till a local landowner, with an eye to the profits he could make from grazing, built an embankment and drained the marshes. The river silted up, the quays were abandoned, and the port moved to where the windmill now stands, much closer to the sea.

Ships were still trading there late in the nineteenth century, though the bigger ones, the steamships, anchored three miles out in the channel of Blakeney Pit. There the freight was transferred to lighters that were poled all the way to Cley: a journey that took seven hours, fourteen there and back.

Then the railway reached Holt, and that was the end. The port simply died, and Cley was left as nothing more than a quiet little village on the edge of the marshland, with the church, the Green and Lubbock's cottage a mile and a half from the sea.

That was how it remained for a full half-century till the last day of January 1953.

On that evening, a Saturday, an immense tidal surge, driven to the south by a force-ten gale, battered down the defences built to contain the sea and devastated the eastern coast of England. From Spurn Head in the north to Margate in the south, great gaps were torn in the sea-walls, the sand dunes and shingle banks, and through them huge seas swept across the land, smashing houses to rubble and chalets to matchwood, flooding towns and villages, scattering like chaff thousands of tons of stone and concrete, blocking the drains with sand and debris, and, as power supplies failed, plunging the coast into terrifying darkness.

On that terrible night, never to be forgotten by those who lived through it, more than three hundred people, helpless in the face of such elemental fury, perished in the wildness of surging water that rose with a frightening speed and engulfed them.

That was the night when boats were torn from their moorings

at Morston and Blakeney; when the storm-driven waters smashed through the shingle bank opposite Salthouse, and white-crested breakers, tossed into fury by a howling wind, surged across the marshlands and broke in a raging torrent of spray against the cottages lining the coastal road, carrying with them scores of heavy pit-props and railway sleepers, that, used years before to shore up the shingle bank, tore into the flint-and-rubble walls of the village like battering rams.

It was the night when a towering wall of water, pouring through a breach in the Blakeney bank, rolled across the marshes, past the windmill and up the Street at Cley, forcing the villagers to take to their bedrooms and then to the roofs of their houses; and when, rolling inland a further half-mile, it surged over the Green and, smashing through the doors and windows of the cottages below the church, flooded their downstairs rooms to a depth of seven feet; and when, as dawn broke on the first day of February, the scattered people of Cley looked out on a scene that had been visible to no one for hundreds of years – the stream that was the Glaven swollen to a tossing, foam-flecked sea that stretched a mile wide all the way up to Wiveton.

That was why Lubbock, returning to his cottage once the waters had receded, found his garden littered with thousands of earth-worms killed by the salt, and a dinghy from Morston washed up against his wall.

In the circumstances, neither of these things unduly surprised him. What he wasn't prepared for was the sight of a young woman lying in the dinghy, naked and with a bullet wound in the middle of her forehead.

I

THIRST

Water, water, everywhere,
Nor any drop to drink.
Samuel Taylor Coleridge: *The Rime of the Ancient Mariner*

1.

Detective Chief Superintendent Hastings laid down his pen and stared at his Chief Inspector. 'Are you telling me, Mike,' he said, 'that this boat wedged itself against the wall of his cottage?'

'That's right, sir,' said Tench.

'With a body inside it?'

'Yes, sir.'

'Shot through the head?'

'Sounds strange, sir, doesn't it?'

'Strange? It's incredible. How long's he been retired now?'

'Close on six years.'

'Six years! He walked out of his office in 1947, and swore that he'd finished with solving murders. All he wanted to do was make a study of windmills. And what's he done since then? He's stumped around Norfolk on his cherry wood stick, tripping over bodies here, there and everywhere, and poking his nose into things that don't concern him. And as if that wasn't enough, murdered women are now floating three miles in boats and landing themselves right on his doorstep . . . I suppose he's already worked out who killed her.'

'Not this time, sir, no. He's got other things on his mind. His cottage was flooded.'

'Was it?' Hastings nodded. 'Then he has all my sympathy. From all accounts it's pretty bad around Cley. Of course, he managed to get out safely himself?'

'Luckily for him, he wasn't there, sir. He'd spent the day here in Norwich, and stayed the night with his sister down at the Riverside because of the storm. He couldn't get back to Cley till this morning.'

'And found the place in a hell of a mess?'

'Uninhabitable, sir. All the downstairs is wrecked and stinks to high heaven. It'll be a couple of months before it's fit to be lived in.'

'So where's he going to stay in the meantime?'

Tench gave a shrug. 'Looks like he'll be here at the Riverside, sir. It's the obvious place.'

15

'Then you'll need to watch your step. He'll be in and out of your office like a jack-in-the-box, telling you what to do.'

'That's possible, sir.'

'Possible? It's inevitable. If I know John Lubbock, and I worked with him for years, he'll already be sniffing around for clues.'

'Let's just hope he's too busy down at the cottage to think about detecting.'

'A vain hope, I'm afraid . . . So remember, Mike, you're in charge of this case, not Lubbock. He may have trained you, and he may still treat you like the son he never had, but that's as far as it goes . . . Now, let's get down to business. What do we know?'

'At the moment, sir, precious little. The woman was naked. No means of identification. According to Dr Ledward, she's been dead for something approaching a week.'

'And that takes us back to before the storm.'

'Looks like it, sir, though we can't be sure till we get the results of the autopsy. We don't know who she is or where she comes from, and we've got no scene of crime, so all we can do in the meantime is trace the boat's owner and hope it leads somewhere.'

'You've got that in hand?'

'Yes, sir. The phone lines are still down, but I've sent McKenzie out to Morston to make some inquiries. It's a toss-up whether he'll be able to get there at all, but he's promised to ring me as soon as he can.'

The Chief Super gave a nod. 'Well, keep me informed, that's all you can do. It's early days yet. But mark my words, Mike. You'll be lucky if you don't get a visit from Lubbock before McKenzie finds a phone that's still in working order. So don't be surprised if he turns up here and gives you chapter and verse about that wandering dinghy, while Mac's still chasing from place to place and swearing fit to turn all the phone boxes blue.'

2.

Detective Sergeant Bill McKenzie was not a happy man.

Nearer fifty than forty, unambitious, overweight and addicted to quaffing pints of Norfolk ale at a couple of gulps, he'd spent three completely profitless hours trailing round those distant parts of Norfolk that he dismissed as 'the sticks'. A confirmed city dweller, he regarded anywhere more than two miles out of Norwich as well beyond the pale of civilization, fit to be inhabited only by those who lacked the common sense to seek healthier climes.

The small village of Morston, on the edge of the marshes, was, by his reckoning, just about as far as one could go into the sticks and, if he hadn't exactly turned every phone box in its vicinity from red to blue, he was ready to turn the Chief Inspector's office to a brilliant scarlet as he flung off his coat and slumped down on a chair.

'It's bloody hopeless, Mike,' he said. 'You'd need a bloody motor launch to get anywhere near the place. I tried ten different phones and there wasn't a squeak from any of them. By then I was closer to Norwich than Morston, so I told myself there wasn't any point in scrabbling through the undergrowth trying to find another, and drove straight back. If you want my opinion, the whole thing's a waste of time. All the records must be lost, washed into oblivion. If you want to trace the owner of that bloody boat, you'll have to put out an SOS on the radio. Barring that, you'll just have to wait till someone shows up and starts asking questions.'

Tench pushed back his chair and stretched out his legs. 'Finished?' he asked.

'Not quite,' McKenzie said. 'I'd just like to add that I'm frustrated, exhausted and dry as the mid-Sahara, but you'll be hard pressed to find a more virtuous officer in the whole of the CID. I've passed twenty-three pubs and never sniffed inside one. The result, as you can see, is a zealous but haggard and desiccated man.'

'You'll survive,' said Tench drily. 'You always have.'

'So what do we do now?'

'Well, waiting's not an option. You know what they say about murder cases. The first forty-eight hours are the vital ones in any search for clues, and that time's long past. The body's in Ledward's lab and the boat's gone to Forensics, but we've still got a nameless victim and no scene of crime. It's a week since the woman died, and so far no one's reported her missing, and that in spite of the worst storm we've had for hundreds of years. We know nothing about her. She may not even come from round here.'

'You think she may be one of the travelling dead?'

'She could be. Who knows? You know what Norfolk's like. It's a million-plus acres of marshes and fens, wild heaths and wood-lands, and long, sweeping roads that run for miles between bare, deserted fields. It's a prime location for dumping unwanted bodies. She could be from anywhere, Mac: London, Penzance, the Borders, you name it. Even if we find the owner of the boat, the odds are that he won't know anything about her. If a man commits murder, the last thing he's going to do is stuff the body inside his own boat.'

'Well, that's true enough . . .' McKenzie seemed unconvinced.

'But what?'

'Well, he might just have taken the easiest course. Panicked and done a runner. It was his boat after all. No one else would be likely to go poking around inside it.'

Tench gave a shrug. 'It's possible, yes.'

'But not probable.'

'No.'

'So what then?'

'We need to put a name to her, and fast, this woman. Other-wise we haven't got a chance in hell of tracing her killer.' He paused and thought. 'You'd better go back,' he said.

McKenzie groaned. 'Oh, come on. Have a heart.'

'Hearts aren't an option either, not at this time. Take a different route, and try for Blakeney. From what I've heard, there's just a chance you'll find a road open down to the quay. Get hold of the local plod. You know him, Steve Harris. It's possible the boat may have been registered there, rather than at Morston.'

McKenzie groaned again. 'Now?'

Tench peered at him. 'You've aged, Mac,' he said. 'Take a ten-minute break. Go down to the canteen and treat yourself to a fizzy lemonade.'

The sergeant heaved himself up. 'Is there no compassion left in the world?' he said. 'If there is, then just do me one last favour. If I drown in the floods on the way to Blakeney, anoint me with ale and lay me out on the bar at the Adam and Eve. Down there, I might at least get a sniff of a pint.'

3.

It was half an hour later that Tench, returning from the CID room, found his office door open, billows of smoke rolling up towards the ceiling, and Lubbock lounging in a chair by the desk, contentedly puffing away at his pipe.

His old Chief didn't move. Teeth firmly clamped on the stem of his pipe, he simply said, 'Bridgeland.'

Tench stared at him. 'Bridgeland?'

'Anthony Bridgeland. That's his name. Chap who owns the dinghy. Thought you'd like to know. He's a retired naval officer. Lives out at Heydon. Should be easy to trace. He must be on the phone.'

Tench pulled out a chair and sat down. He continued to stare. 'Go on,' he said.

'Nothing more to say, laddie. Fish out the phone book and let's take a look.'

'Not yet. First things first. You're itching to tell me, so get on and tell me.'

'Tell you what?'

'Just how you managed to root out his name.'

'Wasn't difficult, laddie. How long have you lived in Norfolk? Six years, seven? Let's just say that I've been here almost ten times as long. You get to meet people over the years. I know an old boatman who lives in Blakeney. Runs a service for trippers in the summer to Blakeney Point. Knows every boat that puts out of there and Morston. The *Spindrift*'s a motorized yacht. It's registered at Blakeney. The word *Morston* on the dinghy's just a quirk on Bridgeland's part. Commanded a corvette or some such of that name during the war. The yacht was anchored at Blakeney. The dinghy must have torn loose and been swept down to Cley . . . Satisfied?'

Tench sighed. 'Yes, but it makes me feel that, even after seven years, I don't know much at all.'

'Well, that's true enough, laddie.' Lubbock was blunt. 'But don't fret, you're learning . . . Now what about that phone book? Heydon's a small place, and Bridgeland's not a common name. Finding him should be simple.'

Tench pulled a battered directory from a shelf, laid it on the desk, flicked through the pages, and then ran his finger down a column. 'Only two Bridgelands,' he said. 'One's at Cromer. The other's a Bridgeland A.J., but he's at Shotton Corner . . . Where the devil's Shotton Corner?'

'Close enough to Heydon as makes no odds. Remember the name, laddie. Stow it away in your memory bank. It's all local knowledge, invaluable in any investigation . . . That'll be him. So what's the address?'

'Two Gables House, Oakengate Road.'

'Oh, that's where he lives, is it?' Lubbock blew out a cloud of particularly pungent smoke.

'You know it, of course.'

'Couldn't miss it, laddie. It's quite distinctive. An old brick farmhouse, timber-framed I'd imagine, but what makes it stand out is the front porch. Odd, very odd indeed. It covers three storeys, with a couple of black-and-white gables, one at the first floor and another at the second. As far as I know, it's all but unique in Norfolk. There's another one like it, but that's at Tacolneston, way south of here on the road down to Diss.'

'You're a mine of information, aren't you?' said Tench.

'We have to be in our job. I've told you that before, Mike. Know the ground. It's an axiom that every good detective should take to heart. If you know where to look, it saves precious time, and it can often be vital when you're searching for clues.' He drew on his pipe and released another rolling billow of smoke. 'It's proved its worth today, hasn't it? You've got a name, an address, a precise location, and a detailed description of what the place is like. What more could you want? So, get off down there, laddie, and see this chap Bridgeland. He may know nothing, but if I were in your shoes I'd want to give him the once-over. And more than that. Since many older men seem to marry young women, I'd want to meet his wife and make sure she's still alive, not waiting for Ledward to carve her up.'

Tench peered at him through another ascending cloud of smoke. His response was ironic. 'Don't tell me you haven't been down there already.'

His old Chief raised a couple of bushy eyebrows. 'Wouldn't dream of going, laddie. That's your job, not mine, and I've got enough to do down at Cley to keep me busy. I just needed to set you on the right track. We've lost a week already. If we're going to solve this case, we can't have you sitting around wasting time.'

4.

There were times Tench admitted, as he drove north from Norwich in the gathering dusk, when the old boy tested his patience to the limit: times when he felt it on the tip of his tongue to remind his ex-Chief that he'd locked up his office and officially retired six years before, and that it was none of his business to be issuing instructions to the present Chief Inspector. And yet he knew in his heart of hearts that he could never bring himself to deliver such a stricture.

He remembered Hastings saying much the same thing. 'It's nothing to do with him, Mike. Isn't it about time that you told him so?'

He'd thought about it. 'Yes, perhaps it is, sir,' he'd said.

The Chief Super had peered at him shrewdly. 'But you never will, will you?'

He'd hesitated. 'No,' he'd said at last, 'I don't think I could, sir. He's irritating, yes, arrogant at times, but I owe him a great deal. He's always treated me more as a son than a subordinate . . .'

'The son he never had.'

'Yes, maybe so, but he's an uncanny gift for tracking down killers, you've said so yourself, and he knows more about Norfolk than I'll ever know.'

'So you'll bite that tongue of yours and let him ramble on.'

He'd nodded. 'I think it's wiser to do that, sir, yes. He taught me to listen. "When you're dealing with a murder," he always said, "listen and learn," and that's what I do. I listen when he talks, and quite often I learn.'

That was true enough. He'd always listened to what Lubbock had to say, ever since the first day he'd started his training, when the old boy had frowned at him over a desk, asked him a question and answered it before he'd had a chance to reply. 'How long have you been here in Norfolk?' he'd said. 'Six months? Less? Well, make no mistake, you've a hell of a lot to learn. You may come from Manchester, the great metropolis, but this is a very different sort of world. D'you know what Norfolk is? It's a broad, flat swathe of medieval England. The population's sparse, and most Norfolk folk live out their lives in rural communities: villages, laddie, and villages that are isolated, small and reclusive. There are seven hundred of them, scattered far and wide, and you'd best be prepared, because in every single one of them you'll be viewed with suspicion. One glance from behind the curtains and they'll know you're a "furriner", and you'll be lucky if you get them to open their doors an inch, let alone their mouths.'

That was the first thing he'd learnt from Lubbock: the first of many things.

The second was patience, because listening to his old Chief in those early days cost a great deal of patience.

He'd marked him down at first as an irascible old devil, difficult to work with, devious in his crab-like approach to a problem, yet intolerant of any step that diverged from his tried and tested procedures; but he'd come, in time and almost imperceptibly, to appreciate that behind the short temper and apparent illogicality there was a thoroughness that laid bare the bones of a case, like a surgeon's knife probing the source of an infection. He got the results, and results, as Tench knew, were what counted in the end.

More than that, Lubbock had seemed to mellow. Or perhaps that wasn't the whole of the truth. Perhaps he himself, as his confidence increased, had found him easier to work with. What he'd first condemned as faults, he'd come to see later as nothing but foibles, and whereas, in the early days, he'd always watched him with suspicion, that suspicion had gradually melted away, to be replaced by a kind of amused affection.

Since Lubbock's retirement, the bond between them had, if anything, strengthened. He'd spent more than a few evenings in the cottage at Cley, drinking the coffee that the old boy kept specially stowed away against such a visit, tapping into his inexhaustible fund of local knowledge, seeking answers to his own unfamiliar problems, and listening to his old Chief, through clouds of pungent pipe-smoke, rambling on about his wonderful windmills.

He owed him more than a little, and though – a DCI himself now for almost three years – there were times when he resented his continued interference, he knew very well, as he'd confessed to the Chief Super, that he'd never be able to bring himself to warn the old boy off.

Old loyalties died hard, old affections persisted and, as he secretly admitted, there always lurked somewhere that weary appreciation that Lubbock's fund of knowledge about his own county was an asset far too valuable to be thrust aside out of sheer exasperation.

So, yes, he'd bite his tongue and let his old Chief ramble on. It was better that way.

As he swung the car on to the Horsford road, he rammed his foot down and gripped the wheel more tightly.

It was ten minutes later that, away to the left, he saw the cluster of lights that was the village of Cawston. The turn-off to Heydon and Shotton Corner was only a mile ahead. He slowed down and relaxed. He'd no doubt that Lubbock's description was accurate. He only hoped that he could pick out those two distinctive gables in the dark.

5.

It wasn't easy. Clouds covered the moon, the few buildings that went by the name of Shotton Corner were widely dispersed, and roads from all four points of the compass appeared to converge there, leading off into the typical Norfolk wilderness of flat and utterly featureless fields.

Twice he took the wrong road, and it was only at the third attempt that he stumbled on the place, though once seen, as Lubbock said, it could hardly be forgotten.

Standing on its own, an even blacker shape against the darkness of the sky, the unbroken landscape stretching all around it, it seemed indeed like a tall ship becalmed on a placid sea, and he wondered for a moment whether this was what had tempted Bridgeland to settle in such a desolate place.

There was no sign of life, no gleam of light from any of the windows. He hesitated briefly, standing by the porch, looking up at the gables, then took a step forward and, raising the heavy iron knocker on the door, rapped three times.

There was no response. He waited, then reached out again for the knocker; but before he could lift it, there were footsteps inside, the rasp and clack of a bolt drawn back from its socket, the creak of a door, and a sudden blinding light shining straight in his eyes.

As he flinched and looked away, the light flashed off, and dimly, as his vision adapted itself, he saw a large black figure blocking the doorway, and heard a gruff voice saying, 'Sorry about that. A fuse has blown somewhere and all the lights are out. I'm having to use a torch.' He peered at Tench. 'I don't know you, do I?'

'No, sir. We've never met. I'm from Norwich. Detective Chief Inspector Tench.' Tench held out his card. 'You're Mr Bridgeland?'

'That's right.' Bridgeland switched on his torch again, took the card, examined it, and handed it back. 'Detective Chief Inspector? You're CID?'

'Yes, sir.'

'I'm intrigued, Chief Inspector. As far as I know I've committed no crime, so why on earth would you want to see me?'

'It's about your boat, sir.'

'Is it indeed?' Bridgeland peered at him again. 'Well, you'd better come in then, and tell me all about it. I've lit a few candles, so just follow me.'

He led the way down a narrow stone-flagged hall, and turned right into a room at the back of the house which had clearly once served as an old farm kitchen. Two candles in tall brass holders flickered in fitful fashion on a long, low refectory table, a log fire in urgent need of replenishment glowed red on a broad, open hearth, and by the dim light they shed Tench could see a vast black cooking range flanked by a pair of ovens and surmounted by a spit. There were a couple of armchairs drawn up by the hearth and, taking one for himself, Bridgeland motioned to Tench to take the other. 'Sorry about the lighting,' he said, 'but I've decided to leave it as it is until daylight. This is an old house. The fuse box is in the cellar, and fiddling with fuse wires by the light of a torch is a tricky sort of job . . . So what's this about the boat?'

'I believe it's a motor yacht, Mr Bridgeland. The *Spindrift*. Is that correct?'

24

'Dead accurate, Chief Inspector. Bought her a couple of years back and sailed her round from Southampton. Kept her moored at Blakeney, though God only knows just where she is now. Must have dragged her anchor last Saturday night. More likely than not, Davy Jones has claimed her. She's probably down on the sea bed somewhere, gathering barnacles. Unless . . .' He paused. 'Unless someone's found her.'

'I'm afraid not, sir,' said Tench, 'but we have found a dinghy bearing that name.'

Bridgeland nodded. 'Have you indeed? And where was it found?'

'It was washed up at Cley, sir. Lodged against the wall of a cottage by the church.'

'But no sign of the *Spindrift*?'

'No, sir. No trace.'

'The dinghy was damaged?'

'Appears not to be, sir. Must simply have broken loose and floated round to Cley.'

'And . . .?'

'And, sir?'

Bridgeland showed some impatience. 'I suggest you come to the point, Chief Inspector,' he said. 'Or at least give me credit for a mite of intelligence. I'm quite sure the police have enough to do at the moment without wasting resources. They're not likely to be sending a high-ranking officer of the CID all the way to Shotton Corner merely to report the finding of a dinghy. So what else have you got to tell me?'

'There was a body in the boat, sir.'

'A body? What kind of a body?'

'A young woman, sir. Shot through the head.'

Bridgeland never moved. All he did was stare. 'Are you seriously telling me, Chief Inspector, that you found a murdered woman inside a boat that belongs to me?'

Tench gave a shrug. 'The inscription on the dinghy was *Spindrift, Morston*?'

'Yes, of course it was.'

'Then those are the facts, sir.'

'And you suspect that I shot this unfortunate woman and dumped her in the boat?'

25

'Hardly that, sir, no. We merely thought that you might be able to help us.'

'Well, I can't.' Bridgeland was curt. 'I know nothing about it. Nothing at all.'

It was difficult to see by candlelight just how old the man was. Tall and broadly built, with a close-clipped beard, he could have been any age between thirty-five and fifty, but Tench thought he discerned a greying at the temples more indicative of the latter. 'Are you married, sir?' he asked.

Bridgeland's answer came swiftly, almost as if he'd been expecting the question. 'No,' he said. 'I'm a widower. Widowed twice as a matter of fact, and married six times. The others, I might add, were amicable partings. We felt that a change of partners had perhaps more to offer.'

Tench said nothing. He waited.

Bridgeland gave a sigh. 'Have you no sense of humour at all, Chief Inspector? No? Then I'll spell it out for your benefit in basic English. I've been wedded to every ship I've served on, and two of them have unfortunately sunk underneath me. But if you need a less cryptic answer to your question, no, I'm not married. I've never been married. I haven't shot my wife. It isn't her body you've found in the dinghy, and though I do have a lady friend, she's busy with plans for our wedding next month. I'm perfectly willing to give you her address. Go and see her. I think you'll find she's still very much alive.'

6.

Tench shook his head. 'That won't be necessary, sir,' he said.

'You're willing to take my word?' Bridgeland showed some surprise.

'Yes, barring any subsequent evidence to the contrary.'

'Then you'll want me to collect the dinghy.'

'Not immediately, sir, no. It's been sent to Forensics for a detailed examination. Once that's concluded, we'll let you know.'

'Then that's all, is it?'

'Not quite, sir, no. You may still be able to help us.'

Bridgeland frowned. 'I'm sorry, Chief Inspector, but I don't see how. I know absolutely nothing about this business, apart from what I've told you.'

'I understand that, sir, yes, but evidence is a very peculiar thing. You may know something vital and not realize you know it.'

'I can't think what.'

'It's possible you may know who this young woman is. The body was naked, and so far we haven't the faintest idea what her name is or where she comes from. And we need to know, Mr Bridgeland, and we need to know fast. Until we can establish her identity, we've very little hope of discovering who killed her.'

'You mean you want me to take a look at her?'

'Yes, sir, we do. If she happens to come from Blakeney, you may have seen her around.'

Bridgeland shrugged. 'Well, fair enough . . . When do you suggest?'

'The pathologist's doing an autopsy this evening. Shall we say tomorrow morning at nine o'clock? You have a car, of course?'

'I'd look well living out here at Shotton Corner without one. Yes, Chief Inspector, I do have a car. It's an old Riley Kestrel, but it serves my purpose. Where d'you want me to meet you?'

'It had better be at my office in Bethel Street. I'll run you from there to the lab.'

'I'll be there,' Bridgeland said. 'Is there anything more?'

'Not at the moment, sir, no.'

'Then I'll light you to the door. I'm sorry we had to talk in little more than a gloaming, but in these old houses the electrics are unpredictable.'

Tench pushed himself up. 'Can I help you?' he said. 'I could at least hold the torch while you mend the fuse.'

Bridgeland gave a laugh. 'No, Chief Inspector, but thanks for the offer. It's easy to see you know little enough about old Norfolk farmhouses. The cellars are death traps. Flights of stone steps without even a handrail, and worn into hollows. I never go down in the dark. It's more than enough for one night to have a dead woman found in my dinghy. I shudder to think of my fate if I were landed with a dead policeman as well.'

7.

Precisely at the moment when the door of Two Gables closed behind Tench, McKenzie lifted the receiver in a phone box at Edgefield, dialled the operator, and asked to be connected to police headquarters in Norwich.

'That you, George?' he said to the Duty Sergeant. 'Put me through to the DCI.'

'He's out, Sarge.'

'He bloody well would be,' McKenzie said. 'Then make it CID.'

In the CID room it was Detective Constable Lock who answered. 'Yes, Sarge?' he said.

'I've a message for the DCI.'

'Right, Sarge.'

'Tell him the man's name is Bridgeland, Anthony James Bridgeland. He lives at Shotton Corner, Two Gables House. It's next door to Heydon.'

'He knows, Sarge,' said Lock. 'He's out there now.'

'He's what?'

'He's out at Shotton Corner. Been gone an hour now.'

There was an explosion on the line, reminiscent, Lock said later, of the sound of an atom bomb dropped in mid-Norfolk, then a string of invective that rattled the phone, tailing off into a series of mutinous growls.

'Then when he gets back,' McKenzie said, 'tell him I'm out in the middle of the sticks. It's pitch bloody black. I'm cold and lonely, and as from now I'm off duty. If he wants me, I'll be in the Fighting Cocks at Saxthorpe, where I propose to consume at least five pints of ale. After that I'm going on to the Black Bull . . .'

'Hang on, Sarge,' said Lock. 'There isn't a Fighting Cocks at Saxthorpe.'

'Isn't there?' McKenzie said. 'Now isn't that just too bad? Tell him I'll be there.'

There was a click, and the line went dead.

8.

Some three-quarters of an hour later Tench pushed open the door of the CID room, and spoke to Constable Lock. 'Any word yet from Mac?' he asked.

'Yes, sir,' said Lock.

'What did he say?'

'Said the name you wanted was Bridgeland, sir. Gave me his address.'

'And what did you say?'

'I told him you knew. You were on your way there.'

'And?'

'He seemed a bit miffed, sir.'

'Miffed?'

'Well . . . yes, sir.'

'I bet he wasn't just miffed. If I know Mac, he swore blue murder, didn't he?'

Lock seemed to hesitate. 'Something like that, sir.'

'Where was he phoning from?'

'Said he was some place out in the sticks, sir, but didn't say where.'

'But he was on his way back?'

'Reckon so, yes, sir.'

'How long ago was this?'

'Round about an hour, sir.'

'And he hasn't reported in?'

'No, sir. Not yet.'

Tench gave a nod. 'Right. Say no more, Des. We both know where to find him.'

'We do, sir?' Lock sounded doubtful.

'Yes. He'll be at the Adam, won't he? Where else would he be?'

'Well, sir . . .'

'What?'

'He did mention a place at Saxthorpe. The Fighting Cocks.'

'The Fighting Cocks?' Tench frowned. 'There isn't such a place.'

'Isn't there, sir?' said Lock.

'No, Desmond, there isn't. If there's one place I do know in Norfolk, it's Saxthorpe, and Mac knows only too well that I know it. He'll be at the Adam. That's his watering hole. He'll be in the snug there, propping up the bar and telling himself that, since he's suffered all the agonies of hell, he doesn't intend to leave until he's drunk the pub dry.'

He was right, but only in part. McKenzie was, as expected, in the snug at the Adam, but he wasn't propping up the bar, nor was he lost in self-commiseration. He seemed, in fact, more than happy with life as, lounging at a corner table, he drained one tankard in a couple of gulps and reached out for a second that, brimming with the Adam's best Norfolk brew, stood waiting his attention.

Catching sight of Tench, he raised it in salutation. 'Hail to the Chief!' he said. 'Take a pew . . . Pint?'

'Why not?' said Tench. 'What's that? Your third?'

'Second,' McKenzie said. 'I'm a model of restraint. But tell me the shop's closed down for tonight and I'll order another.'

'Have it on me.'

'I will,' McKenzie said. 'After all, I deserve it.'

He surveyed his third pint with all the relish of a man retrieved after fifteen waterless days in the middle of the Gobi Desert. 'Who told you about Shotton Corner?' he asked. 'No, on second thoughts, don't bother to tell me. It's a pity he didn't come up with the news a bit sooner.'

'You should know Lubbock. You worked with him long enough.'

'I know him, yes.' McKenzie took a long, deeply satisfying draught from his tankard. 'I respect him, too, but there are times when the old sod gets right up my nose.'

'Then do what I do,' said Tench. 'Sneeze and forget. Take what he has to offer, and think no more about it.'

McKenzie sighed. 'Well, maybe you're right . . . So what did you make of our friend at Shotton Corner?'

'I'm not altogether sure. I couldn't see enough of him.'

'Couldn't, or didn't?'

'Couldn't.'

'Why not?'

'His house had blown a fuse. All the light we had was candles. I need to see him again . . . in daylight.'

'But he talked?'

'Oh, yes, he talked.'

'Then he must have made some impression.'

'He did, but impressions gleaned in a half-light can often be deceptive. Before I say what it was, I'd like a second opinion. He's coming in tomorrow morning to take a look at the body. I want you to be there.'

'You think he might know her?'

'It's always a possibility. If she lived around Blakeney, he may well have seen her.'

'And what if he hasn't?'

Tench gave a shrug. 'Then unless Ledward and Forensics come up with some clue, it's just a case of patience. Apart from issuing a description to the press and forces round the country, all we can do is wait until someone reports her missing.'

'And in the meantime the trail goes cold.'

'It's gone cold already. Most of what there was must have been washed away by the floods, and if there's any left it's still under water.'

McKenzie took another deep draught of ale. 'Well,' he said, 'if you want another opinion, I can give you one now.'

There was a lift of the eyebrows from Tench. 'Go on then. Give it.'

'If you've any doubts at all about this chap Bridgeland, let's give him a grilling whilst he's here tomorrow.'

'We may have to do that sooner or later,' said Tench, 'but it's too early yet. We haven't a scrap of evidence that he's done anything wrong.'

'Well, he's not likely to volunteer any of his own accord,' McKenzie said. 'If he shot her, he's not going to say that he knew her.'

'True enough, but we'll wait . . . Is that all?'

'No.' The sergeant pushed his tankard across the table. 'You can stand me another pint. The sight of all that salt water's given me a thirst.'

II

THE HOUSE

I see . . . blood on my carpet . . . blood in the sky.
James Elroy Flecker: *Hassan*

1.

At twenty past nine the following morning, one of the lab assistants folded back the sheet that covered the body.

'Look very carefully, Mr Bridgeland,' said Tench. 'Do you recognize this woman?'

Bridgeland bent down and studied the face. Then, straightening up, he shook his head firmly. 'No, Chief Inspector, I don't,' he said.

'You've never seen her before?'

'Never in my life, as far as I can tell.'

Tench nodded. 'Well, thank you, sir.'

'Is that all?'

'For the moment, sir, yes. I'll be in touch once Forensics have finished with the dinghy.'

'And when will that be? Have you any idea?'

'Perhaps a couple of days, sir. It shouldn't take more than that . . . You will, of course, be willing to make a statement about the dinghy?'

Bridgeland gave a shrug. 'If you think it's necessary.'

'It's purely routine, sir, nothing more than that.'

'Then of course, if it'll help.'

'It has to be done, sir, and it'll save you time later on.' He nodded towards McKenzie. 'This is Sergeant McKenzie. When we get back to the office, he'll take down your statement. All you need to do is read it through and sign it. Will that be all right?'

'Perfectly all right, Chief Inspector,' Bridgeland said.

It was close to an hour later that McKenzie appeared and tossed two sheets of paper on to Tench's desk. 'Signed and sealed,' he said. 'You still want my opinion?'

'You know I do, Mac, so stop pretending to be modest. It just doesn't suit you . . . What did you make of our friend from Shotton Corner?'

'In brief,' McKenzie said, 'not a lot.'

'And what does that mean?'

'It means that he's either clean as a whistle, or the best liar I've come across in thirty years' service.'

'So how d'you rate him as a suspect?'

'Your guess is as good as mine.'

'And what's yours?'

'If I had to make one, I'd say put him on the list but somewhere down near the bottom . . . His statement rings true. It may well be true, but I wouldn't say for sure that something won't turn up to make it a pack of lies.'

'You're a lot of help, aren't you?'

'Can you do any better?'

Tench read through the statement and pushed it aside. 'No,' he said, 'I can't. The trouble is, Mac, we're working in the dark. We haven't any guidelines. We don't know who she is or where she was killed. We don't know with any accuracy just when she died, and as yet we've no list of possible suspects.'

'And that means we don't know what questions to ask.'

'It means we've plenty of questions, but they may be the wrong ones, and until we get more facts to work on, asking them's just a sheer waste of time.'

'But we can't afford to sit on our hands, so what d'you suggest we do?'

Tench pushed himself up. 'We do what we can to get hold of the facts. If we wait for Ledward's autopsy report, we'll be sitting on our hands for the rest of the day, so let's go and beard the lion in its den.'

A wolfish grin spread over McKenzie's face. 'That's just what I was going to suggest,' he said. 'Leave him to me. I'm in the mood to do some bearding. He doesn't like answering questions from sergeants. Always views me like something unbearably obscene that he's tweezered out of the lower intestine. If I can't rile him into telling me what's what, then the salt from the sticks has dried up my wits.'

'Right,' said Tench. 'You go ahead. I'll give you twenty minutes' start. Maybe by then he'll have found you so unbearable he'll welcome me with open arms like a long-lost brother.'

2.

Dr Reginald Blake Ledward, the Home Office pathologist, had earned a thoroughly deserved reputation as a taciturn man with a caustic tongue, and since he was also a confirmed insomniac, such traits were always most in evidence in the hours before midday. That proved to be so on this particular morning. He hadn't slept well, one of his lab assistants had gone down with the flu overnight, two apparent suicides had already added themselves to the bodies in his fridge, and he'd been plagued by a string of unnecessary phone calls. He was consequently not in the best of tempers, and the sight of McKenzie, a person he viewed as a perpetual irritant, was for him, if not the last straw, at the very least the penultimate one.

McKenzie, on the other hand, was determinedly cheerful. 'A very good morning, Doctor,' he said. 'I hope you slept well.'

Ledward gave him a frosty glare. 'Then your hopes are ill founded, Sergeant,' he said.

'Oh, I'm sorry to hear that.' McKenzie was all contrition. 'A touch of conscience perhaps?'

The glare turned icy. 'No, Sergeant, it was not a touch of conscience. Far from it. I was troubled by the amount of work facing me this morning: work in which I seem to be continually interrupted . . . You have some valid reason for wishing to see me?'

'Oh, yes, very valid,' McKenzie said. 'I'm here on behalf of Chief Inspector Tench.'

'Are you indeed? And where is the Chief Inspector? Don't tell me he's still in bed.'

'Hardly that, sir, no. He's interviewing a suspect.'

'Then tell me this, Sergeant. What is it that's so urgent that he sends one of his minions down to interrupt me?'

'Minions?' McKenzie frowned. 'I'm a simple soul, Doctor. Words of three syllables tend to confuse me. Perhaps you'd explain the meaning of the term.'

Ledward dismissed him with a wave of the hand. 'Never mind,' he said. 'Come to the point. Am I to assume that the Chief Inspector finds it difficult to wait for my autopsy report?'

'He thought you might be willing to summarize the findings.'

'Then he assumes a great deal.'

'We are short of time, sir.'

'So am I, Sergeant. So am I. Every moment you waste defers the report itself.'

'Nonetheless, sir, I'm sure the Chief Inspector would be grateful.'

Ledward sighed in frustration. 'What is it he wants to know?'

'First of all, the cause of death. Was it, as we suppose, a bullet through the head?'

'No, it was not. Let's be accurate, Sergeant. The woman died from a bullet *in* the head, not through it. There was no exit wound. The missile had lodged itself inside the cerebellum.'

McKenzie's face took on a pained expression. 'The cere . . .?'

'Bellum, Sergeant. Bellum. The lower posterior part of the brain. Why can't you people apprise yourselves of even the simplest of medical terms?'

'You removed it, sir?'

'The bullet? Naturally I removed it. I passed it to Forensics.'

'There was no exit wound. So was it low calibre?'

'That's not my province, Sergeant. If you want to know that, you'll have to speak to Mr Merrick.'

'Oh, we will, sir, we will . . . So, in your opinion, when did she die?'

'Sometime between a week and ten days ago.'

'Can't you be more accurate?'

'No, Sergeant, I can't. I'm not a magician . . . Now is there anything else before I'm allowed to get back to my work?'

McKenzie took some time to ponder the question. 'Were there any signs of sexual interference?'

'None that I could see. Nor were there any of recent sexual activity.'

'But she wasn't a virgin?'

For the first time that morning Ledward seemed amused. He even gave a wry smile. 'Oh, no, Sergeant, she was certainly not a virgin. Since she was pregnant, that could hardly be the case.'

'Pregnant?' McKenzie blinked.

'That was what I said.'

'How far pregnant?'

'Three months, I'd say.'

The telephone on the wall broke the silence that followed. The doctor snatched it up in some exasperation, then handed it to McKenzie. 'It's for you,' he said. 'Chief Inspector Tench.'

'Is that you, Mac?'

'Speaking.'

Tench sounded urgent. 'Get back here sharp. We may have got a lead.'

3.

They met on the stairs below the DCI's office, McKenzie going up, Tench coming down. 'Turn round, Mac,' he said. 'We've no time to spare.'

'Don't you want to hear what the old lion had to say?'

'Later,' said Tench. 'You can tell me on the way.'

'On the way where?'

'Blakeney.'

McKenzie groaned. 'Not again.'

'Again and tomorrow and the day after, Mac, or as long as it takes to get at the truth.'

'But why the hell Blakeney?'

'Because,' said Tench, 'we're going to meet a postman. I'm told he's got a little something to deliver.'

The postman was short, stocky and middle-aged, with a voice like gravel running through a sieve.

Steve Harris, the resident constable at Blakeney, introduced him. 'This, sir,' he said, 'is Eli Welt. He's been delivering the post at Breckton since the end of the war. I think you ought to hear what he has to say.'

'Glad to meet you, Mr Welt.' Tench shook his hand. 'What have you got to tell us?'

'Well, sir,' said Welt, 'it come about like this. There's a place up at Breckton name o' The Woodlands. Big place it is, stands on its own, wi' a swath o' trees round it. It were empty for years till three months aback. Then the Kinghams moves in. Man an' his wife. Reginald and Valerie, that were their names. Not short o' money, from what I could see. Did a lot o' renovatin'. Tarted the place up. Ran a brand new Rolls, a Silver Dawn.'

Welt paused and cleared his throat noisily. 'Well, sir,' he said, 'to come to the point, the first time there were a letter for The Woodlands since the storm were yesterday mornin', an' when I go to shove 'em through the flap I see the front door's open. Not much, it's true, a couple of inches maybe, and the Rolls is parked outside. Well, I weren't for thinkin' much of it just at that time – reckoned one of 'em must be some place around – but this mornin' I'm findin' things just the same – door still open, car still parked outside – so I gives the door a nudge, and there's the letter still there as I delivered the day afore an' never bin picked up, an' no sign of anyone round about at all . . . I says to miself, Eli, this is more'n a mite strange, so I pulls the door shut, an' when I finishes mi round I gets on mi bike an' comes straight down here.'

'You didn't go inside the house?'

'No, sir, not an inch. Thought it best not.'

'You did absolutely right, Mr Welt,' said Tench. He turned to Steve Harris. 'The Kinghams. They weren't reported missing in the storm, were they, Constable?'

Harris shook his head. 'No, sir, there was no one missing from either Blakeney or Breckton.'

'Then we'd better go and take a look at the place. You and Mr Welt can come with us in the car.' He turned back to the postman. 'As you say, Mr Welt, it seems more than a little strange. There may be a perfectly innocent explanation, but until we know that for sure, we need to investigate. How far is it to Breckton? A couple of miles?'

'Just about that, sir,' said Welt. 'but on a bike wi' a postbag it gets to be like four.'

'Well, it won't seem four today,' said Tench. He tossed the keys to McKenzie. 'Come on, Mac. You drive.'

4.

At first sight The Woodlands, a square three-storeyed structure of dun-coloured brick, recalled to Tench's mind his father's Victorian vicarage in that run-down part of Manchester where he was born and brought up. Approached by a pitted winding drive through a belt of elm trees, it seemed a bleak, forbidding place, but the sleek lines of the Rolls parked outside on a freshly gravelled standing were enough to dispel the vision as fast as it had formed. No churchman, to his recollection – not even the bishop, and certainly not a canon like his father – would ever have dared to purchase a Rolls, even if they'd had the money to do it.

He pulled the car to a halt on the edge of the gravel. 'Constable,' he said to Harris, 'you and Mr Welt take a look around the grounds. Leave the house to us. I'll do the ground floor. You go upstairs, Mac.'

As he turned the knob and pushed open the door, it was clear, as Welt had said, that the Kinghams had done more than scrub and scour the place. The hallway that confronted them was just about as far removed from that of a vicarage as the entrance to a high-class Soho brothel. The carpet was rich and red, the wallpaper gold, and the foot of the staircase directly ahead of them was flanked by two sculptures of naked young women posed with hands clasped at the back of their heads.

McKenzie stopped and stared. 'Well. I never thought I'd find a whorehouse out in the Norfolk sticks,' he said. 'What the hell are they, these Kinghams? Nudists?'

'Who knows?' said Tench. 'Don't jump to conclusions, Mac. They may be nothing more than connoisseurs of art with eccentric tastes.'

'Well, one thing's for sure. They're not fig-leaf worshippers.' McKenzie stroked one of the statues fondly. 'They're not exactly modest, this pair of charmers, are they?'

But Tench didn't answer. He was down on his haunches, examining the carpet. 'Look at this, Mac,' he said.

It was easy to miss on the deep red pile: a slightly darker stain as if liquid had been spilled and then dried on the surface.

'Blood?' Tench queried.

McKenzie wet the end of his finger, ran it across the stain and then sniffed. 'Could be,' he said. 'Difficult to tell.'

By the foot of the stairs there was a door on the right. Tench flung it open, and what they saw stopped them dead in their tracks. The room bore no resemblance to the hall. The furnishings were far more muted. The panelling on the walls, the table, Welsh dresser and bookshelves were all of dark oak, the carpet was grey, the velvet curtains deep green, but it seemed as if a hurricane had swept it from end to end. The dresser, table and bookshelves still stood intact, but all they'd contained – crockery, Wedgwood plates, vases of flowers and books – lay scattered about the floor, while the curtains had been partially wrenched from their hooks, and trailed across shards of pottery that had once been figurines.

'Hell's bells,' McKenzie breathed. 'What the devil's happened here?'

'I don't know, Mac,' said Tench, 'but we've been searching for a crime scene, and now we've found one.'

'But is it the one we've been wanting to find?'

'Let's hope to God it is. If it isn't, we could well have two murders on our hands.' He pulled the door shut. 'I'll check the rest of the house,' he said. 'There's a phone box in the village. You get on to Norwich. I want the scene-of-crime squad here, and I want them here fast. The sooner we're free to search this place thoroughly, the better.'

5.

Emerging from the house some five minutes later, he took Harris aside. 'Steve,' he said, 'what do you know about the Kinghams?'

Harris gave a shrug. 'Not much at all, sir.'

'Have you ever met them?'

'No, sir.'

'Seen them around?'

'Can't say I've never seen them, sir, but I wouldn't have known them even if I had. I've never had any reason to pay them a visit. They haven't been here that long.'

'Then just what do you know?'

'Only what rumour tells me, sir.'

'And what does rumour say?'

'Virtually nothing, sir. That's the whole point. Since they arrived, they've kept themselves very much to themselves. From what I can gather, they don't seem to have spoken to anyone in the village.'

'They've done a lot to the house. They must have had workmen in.'

'They weren't locals, sir. According to Welt, the firm was from Norwich.'

'Someone they knew?'

'Could have been, sir, yes.'

'Then it's possible that the Kinghams could have moved here from Norwich.'

'Or the firm was recommended by friends already there, sir.'

Tench took a deep breath. 'Yes, I suppose that could be another possibility . . . I think we'd better have a word or two with Welt.'

He turned towards the postman. 'Mr Welt,' he said, 'these workmen who came to refurbish the house. They were from Norwich?'

Welt nodded vigorously. 'That's right, sir. They were.'

'What was the name of the firm?'

'Ah, well.' The postman frowned. 'As to that, sir, I don't really know. It were a dark blue van, but there weren't no name.'

'Then how did you know it was from Norwich?'

'It were the mornin', sir. Icy, an' roads were like glass. I sees this van parked outside wi' ladders on top, an' a chap in white overalls a-fishin' out pots o' paint from the back. Well, we gets to talkin' like, an' I asks him had he had far to drive. "Aye," he says, "Norwich. An' the way out o' Horsford's no better'n a skatin' rink."'

Tench nodded. 'You've been delivering letters here ever since the Kinghams arrived in Breckton?'

'What there were, sir, an' there weren' that many.'

'Were any of them redirected?'

'A couple, sir, aye.'

'Could you see the old address?'

'No, sir, pasted over.'

'But you've been coming up to the house for something like three months?'

'Off an' on, sir, aye.'

'Then you must have seen one of them around at some time.'

Welt shook his head even more forcefully. 'No, sir, never. I never set eyes on a one of 'em, mornin' or noon.'

'Isn't that a bit strange?'

'Strange it may be, sir, but believe me, it's truth.'

'Oh, I'm sure it is, Mr Welt.' Tench stared at the house and drew another deep breath. 'The trouble is, I'm beginning to wonder whether Mr and Mrs Kingham have ever been here at all. Has *anybody* seen them?'

'Oh aye, sir,' said Welt. 'Willie Craske. He's seen 'em.'

There was a pause. Tench shifted his stare to the postman. 'Willie Craske? Who's he?'

'Used to deliver round here, sir. Now he does Stiffkey. Filled in for me, sir, week afore last when I were off wi' a bout o' flu.'

'And you say that he saw Mr and Mrs Kingham?'

'That's what he said, sir. Weren' for very long though. Reckon as they musta given him a good round o' swears.'

Tench frowned. 'What makes you think that?'

'Well, he says to me, "Eli, you got a couple o' right buggers up there at The Woodlands. Wouldn' surprise me if there were blood on the floor afore winter's out."' Welt nodded sagely. 'Looks like he weren' that far wrong, sir, don' it?'

6.

The police car braked to a crunching halt on the gravel, and McKenzie heaved himself out, slamming the door behind him. 'Lester's on his way,' he said.

Sergeant Jim Lester was head of the scene-of-crime squad, young and enthusiastic, but experienced, perceptive and always efficient.

'Good,' said Tench. He turned back to Welt. 'Where does Willie Craske live?'

'Warham, sir,' said Welt. 'Cottage by the crossroads, name o' The Homestead.'

'Right . . . Steve,' he said to Harris. 'Take the car. Drive Mr Welt back to Blakeney and take a statement from him. Then come back here . . . Mac, you come with me. There's something upstairs I think you should see.'

The rich red carpet continued up the stairs and on to a spacious landing where there were five closed doors. Tench opened two of them. 'Separate bedrooms,' he said. 'Take a look, Mac, but don't go inside.'

There was nothing particularly gaudy about them. They'd been tastefully furnished, but in appearance they were very different indeed. The first was clearly a man's room. The carpet was dark green, the curtains gold. The single bed lacked a coverlet, and the mahogany dressing table was bare save for a hairbrush and comb, and a single framed photograph of a group of four men in open-necked shirts and shorts leaning on what appeared to be polo sticks.

The second, with its pink flowered carpet and royal blue curtains, could only be a woman's, but the same hurricane that had swept through the downstairs room had left it in a state of equal devastation. The floor was littered with pots and tubes of make-up, a set of pearl-backed brushes and combs, and a sea of assorted underwear tossed from an upturned drawer, while, almost within reach of the two detectives, lay a framed wedding photograph, the glass of it splintered as if someone had wantonly ground it underfoot.

McKenzie cocked his head on one side to get a better view, but the glass had been broken into so many pieces that the picture itself was difficult to see. 'The Kinghams?' he queried.

'Must be,' said Tench.

'Then it looks as if their marriage was in the same sort of state. Smashed beyond redemption.'

'Looks like it, Mac.'

'And if she was the woman dumped in Bridgeland's dinghy, then where's Mr Kingham?'

'That's a very good question. I wish I knew the answer.'

'There's only one answer. Can be only one. He's skipped it, hasn't he? And he's already had a week to make himself scarce. We need to put out a call, Mike, and fast.'

Tench was more cautious. 'Maybe,' he said.

'Maybe?' McKenzie found it difficult to contain himself. 'It's plain as a plate-glass window. The man's smashed up the house and shot his wife. He's done his best to hide the body and made off God knows where. We need to track him down.'

'Oh, we'll track him down,' said Tench, 'but you're jumping to the obvious conclusion, Mac.'

'Obvious is right.'

'There could be other explanations.'

'Then name one.' McKenzie was fast losing patience. 'Just do me a favour. Name one.'

'A jealous lover? Someone we don't know about? Look, Mac, we've absolutely nothing as yet to connect this case with the woman in the boat. We need more facts about this couple, the Kinghams.'

'And where do we find them?'

'We need to talk to Willie Craske.'

'Ah, yes,' McKenzie said, 'the elusive Mr Craske. Just who the hell is he?'

'He's another postman, Mac. A friend of Eli Welt.'

'And why the devil do we need to talk to another postman?'

'Because,' said Tench, 'he's the only one so far who claims to have seen the Kinghams, and before we take any firm decisions we need to hear what he has to say.'

7.

Returning from Blakeney, Steve Harris was immediately followed up the drive by the vans of Sergeant Lester's scene-of-crime squad. They rolled to a halt on the verge of the gravel.

'You made good time,' said Tench.

'No hold-ups for once, sir. Had a clear road.' Lester swung the door open and dropped to the ground. 'What have we got here, sir?'

'Possibly a murder, still to be confirmed. No sign of a body, but blood on the hall carpet. A couple of rooms that look as if a whirlwind's hit them. Tape the house off. The whole place needs treatment from top to bottom. Photographers, printmen, the whole of the team. You know what to do.'

'Right, sir,' Lester said.

'Oh, and one thing more. In the bedrooms you'll find a couple of photographs. Dust them and bag them before anything else. I need to take them away.'

'Will do, sir.'

'Good.' Tench turned to Harris. 'Steve, you come with us.

We'll drop you back at Blakeney . . . You drive, Mac. Warham.
The crossroads.'

McKenzie didn't need to drive all the way to Warham.
Approaching the village on the road from Binham, they overtook
a visibly toiling cyclist: a tall, gangling man in a postman's
uniform. 'That'll be him,' said Tench. 'Pull into the side, Mac.'

He stepped out of the car and held up his hand. The cyclist
wobbled and stopped.

'Willie Craske?' said Tench.

The man looked dubious. 'Mebbe. Mebbe not. What d'ye want
ter know fer?'

Tench pulled out his card. 'Detective Chief Inspector Tench,'
he said. 'I think you can help me.'

An expression that was almost mutinous crossed the man's
face. 'I ent done nothin' wrong.'

'I'm well aware of that, Mr Craske.' Tench was curt and yet
soothing. 'I simply want to ask you about something you may
have seen. Just lay your bike down and step inside the car.'

Craske complied, with some reluctance.

'Now,' said Tench, 'am I right in thinking that a fortnight ago
you delivered the post in Breckton?'

'That's right. So what?'

'I'm investigating an incident at The Woodlands, Mr Craske.
You delivered a parcel there?'

For the first time the postman's eyes showed a gleam of
interest. 'What's up then?' he said. 'Has he done her in?'

'Did you deliver a parcel?'

'Aye. Wednesday mornin'.'

'Tell me what happened.'

The postman gave a shrug. 'Well, there's a hell of a ruckus
goin' on, ent there? Kingham, he's swearin' fit ter rouse the
whole village, an' she's spittin' an' screamin' back at him like.'

'Had you seen them before? Mr and Mrs Kingham?'

'No, they weren' never around.'

'Then how did you know it was them?'

Craske gave him a look of exasperation, as if he were a
somewhat dim-witted child. 'Who the hell else could it be?'

Tench raised his eyebrows. 'Go on, Mr Craske. So what did
you do?'

'Well, there were only one thing ter do, weren' there? I knocks on the door.'

'And?'

'Well, the ruckus stops, don' it? An' he yanks the door open like ter snap it off its hinges. There's a crack as it hits the wall. Big chap he were. Stands there lookin' down at me, face like a bloody black thunder cloud. "What the devil do *you* want?" he says.'

'And what did you say?'

'I ent fer sayin' nothin'. Just gives him the parcel, an' he snatches it an' slams the door wi'out so much as a word o' thanks, never mind a Gawd bless. An' afore I turns away, the same ol' ruckus it starts up agen.'

'And you left?'

'Too bloody true I did. I ent fer gettin' mixed up in a ruckus like that.'

'So you never saw the woman you thought was Mrs Kingham?'

Craske shook his head. 'No, not ever. Not so much as a glimpse.'

Tench gave a nod. 'If you saw the man again, would you recognize him?'

'Too bloody true I would.' Craske didn't hesitate. 'I can still see him now, a-standin' there glowerin' down at me like fer two pins he'd reach out an' wring my bloody neck. If he's done his missus in, then tek my word fer it, he needs stringin' up like a dead bloody crow on the end of a pole.'

8.

They watched him pedal away towards Warham.

'Looks like I was right,' McKenzie said. 'We need to put out a call for Kingham just as soon as we can.'

'Not yet,' said Tench. 'Back to Breckton, Mac. I want to take a good hard look at those photographs.'

'We're just wasting time.'

'I don't think so.' Tench was adamant. 'If Kingham shot his wife, he's had a week to put distance between himself and here.

Another hour's not going to make any difference . . . Back to Breckton, Mac.'

At The Woodlands the scene had changed. The house was taped off, and inside all was alive with activity. Lights flashed as photographers turned their lenses on every object that might provide a clue; fingerprint experts dusted doors and windows, furniture and fittings with brushes that they hoped would reveal a vital touch; and men on their hands and knees, armed with tweezers, examined carpets and rugs and dropped minute findings into plastic bags.

Lester had worked with his usual swift efficiency. The photograph frames had already been dusted, and the prints removed and placed inside plastic folders. Tench checked them, then took them out to the car so that he and McKenzie could study them more closely.

The wedding portrait had been scarred by the broken glass, but its main features were untouched. It showed the bride and groom in conventional pose, smiling happily arm-in-arm before a church door: both of them young, possibly in their twenties, the man taller than his bride and heavily built, with a shock of dark hair and a dark moustache, while the woman was short and slim with a delicate face that was pretty and might in repose have been beautiful.

Tench peered at her and passed the print to McKenzie. 'What d'you think, Mac?' he asked.

McKenzie held the print to the light. 'Looks like her,' he said, 'but it must be, mustn't it?'

'Not unless that's Kingham and he was the one who killed her . . . And even then we can't be sure.'

'Well, Craske'll be able to tell if it's Kingham.'

'But he won't be able to tell if it's the woman in the boat. He never saw Mrs Kingham, did he? We need a positive identification, Mac.'

'And that means we have to find Kingham himself.'

'Or someone who knew her, and knew her well enough to say.' Tench picked up the other print, and laid a finger on one of the four men in the group. 'That's Kingham,' he said, 'and it's clearly been taken at a polo match. But where?'

'Well, it's not in England for sure.' McKenzie pointed to a tree in the background of the picture. 'I've never seen a tree like that in this country. What the hell sort of tree sprouts branches like that? They're growing back into the ground.'

Tench in his turn held the print to the light. 'I'm not sure, Mac,' he said, 'but I think it's called a banyan.'

'Never heard of it.' McKenzie frowned. 'Where does it grow?'

'It's a tropical species, Asia, but I wouldn't like to try and pinpoint the country. India, Burma, Malaya, Singapore?'

'Well, it does give us one solid fact about Kingham. He's been out in the East.'

'One fact's not much use, Mac. We need a lot more. We need to match fingerprints. We need to match the dead woman's with those that Lester's gathering in the house, and we can't do that till he's finished his work.'

'So what d'you suggest we do until then?'

'We go back to Norwich,' said Tench. 'We need to get things organized. According to Welt, the decorators came from Norwich, so it's a pretty fair bet that the Kinghams lived there before they moved to Breckton. Let's gamble on the chance that they sold a house in Norwich and bought this one here. I want to know which estate agents dealt with the sales. That's your job, Mac. Get on the phone as soon as we get back and make some inquiries. Start off at Holt. It's the nearest town to here. It was probably a Holt firm that dealt with The Woodlands.'

'And what about Kingham?'

'Forget about Kingham. We can't go putting out a call for the man till we know for sure that the woman Lubbock found in the boat is his wife. First things first. I want to find someone who knew Mrs Kingham, and for that we need the whole team on the job. Lester's men'll be here for the rest of the day, so get moving, Mac. The sooner we get back to Norwich, the better.'

9.

McKenzie switched on the engine, then switched off again.

'We've got a visitor,' he said.

A low-slung white sports car came snarling up the drive. It slewed to a halt by the edge of the tapes that read 'POLICE. DO

NOT CROSS', and a tall, powerfully built young man flung open the door and stood for a moment staring. Then he lifted the tape and ducked underneath it.

Tench was out in a flash. 'Stop, sir,' he said. 'You can't go in there. The place is a crime scene.'

The young man seemed to sway for a moment on his feet, then he steadied himself. 'Oh, God, no,' he said. 'The bastard's killed her, hasn't he? I told her he would, but she wouldn't believe me.'

III

THE VISITOR

I have eyes upon him,
And his affairs come to me on the wind.
William Shakespeare: *Antony and Cleopatra*

1.

Tench gripped him by the arm. 'Who are you, sir?' he said.

'What does that matter?' The man tried to shrug him off. 'He's killed her, hasn't he?'

'Your name, sir.' Tench was curt.

'Meredith. Giles Meredith. Let go of me, will you?'

'Come and sit down, Mr Meredith. We need to have a talk.' He led the man to the car, pushed him down on the back seat and took the one beside him. 'Now, sir,' he said, 'let me introduce myself. I'm Detective Chief Inspector Tench, and this is Detective Sergeant McKenzie. We're investigating a possible crime at this house, and it seems like you may be able to help us. Where d'you live, Mr Meredith?'

'Blickling.' The man turned on him fiercely. 'What's happened in there? Tell me.'

'We don't know what's happened, Mr Meredith, not yet. That's why we need you to answer some questions . . . You say you live at Blickling. That's twenty miles away, as near as makes no odds. So what brought you here?'

Meredith breathed deeply. 'You're not going to tell me, are you?'

'I've already told you, sir,' said Tench. 'We're not certain what's happened, so please answer my question. What was it that brought you here?'

'What the devil d'you think it was? I was worried about her.'

'You mean Mrs Kingham?'

'Yes. Her name's Val. Valerie Kingham.'

'You're a relative of hers?'

'No, just a friend. A very concerned friend.'

'And a friend of her husband's?'

'Hardly.' Meredith all but spat out the word.

'I see.' Tench frowned. 'Then I think we'd better start at the beginning, Mr Meredith. How did you come to know Mr and Mrs Kingham?'

Meredith sighed. 'Is all this really necessary? Why can't you tell me just what you do know?'

'All in good time, sir, but first of all we need you to put us in the picture.'

'All right.' Meredith turned to face him. 'I'm a partner in a publishing firm in Norwich. You may have heard of it: the Norwick Press. I have a large house at Blickling, not far from the Hall. It stands in its own grounds, and has a lodge on the Aylsham road that I let from time to time. Twelve months ago I let it to the Kinghams. They'd just arrived from abroad, and they rented it until they could find a suitable house of their own. They moved out three months ago when they bought this place at Breckton . . . That's how I know them. Now tell me what's happened.'

Tench ignored the question. 'You say you were worried about Mrs Kingham. Why was that?'

'Because the man was a drunkard with a violent temper. He'd assaulted her more than once.'

'How d'you know that?'

'Good God, man!' Meredith took another deep breath. 'Do I have to spell it out? She told me. That's how.'

'I'm afraid you'll have to be more precise, Mr Meredith. When and where did she tell you?'

'Soon after they moved in. She came to my house.'

'Why did she do that?'

'She was frightened.'

Tench waited. 'Go on, sir,' he said.

'You want to know every detail?' Meredith was close to exasperation. 'Right, then. I'll tell you. She came knocking at my door about eleven o'clock at night. She was weeping and terrified. There was blood on her face and a cut above her eye. It was a deep cut. I ran her into Aylsham and had it stitched. Then I took her back to my place, and made up a bed for her in the room next to mine. She wasn't in any fit state to answer questions, so I didn't press her with any till the following day, but from what little she did say I gathered that he'd come home savagely drunk, picked a quarrel and hit her. And it wasn't the first time . . . And believe you me, Chief Inspector.' Meredith paused. 'It wasn't the last.'

56

2.

McKenzie had been listening intently to what was said. Now he turned in his seat.

'Are you telling us the same thing happened again?'

'Yes, of course it did. The man drinks, and when he drinks he gets violent, and when he gets violent he loses control. I wanted her to leave him. I said I'd take her in, provide her with a refuge. I told her if she didn't, then one day he'd kill her . . . And he has done, hasn't he? The bastard's killed her.' Meredith was all but shouting.

Tench, on the other hand, was quiet and still deliberate. 'At the moment, Mr Meredith, we've no conclusive evidence to support such a crime.'

'Then what the hell are you doing here? You said you were investigating a possible crime. What crime?'

Tench slid the wedding picture out of its folder, and handed it to him. 'Tell me, sir,' he said. 'Do you recognize the people in that photograph?'

Meredith barely glanced at it. 'Of course I bloody well do. It's him and Val, isn't it?'

'Mr and Mrs Kingham?'

'Yes.'

Tench removed the other picture. 'And in that one?' he said.

'Well, he's there, the smug bastard. The one on the left. I don't know the others.'

'You said Mr and Mrs Kingham arrived from abroad. Have you any idea where that photograph might have been taken?'

Meredith gave a shrug. 'India, I should think. That's where they came from.'

'And the other?'

'India again. They were married out there. I don't know where exactly.' He tossed the pictures back. 'How many more questions? Get to the point, Chief Inspector. What's happened here?'

Tench slipped the photographs back in their folders, then he paused for a moment. 'We need your help, Mr Meredith, on one vital point. Both Mr and Mrs Kingham appear to be missing, there are signs of violence inside this house . . .'

'That's not surprising.'

'And I have to tell you that we've found a woman's body.'

'Oh, no.' Meredith closed his eyes. When he opened them again, he turned on Tench savagely. 'I thought you said there was no evidence of murder.'

'There isn't . . . in the house. The body was found three miles away, at Cley, and we've no conclusive evidence that the woman is Mrs Kingham.'

'Of course it's her. It must be. I told her what would happen. What more evidence d'you want?'

'Evidence of identification, Mr Meredith. As far as we're concerned there could be no connection between what was found at Cley and what's happened in this house. We need to be sure that the body is indeed that of Mrs Kingham.'

'Where is she?'

'You're willing to make an identification?'

'I want to see her. Where is she? What did he do to her?'

'The woman was shot through the head, Mr Meredith.'

Meredith groaned and closed his eyes again. 'Oh, the bastard!' he said. 'The murdering bastard!' He looked straight at Tench. 'I should have taken her with me. I should never have left her alone here with him.'

'You're willing to view the body?'

'Yes. I *need* to see her.' Meredith spoke fiercely. 'But I'll tell you this now and for free, Chief Inspector. If the woman you show me turns out to be Val, you'd better find Kingham and find him quickly, because if I lay hands on him, I'll be sorely tempted to purchase a gun and shoot him straight through the head myself.'

3.

At half past four that same afternoon, the same lab assistant folded back the sheet that covered the body.

Meredith took one look, then he turned away. 'Yes,' he said, 'it's Val.'

'We need you to be absolutely sure, sir,' said Tench. 'Please look again.'

'I don't need to look again.'

'For the record, sir. Please.'

Meredith turned back.

'You're certain this woman is Mrs Valerie Kingham?'

'Yes, Chief Inspector. How many more times?'

'Thank you, sir,' said Tench.

Half an hour later they sat in his office, he and McKenzie on one side of the desk, Meredith on the other.

'I realize, sir,' he said, 'that this has not been a pleasant experience for you.'

Meredith barely glanced at him. 'I'd say that was something of an understatement, Chief Inspector.'

Tench nodded. 'Nonetheless, sir,' he said, 'I hope you'll be willing to help us a little more . . . We need to find Mr Kingham.'

'That's stating the obvious. Get on with it, Chief Inspector.'

'We need a description.'

'Six foot two or three, heavily built, dark wiry hair, thick black moustache, swarthy complexion, with a two-inch scar above the left eye. Got it in a polo match, so I'm told. Evil-tempered, swills whisky by the bottle, easily provoked to violence. In a phrase, a drunken bully . . . How much more d'you want to know?'

'Where did he work?'

'He didn't, not since he got back here. He didn't need to work. His parents left him a packet. Enough to buy the house and a Rolls Silver Dawn, and have plenty left over. Val always said he was looking for a job, but he never seemed to me to be bothered about finding one.'

'What about India?' McKenzie said. 'He must have worked there.'

'Yes, he did. Something to do with jute, but I don't know what precisely. They lived in Calcutta.'

'Mrs Kingham's relatives.' Tench spoke again. 'They need to be informed. Where do her parents live?'

'They don't. They're both dead. Killed in a car crash on a mountain road. That was what she told me.'

'Had she any other relatives?'

Meredith gave a shrug. 'She never mentioned any.'

'Have you any idea where Mr Kingham might have gone?'

'No, not the faintest. I wish to God I had.'

'Had he any other car apart from the Rolls?'

'Not as far as I know, but a car like that should be easy enough to trace. There aren't that many Silver Dawns around.'

'That's true sir,' said Tench, 'but it isn't likely to help us. The Rolls is still parked outside the house at Breckton. Surely you must have seen it.'

Meredith seemed bewildered. He closed his eyes for a moment. 'Yes,' he said, 'of course I did. I must have forgotten. Thinking about Val must have blotted it out completely.'

'Only natural, sir. Just a memory lapse. We all get them from time to time.'

'I suppose so.' Meredith still seemed a trifle confused. He stared at Tench. 'But why would he make off and leave the car behind?'

'Panic?' said McKenzie. 'Murderers often do.'

Meredith shook his head. 'Not Reg Kingham. He's not the type to panic. He's more likely to have left it simply because he knew it'd be easy to trace.'

'Maybe.' Tench was thoughtful. 'A week ago today, sir,' he said, 'where were you exactly?'

Meredith stared at him again. 'What the devil's that got to do with Reg Kingham?'

'You said you should never have left Mrs Kingham alone at The Woodlands. You should have taken her with you . . . Taken her where, sir? . . . Where were you last Friday?'

4.

'I was in France. Does it matter?'

'When did you go, sir, and when did you come back?'

'I went a week last Wednesday, and I came back last night . . . I repeat, does it matter?'

'Yes, I'm afraid it does, sir.'

'Why?'

'It may help us to establish the time of Mrs Kingham's death. When did you last see or speak to her, Mr Meredith?'

'I spoke to her on the day before I left for France. I've had no contact with her since then.'

Tench frowned at him. 'Isn't that rather strange?'

'No. Why should it be?'

'You were very concerned about the lady's safety. Yet you spent eight days in France, and made no effort to find out whether she was safe?'

'I can see that it may seem strange to you, Chief Inspector, but I had my reasons.'

'Then share them with us,' McKenzie said.

Meredith looked at him sharply and then back at Tench. 'Tell me,' he said. 'Am I right about this?' He sounded incredulous. 'You surely don't think I had anything to do with Val's murder?'

'No, sir, we don't.' Tench spoke smoothly. 'We're simply trying to establish the facts, but to do that we need to know the whole of the truth. So bear with us, sir, if we seem to be probing a little too deeply.'

Meredith drew breath. 'All right,' he said. 'Go on.'

'Just how close was your relationship with Mrs Kingham?'

'We were friends.'

'And that's all?'

'Yes, that's all.'

'Then what were your reasons for not making contact while you were in France?'

'Kingham suspected we might be more than friends. Wrongly, of course, but if he knew I'd rung her up, he might well have turned violent.'

'So you arranged with her not to phone?'

'We had no option. There was no telling when he might be at home.'

'Did you ring her when you returned from France last night?'

'No, I didn't get back until midnight. She knew I was coming back, and said she'd ring me this morning.'

'And when she didn't?'

'I was worried, so I drove over to Breckton.'

Tench nodded. There was a pause. 'Why did you go to France, Mr Meredith?'

'I had business there.'

'Would you care to tell us what that business was?'

'I went to negotiate a contract with a Paris publisher. There's no secret about it.'

'And that took you eight days?'

'No, it took me two, but I had other business in France. I'm buying a cottage at a little place called Coursac down in the Dordogne. I went down there to finalize the arrangements . . . And, Chief Inspector, if you're so anxious to check on my movements, I'm quite prepared to offer you chapter and verse. I travelled by car, took the ferry to Calais, drove from there to Paris and then down by Châteauroux and Limoges to Périgueux. I stayed in hotels in Paris, Châteauroux and Périgueux. If you want to know the names and dates, I can give you those too. And if you need to pinpoint exactly where I was on the day that bastard killed her, just tell me when it was.'

'That's the trouble,' McKenzie said. 'We don't know when it was . . . You say the last time you spoke to her was a week last Tuesday?'

'Yes, in the evening. Kingham was out drinking, and she phoned me.'

'Then at the moment all we can tell you is this. She was alive on the Tuesday evening and dead by the time the storm broke on Saturday. And that brings us to another point. When you heard about the storm, why weren't you worried enough to try and get in touch with her? . . . Was it perhaps because you already knew she was dead?'

5.

Meredith pushed himself up and kicked back his chair. For a moment he stood there glaring at McKenzie, but when he spoke, it was to Tench. 'When I agreed to help you, Chief Inspector,' he said, 'I didn't expect to be viewed as a suspect. I strongly resent your sergeant's insinuations. I've told you where I was and what I was doing. If you're not prepared to accept my word, then I suggest you seek assistance from some other source.'

Tench raised a hand. 'Please sit down, sir,' he said. 'You have my assurance that you're under no suspicion, and we're grateful for your help.'

'So you should be.'

'Yes, indeed, sir' – Tench spread a little oil – 'but the fact still remains that Sergeant McKenzie's first question was a reasonable one. You say you were deeply worried about Mrs Kingham's safety, and I've no cause to disbelieve you. Yet that in itself poses a problem. I need hardly remind you that, while you were away, the worst storm in living memory struck the Norfolk coast. A hundred people were drowned, but you made no attempt to discover whether or not Mrs Kingham was safe. Sergeant McKenzie naturally finds that strange, and so, to be frank, do I. Can you tell us why you didn't?'

Meredith's lips tightened. 'I don't see why, as an innocent bystander, I should have to account to you for everything I did.'

'I understand that, sir, but before we take any action we need to clarify your position and that of Mrs Kingham.'

Meredith took another deep breath. He sat down. 'Very well, Chief Inspector,' he said, 'I'll give you an answer. It's a very simple one. When I travel abroad, I rarely buy a newspaper. The English ones available are already a day old and the news is stale. On the night the storm broke, I was driving down to the Dordogne. I knew nothing about what had happened here till I reached Périgueux, and even if I had I wouldn't have been unduly alarmed. The Woodlands is a couple of miles from the coast and stands on higher ground, and as I told you, I was reluctant to ring in case Kingham himself might pick up the phone . . . Have I made myself clear?'

Tench inclined his head. 'Perfectly, Mr Meredith.'

'I've clarified my position?'

'You have, sir. Thank you.'

'Then perhaps' – Meredith's tone was caustic – 'since, as I understand it, our good friend Mr Reginald Kingham has already been missing for something like a week, you can tell me what steps you propose to take, belatedly it seems, to track the bugger down.'

'Now that we know the facts, sir, you can rest assured that we'll find him.'

'You'd better, Chief Inspector, because if the murdering bastard crosses my path, he'll like as not be under the wheels of my car.'

'Leave him to us, sir. Go back to Blickling. We'll keep you

informed of any developments. It would be most inadvisable for you to take any precipitate action of your own.'

Meredith seemed to hesitate. 'There's nothing else?' he said.

'Not at the moment, sir, no.'

'Very well, Chief Inspector. But I want the man caught.'

'So do we all, sir . . . And he will be.'

Meredith got to his feet. 'I wish I were as confident as you, Chief Inspector. He's probably halfway across Europe by this time, or holed up in some fancy hotel in the tropics. He's got money, and he's a pretty cool customer when he's sober. Finding him may not be as easy as you think.'

6.

McKenzie watched the door close behind him. 'If you want a second opinion on that one,' he growled, 'I'll give you one now. I wouldn't trust him as far as I could spit a flint pebble.'

'You think he's lying?'

'No, but I think he's only telling us half the truth. I reckon there was more between him and his precious Val than he cares to make out.'

Tench gave a nod. 'I wouldn't argue with that. The question is, just how much?'

'My guess would be there's a hell of a lot. He never chose to mention she was way up the spout.'

'He may not have known. Three months, Ledward said. That's not very long. It's conceivable she may not have known herself.'

'Conceivable's the word. Answer me this. Whose was it?'

'That's another question.'

'It's a damned important question. Suppose it was his, and Kingham found out.'

'Why would he do that?'

'Why not? It could have happened. To use your word, it's conceivable, isn't it? He comes home late at night as drunk as a skunk, picks his usual quarrel, and in the heat of it all she loses control and spits out the truth. For a man like Kingham, that's more than enough to drive him clean off his rocker. He rages through the house, smashing everything in sight, and then, bang! He shoots her. She lies there, dead, on the floor of the hall, and whether he panics or not, he disappears somewhere into the night . . . No, he may not be lying, but I reckon our Mr Meredith's hiding a good deal more than he's chosen to tell us. He needs checking on, that one, and then double-checking. And so does our naval hero from Shotton Corner.'

'You'd have both of them on the suspect list?'

'For the time being, yes. And that makes me query another thing, too.'

'And what's that?'

'Whether that woman who's lying on a trolley in Ledward's lab *is* Valerie Kingham . . . Look, Mike. Two men have taken a look at her, Bridgeland and Meredith. Bridgeland said he didn't know her, and Meredith said he did, but as far as I'm concerned they're both of them suspects, and neither can claim to be a close relative. They could both be lying. If Bridgeland's mixed up in this case after all, then he wouldn't want to say that he knew her, would he? And as for Meredith, well, if he's something to hide, he'd want to see her dead and buried as soon as possible . . . We don't know much about him yet, do we? Has he got a wife? If he has, then that could cast a very different light on everything he's told us.'

'And what about Kingham?'

'He's still the prime suspect, isn't he? Has to be. All the evidence we have points towards him, and he's the one who's legged it. The other two haven't. So, if he's innocent, why has he legged it, and where's he legged it to? I'm not one for trusting Mr Meredith overmuch, but he's right about one thing. Finding the bastard's not going to be easy, and the longer we leave it the harder it's going to be. We need to put out a call, Mike, now. Never mind waiting for Lester and Merrick to match finger-prints. Get the Chief Constable to put out an express message. All forces in the country, all ports and airports.'

Tench seemed to ponder the point, then he nodded. 'You know, Mac,' he said, 'I've a feeling you may be right.' He pulled the phone towards him. 'Put me through to the Chief Super-intendent Hastings,' he said. 'It's urgent.'

IV

QUESTIONS OF TRUTH

What is truth? said jesting Pilate; and would not stay for an
answer.
Francis Bacon: *Of Truth*

1.

The call went out that evening at half past six, but it was close to midnight before Tench turned up the drive to his house at Cringleford, and McKenzie unlocked the door of his bachelor flat in the heart of the city.

A further couple of hours spent searching the house at Breckton, making contact with the local rector, with Sergeant Lester and with Constable Harris at Blakeney had provided Tench with most of the additional details he needed to brief his team early the following morning.

He faced them assembled in the CID room, rapped the table in front of him, and waited for the babble of voices to subside.

'As you already know,' he said, 'on Thursday morning a dinghy was found washed up against the wall of a cottage at Cley. It contained the body of a woman, shot through the head. We now have information that leads us to believe the victim was a young married woman named Valerie Kingham, who lived at The Woodlands, a large detached house in the village of Breckton. A search of the house has revealed traces of blood on the hall carpet and considerable devastation in a couple of the rooms. It has not, however, revealed any trace of the victim's husband, Reginald Kingham, though we've since been apprised of certain details about both him and his wife: details that we have, at the moment, to take on trust, and will require confirmation.

'What we've gathered so far is this. Mr and Mrs Kingham arrived in this country from India twelve months ago, and rented a lodge in the grounds of a house in Blickling, owned by Giles Meredith, a partner in the Norwick Press, a publishing firm with offices here in Norwich. Mr Kingham had had a job in the Calcutta area, apparently in the jute industry, and he and his wife rented the lodge at Blickling until they could find a more suitable place of their own. This they did three months ago, when they bought The Woodlands.

'It appears that the Kinghams were not short of money. They carried out extensive alterations to the house, but Kingham, so

69

we're told, was a violent drunkard who subjected his wife to physical abuse, so much so that from time to time she sought refuge with her neighbour and landlord, Mr Meredith.

'According to Dr Ledward, who performed the autopsy on Mrs Kingham's body, she died between eight and eleven days ago, and since then nothing has been seen or heard of Mr Kingham. Because of that, as you also no doubt know, the Chief Constable has put out a general call for information about him to all forces, ports and airports in the country.

'Sergeant Lester and the scene-of-crime squad have made a detailed examination of the house, and taken fingerprints which Ted Merrick, at the lab, will compare with those taken from the body of the woman. We're awaiting his report, and also one from him on the bullet found lodged in Mrs Kingham's brain, but it seems likely that the weapon used to kill her was one of low calibre, possibly a small pistol. This has yet to be found.'

He paused and looked around him. 'Now, to bring you up to date. The house has been under guard all night by two officers from Wells. They've already been replaced this morning by two from the city force, and they and their reliefs will be responsible for the security of the place until further notice. As far as we know, the Kinghams possessed only one car, a Rolls Royce Silver Dawn. This we found parked outside the house, and it has now been passed to Forensics, along with the dinghy, for closer inspection. Here again, we're still waiting for results.

'There's one further point which may well be significant. Once Sergeant Lester and his team had finished their work last night, Sergeant McKenzie and I went back to the house. In the course of our search we found Kingham's passport in one of the bedroom drawers, so he could still be somewhere within the country, if not in this immediate locality . . . Any questions so far?'

No hands were raised.

'Right,' he said. 'Now, as you'll realize, there's little we can do at this time except double-check the statements we've already received and gather more evidence, but that in itself is a considerable task, and one for which we shall need reinforcements. I've spoken to the Chief Super and he's agreed to provide whatever we need, so I'll outline the situation as it stands at the moment, and detail exactly what we have to do.'

2.

There was another short pause. Tench glanced at his notes.

'First of all,' he said, 'since Breckton is twenty-five miles from here, we're going to need an incident room close to the scene of crime. Apart from the church and The Woodlands itself, the only building of any size in the village is the church hall, but the rector has agreed to make it available for a limited period, and Constable Lock is already down there, making all the necessary preparations with the help of three uniformed officers from the city, who'll assist in the running of the place once it's fully established. A phone line will be laid, and those of you working in and around the village will operate from there and report any findings to Lock.

'Now the prime suspect in this case is, of course, the woman's missing husband, Reginald Kingham. We need to find him, and to do that we need to know more about him, and that means pursuing every scrap of information that may give us a clue to his present whereabouts. In the first place, it means making house-to-house inquiries in Breckton itself . . . George and Steve,' – he turned to Detective Constables Rayner and Spurgeon – 'that's your job. It may prove unproductive. The Kinghams appear to have kept themselves very much to themselves, and just how many of the villagers ever set eyes on them is difficult to say. Possibly few, if any, but we need to question everyone just to make sure. We know that Kingham drank heavily, but we're not yet certain just where he drank. There is a pub in Breckton, the Plume of Feathers, but he may have used a favourite watering hole outside the village, possibly in Blakeney. Wherever it was, he must have made himself known to the barmen and the regulars. We're particularly interested in his movements between Tuesday and Saturday of last week, and any casual remark he may have dropped that could give us a clue to where he is now.'

He paused again, and turned to Inspector Gregg. 'Andy,' he said, 'you've got a much more difficult job. I want to know everything about the Kinghams that it's possible to uncover. You'll have to start with the basic facts, and build on the little we so far know. Their passports, bank books, and a number of other documents we found in the house are in these three box files.

I want to know the firm Kingham worked for in India, what his job was, where he lived, how long he worked there, and why he left. I suggest you contact the banks concerned, the estate agents who sold him the house at Breckton, the firm of decorators from Norwich who worked on the place, and pubs in the Blickling area that he might have frequented while he lived there. I also want any details you can find about Mrs Kingham, particularly whether she has any living relatives. We've been told that her parents died in a road accident in India, but that needs checking . . . OK?'

'Right, sir.' Gregg nodded.

'Kingham, as I said, is the prime suspect,' – Tench glanced round his team again – 'but there are two other men that we can't entirely rule out at the moment. The first of these is the owner of the dinghy, a retired naval officer, Anthony Bridgeland, who lives at Two Gables House, Oakengate Road, Shotton Corner, near Heydon. The other is Giles Meredith, the Norwich publisher, who has a large house at Blickling by the name of Green Park, and who rented one of his lodges to the Kinghams. It isn't likely that either of them shot Mrs Kingham, but it isn't entirely impossible that they might have done, and we need to rule them out as suspects as soon as we can.

'Bob,' – this was Detective Constable Ellison – 'I want you to check on Bridgeland.' He held up a sheet of paper. 'This is a copy of the statement he made to Sergeant McKenzie. I'd like you to pay him a visit and go through it again with him. Make some suitable excuse, and check that he doesn't contradict himself. Right?'

'Right, sir,' said Ellison.

'And before you see him, it might be worthwhile driving down to Blakeney. There's an old boatman there called Isaac Jacks. According to rumour he knows every boat that puts out of there and Morston, and he certainly knows Bridgeland. He might be able to give you some useful information . . . Oh, and Bridgeland's got what he calls "a lady friend". Says he's marrying her next month. Try to find out who she is and where she lives . . . And a word of warning. He can be a prickly customer, so be prepared to tread carefully.'

There was a nod from Ellison.

'Good,' said Tench. He turned to Sue Gradwell, the only

72

feminine member of his team. 'Sue,' he said, 'I need you to check on some details that Meredith gave us. According to what he says, he was in France last week, and he's given us a list of the hotels he stayed at and the dates. This is the list.' He held up another sheet of paper. 'How's your French?'

'Schoolgirl, sir,' she said cheerfully.

'Not good enough to hold a conversation on the phone?'

'Hardly, sir, but I can always try.'

'Well, these places and dates need checking,' said Tench. 'We need to be sure that Meredith actually was where he claims to have been. But don't worry, you'll have some help. There's a handsome young officer serving with the city force, Constable Jules Winterton. His mother's French, and he spent a lot of his early childhood on a Brittany farm. He speaks the language fluently, and he'll make himself available just as soon as you need him. I gather he's got something of a roving eye when it comes to the opposite sex, so see that he keeps his mind on the job.'

'He'd better,' she said. 'If he tries anything on with me, he'll get an elbow where it hurts.'

A ripple of applause ran through the team. Tench waited, then raised a hand. 'A couple of things more,' he said. 'There'll be a team of twenty officers drawn from various parts of the county reporting any time now to Constable Lock at Breckton. They'll be searching the grounds of the house for the murder weapon . . . And last point – Sergeant McKenzie will be here in Norwich with me. We'll be taking any urgent calls until such time as the phone line to the incident room's set up . . . Now, are there any questions?'

He looked round the room. 'No? Then it's time to make a start. Let's see if we can get a valid line on this case before what's left of the trail disappears under a load of snow.'

3.

He waited till the team had dispersed, and then turned to McKenzie. 'Get down to the *EDP* offices, Mac,' he said, 'and have a word with Dave Ransome. I rang him last night and promised him a story, and he said he'd give us a spread in tomorrow morning's edition.'

Ransome was crime reporter for the *Eastern Daily Press*, and a man with whom Tench had had a working relationship for a number of years.

'Right.' McKenzie nodded. 'Just how much d'you want me to tell him?'

'Give him the bare bones, nothing more than that. There's no cause to mention Bridgeland or Meredith, and don't tell him about the pregnancy. I don't want that made public. We'll keep it up our sleeves. Say that at the moment we've no sound reason to connect the woman's death with the findings at The Woodlands, but we'd like to speak to Reginald Kingham, the dead woman's husband, as we think he may be able to help with our inquiries. Give Ransome a physical description of him, but say nothing about his drinking. Ask him to put out an appeal for information. Anyone who's seen Kingham or knows anything about his movements over the last ten days to contact us here. You know the kind of thing.'

'Well enough,' McKenzie said.

'And promise him he'll be the first to know of any future developments. We need to keep him running with us every inch of the way. He's a useful ally.'

He watched his sergeant drive out of the compound and disappear into the midst of the city traffic, then he pulled out a chair and began to read through Ledward's autopsy report for the second time that morning.

Couched in the doctor's medical phraseology, it made no concessions to the layman, and after the first few sentences Tench found himself, as usual, struggling to understand just what Ledward was saying, but after reading it a third time he felt that he'd grasped most of the vital points.

The body was that of a woman aged between twenty-eight and thirty-two. She was five foot four inches tall, and weighed 117 pounds. She had dark hair, blue eyes, a mole below her left breast and an appendectomy scar. She'd died from a gunshot wound some seven to ten days prior to the autopsy, the bullet entering through the middle of the forehead and lodging itself in the lower posterior part of the brain. It had been extracted and passed to Forensics for detailed examination. There were no burn marks around the entry wound.

There were no signs of sexual interference on the body, nor of any recent sexual activity, but the woman was approximately three months pregnant. The stomach contents revealed that she'd taken a meal of orange juice, white toast, marmalade and coffee some two hours before her death. Apart from the bullet wound, there were no signs of physical injury on the body, nor any that might indicate involvement in a struggle, and no blood, skin or fibres had been found beneath the fingernails.

The doctor, true to form, had not indulged in any guesswork about the circumstances of Valerie Kingham's death, but it seemed clear enough to Tench that, unless the woman's diet had been somewhat eccentric, she must have been killed roughly a couple of hours after breakfast, and without any warning. Whether the bullet had been high calibre fired from a distance or low calibre from closer range could only be determined once he received Merrick's report from the lab. Given the accuracy of the shot, the latter, he felt, was probably the more likely.

Apart from that, there was only one thing in the whole of the report that might yield a worthwhile clue to the killer's identity. Ledward had found some minute fibres adhering to the body, but, true to form again, he'd ventured no opinion as to what they might be, and had simply sent them to Forensics for further inspection.

Tench knew only too well that to ring him would elicit nothing but the usual response: that speculation wasn't a part of his job.

With a sigh that signalled his growing frustration, he dragged the phone towards him and asked to be connected to Merrick at the lab.

4.

If the doctor was reluctant to share his information – McKenzie always said that dealing with him was like wrestling with a clam – Ted Merrick, the young analyst in charge of day-to-day work at the lab, was his direct antithesis. He'd never been addicted to morning melancholia, nor was he inclined to regard his findings as classified material; and since he was, in addition, genuinely cheerful, the atmosphere around him was much more relaxed.

Tench heard his voice on the end of the line. 'Laboratory. Merrick speaking.'

'Ted,' he said, 'it's Mike Tench . . . This case of the woman found dead in the dinghy. Any news on the fibres Ledward found on the body?'

'Oh, I think we can tell you a little bit about them, sir, yes.' Merrick sounded even more cheerful than usual. 'Would you like to come down and take a look for yourself?'

'Give me ten minutes,' Tench said, 'and I'll be with you.'

Merrick had set up two microscopes side by side. He placed a slide under each, adjusted the focus and then stood back. 'Have a look, sir,' he said.

Tench peered into each in turn, and then repeated the process. 'They both look exactly the same to me, Ted,' he confessed, 'but then I'm no expert. Is there a difference?'

'No,' Merrick said. 'You're correct. They're identical.'

'I take it one of them's a sample of the fibres found on the body.'

Merrick nodded. 'Yes. That's the one on the left.'

'And the one on the right?'

'It's a shred of fibre I took from a case when I was training up in Edinburgh. A woman was stabbed. It was found beneath her fingernail.'

Tench peered at it again, and then frowned. 'What is it?'

'It's cotton. A fragment of a soft cotton yarn known as candle-wick. The woman in Edinburgh was stabbed in her bed. She dragged her nails across the bedspread . . . I knew I'd seen it somewhere before, so I went through my samples and fished out the slide. It's strange. The colour's exactly the same, too. A delicate shade of pink. It was probably made by the same firm . . . And there's something else for you to think about. When we examined the dinghy, we found the same fibres there. So what d'you make of that?'

'What do *you* make of it?'

Merrick scratched his head. 'You say the woman was naked when she was found?'

'Yes, she was.'

76

'D'you know where she was when she was shot? The precise location? Was it in the house?'

'Yes, but not in the bedroom. Downstairs in the hall.'

'Then if I had to make a guess, I'd say that whoever killed her stripped the bedspread from her bed, wrapped her inside it, took her down to the boat, and then pulled it roughly from underneath her, dragging it across the planking.'

'That fits.' Tench nodded. 'There was a lot of wanton damage in the bedroom, and as far as I remember, no bedspread on the bed.'

'Then that's what you're looking for,' Merrick said. 'One pink, tufted, candlewick bedspread.'

'And some kind of a car with candlewick fibres on a seat or in the boot.'

'Almost certainly, yes.'

'But there were none in the Rolls?'

'None that we could find.'

'Then what about fingerprints?'

'You mean hers? The dead woman's? Oh, yes, we found those.'

'In the car?'

'And all over the house. Mainly hers and what we took to be her husband's. There were some errant ones, too, but we're still in the process of sifting and listing. You'll get a complete rundown in my report.'

Tench took a deep breath. 'Well, thanks a lot, Ted. You've been a great help . . . Now what about the bullet? Any news on that? Has Alex taken a look at it yet?'

Alexander Carson was the ballistics expert at the lab, a man of long experience and considerable talent.

'Yes, he has.' Merrick removed the slides from the microscopes and locked them in a drawer. 'I was going to ring you about it. I think he's pretty sure what type of gun fired it, but he wants to have a word with you about it himself. Have you time to see him now?'

'Just as much as he needs,' said Tench.

Merrick reached for the phone. 'Then I'll call him in,' he said.

5.

Carson was a large, keen-eyed, slow-moving man, with hair that had long turned grey at the temples. He spoke as he moved, slowly and deliberately, as if a lifetime of dealing with precision mechanisms had impressed on him the need for precision of statement. 'This bullet of yours, Mike,' he said, holding it up in its plastic bag.

'Yes,' said Tench. 'What calibre is it?'

'It's a .25 automatic – pistol cartridge.'

'Can you tell the type of pistol that fired it?'

'Well enough, I think, to eliminate doubt.' He removed it from the bag, and turned it round and round between his finger and thumb. 'But before I say any more about it, let me put you in the picture. Immediately after the war I was working for a time in India, and I've seen this kind of bullet before. It's the same kind that was used to assassinate Mahatma Gandhi.'

Tench peered at it closely. 'Now that's interesting,' he said. 'The dead woman and her husband only came back from India twelve months ago.'

'Then the pistol probably came back with them,' said Carson. 'It's an Italian Beretta. 6.35 millimetre. There are thousands of them around out there. They're a legacy of the war.'

'A Beretta.'

'That's right. It's a vest-pocket pistol. The barrel's only two and a half inches long. It's an under-powered gun.'

'How much under-powered?'

'Considerably so.'

Tench frowned at the bullet. 'Can you give me some figures, Alex? How does it compare with other types of gun?'

Carson looked at him quizzically. 'Figures may not help, but I can always quote them.' He thought for a moment. 'The simplest way is to compare muzzle energy and muzzle velocity, so let me put it like this. The two most effective pistols for killing a man are both Smith and Wesson Magnums, the .44 and the .357. Now take the .357. It has a muzzle velocity of 1515 feet per second. The muzzle velocity of the small Beretta that fired your bullet doesn't amount to fifty per cent of that. It's only 750 feet per second. The muzzle energy of the Smith and Wesson's about

807 foot pounds. The Beretta's is only a fraction of that: 63 foot pounds. It's not what I'd describe as a killing weapon.'

'But it can kill, can't it? It killed the Mahatma.'

'Oh, yes, it can be a killer, if you hit the right spot at very close range. The man who killed Gandhi was close enough to touch him, just a couple of feet away. He fired three shots. One passed clean through the heart, and another embedded itself in a lung. And Gandhi, don't forget, was nearly eighty years old.'

'So if he'd been a younger man, and his assassin had fired from yards and not feet, he might well have survived?'

'Barring a lucky shot, yes, he very well might.'

Tench gave a nod. 'You've read Ledward's report?'

'Yes.'

'Then let's take a step further. In view of what he said about the lodgement of the bullet and its possible trajectory, can you estimate the range from which the shot was fired?'

'I can make a logical estimate,' Carson said. 'From the point of entry, the track of the bullet, its point of lodgement, the absence of burns or powder abrasions on the skin, and from what I've seen of it under a microscope, I'd say it was fired from more than arm's length, but not a great deal more. A couple of yards, maybe three . . . And talking of microscopes, is there another woman somewhere in this case?'

Tench stared at him. 'Not that I know of yet. Why?'

'Just a joke among gunsmiths,' Carson said. 'They call this Beretta a lady's gun, so if there is another woman, it might be a good idea to put *her* under one of your microscopes as well.'

6.

At the very same moment that Tench started up his car to drive back to police headquarters, Detective Constable Bob Ellison stepped out of his on to the quayside at Blakeney and, shivering in a breeze that was blowing straight across the marshes from somewhere in the Arctic, approached a short, weatherbeaten scrap of a man who'd been pointed out to him as Isaac Jacks.

'Mr Jacks?' he inquired politely.

'Mebbe.' The man looked him up and down with obvious

mistrust. 'Then agen, mebbe not . . . Depends like,' he added. 'Wha' d'ye want ter know fer?'

Ellison was, apart from Sue Gradwell, the youngest member of Tench's team, but he was sufficiently well versed in the foibles of Norfolk villagers to deflect the question. Instead of answering, he produced his card. 'Detective Constable Ellison,' he said.

'Oh aye?' Jacks peered at the card.

'I'm from Norwich.'

'Are ye now? Tha's a mite fur away.'

Ellison ignored the comment. 'You know a yacht called the *Spindrift*?'

'Could do. Depends.'

'It's owned by a man named Bridgeland. He says it was moored here in Blakeney before the storm. Is that true?'

Jacks gave a shrug. 'If he tells as it were, then mebbe it were.'

'Did you see it?'

There was a pause. 'Wha' d'ye want ter know fer?'

For all his natural courtesy, Ellison's patience was beginning to wear thin. 'Because, sir,' he said, 'we're investigating a murder, and we need to be absolutely sure of our facts. So did you see the *Spindrift* moored here before the storm?'

'Aye, she were moored.' Jacks gave the answer grudgingly. 'Wha's ter do wi' a murder?'

'We found the *Spindrift*'s dinghy washed up at Cley. There was a dead woman inside.'

Jacks raised a couple of shaggy grey eyebrows. 'Was there now?'

'Yes, there was, Mr Jacks.'

The boatman seemed to ponder the statement, then he sniffed. 'Nowt ter do wi' th'*Spindrift*.'

Ellison gave a sigh. 'It was the *Spindrift*'s dinghy, Mr Jacks.'

'I ent deaf, mister policeman, an' I ent shanny, not yet. I'm a-tellin' ye once an' I'm tellin' ye agen. It were nowt ter do wi' th'*Spindrift*.'

Ellison drew on every one of his reserves of patience. 'Let me explain, Mr Jacks.'

'Ent no bloody need.' Jacks was dismissive. 'I got lugs as can hear a kittywitch as fur off as Cley.'

Ellison bit his tongue. 'Please listen, Mr Jacks. I need to get things clear. Mr Bridgeland says the *Spindrift* was moored here at Blakeney, and you say you saw her. We've discovered her dinghy washed up against the wall of a cottage in Cley. How can you possibly say it's not connected to the *Spindrift*?'

'Cos that's what it were. Not connected,' said Jacks.

'What d'you mean, not connected?'

Jacks turned aside and spat on the quayside. 'Means as I tells it, don' it? Dinghy weren' connected ter th'*Spindrift*, were it?'

'I don't know,' said Ellison. '*You* tell *me*.'

'Well, it weren', were it? It weren' here at all.'

'Then where was it?'

'Reckon it were at Morston,' Jacks said blandly.

Ellison's patience at last ran out. 'Why the hell should it be at Morston?'

'Cos tha's where he allus lays it up wintertime. Foreshore at Morston.'

'So if Mr Bridgeland said that the yacht and the dinghy were both moored here at Blakeney, he wasn't telling the truth.'

'I ent sayin' that.' Jacks turned and spat again. 'But it weren' here, were it? I ent ruddy blind. So reckon ye'd best go an' ax him yerself.'

7.

If Ellison was frustrated, so was Sue Gradwell, but for a very different reason.

She was bored, and she resented being bored.

When she'd joined the CID some three years before, she'd envisaged herself as a kind of pioneer, bringing something to a totally masculine squad that had till then been lacking; solving the odd intractable case by a typical flash of woman's intuition; appraised as an asset in the fight against crime, and possessing a talent unique in itself that no one would possibly dare to misappropriate.

But it hadn't turned out like that. She'd spent most of her time proving her male associates' all too plausible thesis that the most mundane, petty and boring tasks were purposely designed to be done by women. She'd held the hands of bereaved wives and mothers, tended weeping sisters and calmed bewildered children. She'd returned victims' clothes to grieving relations, answered the phone in the CID room, typed out innumerable statements from suspects, and done little else but run errands for those who refused to bother themselves with the routine chores; and when, at last, more out of boredom than anything else, she'd decided it was time to use her own initiative, she'd been left battered and bound on an airfield runway, lucky to escape death at the hands of a man who'd revealed himself as a multiple killer.

For a few days, lying in a hospital bed, she'd been a heroine, if a misguided one; but, once back with the squad, nothing seemed to have changed. All the men she worked with, McKenzie, Gregg and Lock, Ellison, Rayner and Spurgeon, even the Chief himself, if not misogynistic, still clung to the belief that God had designed women to do this and men to do that, and this was always the most tedious, uninspiring and unproductive. And here she was again, three years on, still fobbed off with a boring assignment that could just as well have been done by a girl in a gymslip.

It wasn't that Constable Jules bloody Winterton wasn't handsome. He was. It wasn't that his roving eye was roving a little too much for comfort. It wasn't. It was simply the fact that, seated beside her, he was far too capable to need her at all. His French was fluent to the point of being colloquial, his knowledge of the country extended from Calais all the way down to Cannes, and he'd come prepared with a Michelin guide that listed, so it seemed, the telephone number of every hotel available to Meredith in Paris, Châteauroux and Périgueux. All she was required to do was to read out the name of the hotel and the dates of his stay, and then sit twiddling her thumbs while her capable colleague dialled a number, jabbered away in French, and then turned to her and said, 'Right. That one's checked. What's next on the list?'

Meredith had set out for France on the morning of Wednesday the 28th of January. He'd spent that night and the following two in Paris, and had then driven south. He'd stayed at Châteauroux on the night of Saturday the 31st, spent two nights in Périgueux, and then returned to Châteauroux on Tuesday the 3rd. On the

4th he'd once again been in Paris, driving home from there on Thursday the 5th.

For some peculiar reason best known to himself, Winterton chose to start in the south and work to the north. He rang the two hotels in Périgueux and Châteauroux, and checked with them the dates of Meredith's stay. Once he was through to them, it didn't take him long. 'Right,' he said. 'They're confirmed. Now where did he stay in Paris?'

Sue consulted the list. 'Some place called the Martinique on the Rue Vermet.'

Winterton ran his finger down a column in the Michelin guide, and then dialled a number. Getting through to the Martinique seemed to take a long time, and the subsequent dialogue even longer. She soon gave up trying to follow what was being said, and confined herself to scrawling doodles on the list, but at last, after what seemed an interminable conversation, he set down the phone. 'That's interesting,' he said.

Sue dragged herself back. 'What is?' she asked.

'Well . . .' Winterton scratched his head. 'He certainly stayed there coming back. It's the outward journey that's the problem. He booked in for three nights, the Wednesday, Thursday and Friday, but he only slept there for two. According to the manager, he left on the Friday morning, but insisted on paying for the night that he'd booked; and we know he didn't turn up at the hotel at Châteauroux until late on the Saturday. So where did he sleep on the Friday night?'

'That's Friday the 30th. The night before the storm.'

'Absolutely right.'

'Well, there's only one person can tell us,' Sue said, 'and that's Meredith himself.'

There was a nod from Winterton. 'Shall I give him a ring? What's his telephone number?'

But WDC Gradwell had already made up her mind. She was itching to do some real detecting for a change. 'No,' she said swiftly. 'It's important to see him. We need to watch his face. He's got an office here in Norwich, the Norwick Press. I think it's time we took a little drive round the city, and asked Mr Meredith just what he was doing for the rest of that Friday that he seems so anxious not to tell us about.'

8.

If Bob Ellison and Sue Gradwell, for all their frustrations, had reason to feel they were close to uncovering secrets that might be vital, George Rayner and Steve Spurgeon, trailing from house to house in Breckton, were finding no such consolation.

By mid-morning they'd knocked on every door in the village, and their efforts to learn more about Kingham and his wife had proved just as unproductive as Tench had warned them they probably would be.

The Woodlands, it was true, was hidden behind trees at the very end of Breckton, but in spite of the fact that the Kinghams had lived there for all of three months, the place might well have stood empty for all that the villagers had seen of the pair. The landlord of the Plume of Feathers had never set eyes on Kingham; the young couple who ran the post office and general store were adamant that Mrs Kingham had never set foot in the place; and though half a dozen people had nodded and said yes, they had seen them, it was only because they'd noticed the Rolls turning into the drive or turning out towards Holt, sometimes driven by a woman they took to be Mrs Kingham, or more often, faster and more erratically, by a man who could only have been Kingham himself.

There were, in consequence, only two conclusions that Rayner and Spurgeon could possibly draw: that if Mrs Kingham had shopped, as she surely must have done, she must have done so in Holt, or maybe even in Norwich; and that if Kingham had drunk heavily, as he obviously had, he must have downed his whiskies in some pub other than the Plume of Feathers.

'But where the hell do we look?' said Spurgeon. 'There must be a hundred pubs within ten miles of here.'

George Rayner, square-built, solid and eternally phlegmatic, thought for a moment. 'The Chief suggested Blakeney. Let's take a look there.'

They took a long look, but without success. They drove from there by way of Langham, Field Dalling and Saxlingham as far as Holt, and then back by Glandford. They drove as far along the coast in both directions till the still-flooded roads forced them back inland. They drove round in what seemed to be repetitive circles, stopping at every village pub they could find, without discovering a single barman who claimed any knowledge of a hard-drinking man over six feet tall, with a thick black moustache, a swarthy complexion and a two-inch-long scar above his left eye; and it was mid-afternoon and near closing time when, by mere serendipity, two miles from Breckton, on a narrow side road in the middle of nowhere, they stumbled across a shabby little pub called the Bottle and Glass.

Rayner wasn't impressed. 'No,' he said, 'I don't think so. It's not Kingham's scene.'

'We may as well give it a call,' said Spurgeon.

'I suppose so.' Rayner drew a deep breath. 'But it's the last,' he said flatly. 'After this, we pack it in. I've seen enough bottles and glasses for today.'

The bar was cramped and dingy with a solitary drinker still lingering over his last pint of ale, but the landlord, despite his apparent lack of trade, was cheerful enough.

A broad, ruddy-faced man with fists as big as hams, he placed both of them on the bar. 'An' what'll it be fer you two gen'le-men?' he asked.

Rayner produced his card. 'A large glass of help, to begin with, sir,' he said. 'We're trying to trace a man, and we believe he may well have been one of your customers. A swarthy chap, six foot odd, with a thick black moustache and a scar two inches long above his left eye. According to what we've been told, his tipple was whisky. Drank it by the pint. And he's not short of money. Drives a Rolls Silver Dawn . . . Does he ring any bells?'

The landlord seemed amused. 'Black moustache? Scar? Drinks whisky?' he said. 'Let's be askin' Jake . . . Hey, Jake!' he shouted to the man with the pint. 'Do we know a chap wi' a black moustache an' a scar as drinks whisky?'

The man lowered his glass. 'Oh, 'im,' he said. 'Aye.'

'There ye be, sir.' The landlord stood back and straightened up. 'Tha's as fair an answer as ye'll get this side of Lynn. If old Jake says aye, then he don' ring a bell, he rings a whole bloody peal.'

'Then you know him?' Rayner could hardly believe his luck.

'Oh, we knows him all right.'

'Causes trouble, does he?'

'Trouble?' The landlord seemed vastly entertained at the very suggestion. 'Lord no, sir, never a mite. If he caused any trouble he'd be out on his neck. Jus' sits an' drinks an' never says a word. Comes in every night. Orders a bottle o' Scotch, teks it ter tha' table ovver there i' th'corner, pours hisself a glass, an' does nothin' but drink. We calls him th'Black Monk, cos of his tash and arter they fellers as teks a vow o' silence. Drinks till it's closin', then ups an' goes an' never says so much as a wish-ye-bloody-well. An' if th'bottle ent finished, it goes away with him . . . Ent seen him though now, not since afore th'storm. Not drowndead, is he?'

'Not that we know of, sir,' said Spurgeon. 'Can you remember exactly when he was last in here?'

The landlord stroked his chin. 'Tha's a bit of a poser, that is, an' tha's a fact . . . Reckon as Jake'll know.' He turned and shouted again. 'Jake! What night were th'Monk last in?'

Jake pondered the question, and counted on his fingers. 'A week agone,' he said. 'Thursday.'

'Is he sure about that?' Rayner clearly had his doubts.

The landlord nodded. 'Wouldn' say 'less he were.'

'But it's more than a week ago. How *can* he be sure?'

The landlord tapped the side of his prominent nose. 'Domino night,' he said.

'Domino night?'

'Jake allus counts forrard from domino night. If he says it were Thursday, then it *were* bloody Thursday. He ent never wrong . . . Now are you two gen'lemen drinkin', or not?'

9.

Detective Inspector Andrew Gregg, instructed to find out all that he possibly could about the Kinghams, was also suffering the frustrations that seemed to be attending every member of Tench's team.

Tall, slim and recently promoted, Gregg was, at times, decep-tively casual. His initial approach to witnesses, and indeed to suspects, was always one of polite inquiry, and this, in some quarters, created the impression that he was most unlikely to be anything more than gentle, well-mannered and mildly ineffectual.

But those who inadvertently jumped to this conclusion were deceiving themselves. As they later discovered to their considerable cost, Gregg could, on occasion, be intimidating, caustic and utterly ruthless in pursuit of the evidence he was determined to acquire.

Having first established from the contents of the box files that Kingham had been employed in India by Mitchison and Blake, a trading company based in Calcutta, but with offices in London, he rang them, introduced himself, and said he was making inquiries about one of their ex-employees, a Reginald Kingham. 'Can you connect me with someone who'll be likely to help?' he asked.

There was a pause, then the girl on the company switchboard said doubtfully, 'I think I'd better put you through to Mr Dauncey.'

There was another long pause before a gruff voice said, 'Dauncey.'

Gregg went through the formalities again. 'I gather you may be able to help me, Mr Dauncey.'

'So I was told, Inspector. What is it you want to know?'

'I believe your firm is based in Calcutta.'

'Yes, that's correct.'

'And deals mainly in jute.'

'Yes, we have mills on the banks of the Hooghly.'

'I'm informed that you employed a Mr Reginald Kingham.'

'Yes. We did.'

'Can you tell me how long for?'

'If I remember correctly, it was roughly nine months.'

'Can you give me the precise dates of his employment, Mr Dauncey?'

The man seemed to hesitate. 'I can't recall the exact dates. Do you really need to have them?'

'They'd be much appreciated, sir.'

There was a sound of drawn breath on the end of the line. 'Hang on for a moment. I'll have to look them up in the files.'

There was another pause that seemed to Gregg to be excessively long. Then Dauncey spoke again. 'We employed Mr Kingham from the 10th of February 1951 till the 15th of November that same year.'

'Thank you, sir,' said Gregg. 'What was his job?'

'He was training as a clerk to be in charge of the office at one of our mills, the Empire Mill.'

'And where did he live at that time?'

'With other trainees. The company has a house called the Battery in one of the Calcutta suburbs.'

'I take it that he wasn't married at that time.'

'Not as far as I know.'

'How long does the period of training last?'

'Normally twelve months.'

'Then he never finished the course?'

'No, he didn't.'

'Why was that, sir?'

Dauncey cleared his throat. 'I'm afraid I'm not at liberty to divulge that information.'

This time it was Gregg who paused. 'I see,' he said. 'Would you care to tell me why?'

'The company has certain rules. I'm not in a position to be able to tell you more.'

Gregg was not to be deflected. 'Then who is?'

'No one here, I'm afraid. You'd have to speak to Calcutta.'

'Let me put you in the picture fully, Mr Dauncey.' Faced with such intractability, Gregg, on his part, could be just as intractable. 'We're conducting an inquiry into a case of murder. Mr Kingham is a suspect, and we're unable to trace his whereabouts. It's essential we learn everything possible about him.'

Dauncey was unmoved. 'Then all I can do, Inspector, is repeat what I said. Company rules preclude me from saying any more. I can only suggest you address any further inquiries to Calcutta.'

There was a click, and the phone went dead.

Gregg replaced the receiver, picked it up and rang again. 'Put me through to Mr Dauncey,' he said with all the curtness he could muster.

This time there was no pause. 'I'm sorry, sir, but Mr Dauncey is unavailable.'

'How very convenient!' Gregg replied.

He slammed the phone down.

10.

If Mike Tench had been aware of that morning's developments, he might well have wondered just where the case was leading. A woman was dead, shot at close range in the hall of her house by someone armed with a vest-pocket pistol. Her husband, a man who reputedly drank to excess and violently abused her, was missing, and all efforts to trace him had thus far failed.

Added to that, his two other suspects had apparently both been lying to the police, one about the whereabouts of the dinghy in which the dead woman had been found, and the other in respect to his travels in France. And, to top it all up, the husband now appeared to have left his job in India because of some seemingly sinister incident that his former employers, for some reason or other, refused to discuss.

That being so, it might well have appeared to Tench that the members of his team, far from solving his problems, had merely confronted him with a set of new questions. Why had Bridgeland deliberately implied that his boat had been moored at Blakeney, when he knew without doubt that it was laid up at Morston? Why had Meredith given a purposely deceptive account of his journey through France? Why had he left his Paris hotel early on the day before the storm? What had he been doing for the rest of the day, and where had he slept that night? And what had happened six thousand miles away in India that had cost Kingham his job, and made his firm so reluctant to say a word about it?

Perhaps it was as well that word of his team's frustrations never reached Tench that morning, because by the time he returned home to Cringleford late that night, the whole pattern of the case had changed, and what had seemed at first to be a purely domestic tragedy was turning into something very different indeed – an international conundrum.

V

THE TOWER

What in the midst lay but the Tower itself?
Robert Browning: 'Childe Roland to the Dark Tower Came'

1.

Bob Ellison was a young man of many varied interests, not the least of them place names, a subject in which he'd made himself something of an expert.

Approaching Shotton Corner, he braked the car to a halt and surveyed the flat landscape that lay all around him. The name Shotton, he knew, was derived from a couple of Old English words that signified a farmstead on a steep slope, and this presented a problem that appeared to have no immediate solution. There were certainly farmsteads – he could see three or four – but no sign of a slope, let alone a steep one. Furthermore, as he knew, anybody searching for a steep slope in Norfolk would be hard put to find one, save perhaps on the coastal ridge between Salthouse and Cromer; and the only alternative explanation of the name – that Shotton might be a corruption of two words meaning a Scottish village – was equally outrageous.

It was a problem he'd have to solve, but one for the future.

He shrugged and drove on.

If there was no steep slope, there was a farmhouse plainly visible with a three-storeyed porch, and beside it, on a concrete standing, a man with a close-clipped beard was seated at the wheel of a small open sports car that had seen better days. He was wearing a heavy topcoat, a muffler and a pair of goggles. As Ellison approached, the engine rattled into life, and the car began to move, though with some hesitation, towards the road.

He raised a hand. The car stopped. 'Mr Bridgeland?' he inquired.

The driver raised his goggles, and looked Ellison up and down with obvious disfavour. '*Commander* Bridgeland,' he said. 'And who the devil are you?'

Forewarned that he was dealing with a prickly customer, Ellison remained unperturbed. Nonetheless, he trod carefully. 'My apologies, Commander,' he said. 'Detective Constable Ellison, Norwich CID. I'm here at the request of Chief Inspector Tench.'

'You mean you're here on his instructions.' Bridgeland's words were a statement of fact, not a question.

'Yes, sir. That's correct.'

'Then be accurate, Constable. Superiors never make requests of subordinates. They issue instructions, give orders. Am I right?'

'Yes, sir.' Ellison nodded.

'Then pray tell me. Precisely why has Detective Chief Inspector Tench ordered you to come and see me?'

'It's the statement you made to Sergeant McKenzie, sir.'

'Is it? Tell me more . . . And be quick about it, Constable. I've an appointment to keep at Cawston.'

'We've received new information, sir, that seems to conflict with it.'

'Then tell Chief Inspector Tench from me that there's only one possible explanation. His new information's wrong.'

'It comes from a very reliable source, sir.'

'What source?'

'At the moment I'm not at liberty to say, sir.'

'Indeed?' Bridgeland glared. 'Then perhaps you'll be kind enough to tell me, Constable, just what this very reliable source has had to say that conflicts with my statement.'

'It's about the dinghy, sir.'

'*What* about the dinghy?'

'Our source maintains that it wasn't moored at Blakeney. It was laid up at Morston.'

'Then your source is right, isn't he?'

Ellison was baffled. 'Are you saying, sir, that the dinghy *was* laid up at Morston?'

'Of course it was. I laid it up there last October.'

'But in your statement you said it was moored at Blakeney Quay.'

'You're wrong, Constable. I didn't. I said the *Spindrift* was moored there.' Bridgeland lowered his goggles and revved up the engine. 'You're just wasting my time. There's no conflicting statement. Go back to the Chief Inspector and tell him so from me.'

'But . . .'

'No buts, Constable. The problem's solved. So go back and say so . . . Now step out of my way. I'm already late for my appointment.' He revved up again, the car jerked into motion and, reaching the tarmac, turned to the right and rattled away in a cloud of blue smoke on the Cawston road.

But the problem wasn't solved, and Ellison knew it. He wasn't any closer to finding an answer than he was to discovering just why there wasn't a steep hill at Shotton Corner, when the name of the place implied that there was.

For a moment he sat at the wheel of his car, deciding what to do. Then he too revved up and, moving forward smoothly and gathering speed, set off towards Cawston.

2.

His frustrations were not the only ones that persisted that morning. Events seemed to be following a similar pattern for Sue Gradwell and Winterton.

Not that Sue felt unduly frustrated. The facts, first that Giles Meredith was not in his office at the Norwick Press, second that his secretary didn't expect to see him for the rest of the day, and third that she had no idea just where he might be, all failed to deflect her from the purpose she'd chosen – to track down Mr Meredith and demand an explanation of what he was doing on the day before the storm.

'He must be at home,' she said.

'And where's that?' Constable Winterton had had sufficient experience of the opposite sex to be more than a little wary of their misdirected enthusiasms.

'Blickling.'

'That's fifteen miles away.'

'So what?' she said. 'Come on, Jules. We've a job to do. Take the Aylsham road. It's a large house, Green Park. Stands in its own grounds somewhere close to the Hall. There's a gated drive with a lodge. Should be easy to find.'

It wasn't.

The drive had no gates, and the lodge, set back from the road, was partly concealed by a cluster of cedars, but after driving past it twice they eventually found it.

The drive itself wound for several hundred yards between clumps of rhododendrons till it opened out on to a broad stretch of parkland and a large, red-brick, neo-Tudor house, three bays in width and three storeys high, crowned by two rows of polygonal chimneys.

Winterton braked the car to a halt and stared. 'Publishing?' he said. 'What does he publish? Erotic magazines?'

'Maps and guidebooks, I think. And anything with a local flavour.'

'And something a hell of a lot more profitable. He must do. You don't build a place like that out of maps and guidebooks. There couldn't have been much demand for them during the war.'

'What does it matter?' Sue wasn't to be deflected by Constable bloody Winterton any more than she had been by Meredith's secretary. 'We're concerned with his travels, not with his money. Just drive on, and let's do what we came to do.'

Three pristine white steps led up to the front door. The knocker was iron and shaped like a Tudor rose. She raised it and rapped three times.

There was no response. She rapped again and waited. There was still no sound from inside.

'There's no one in,' said Winterton. 'We're just wasting our time.'

'No, we're not.' Sue was adamant. 'Listen,' she said.

There was a faint sound of footsteps, then the door was opened, not without some caution, by a woman, a faded blonde. She wore a dressing gown, slippers and a look of weary, almost desperate, resignation. 'Yes?' she said. 'What do you want?'

Sue showed her card. 'I'm WDC Gradwell and this is Constable Winterton. We're here to see Mr Meredith. Mr Giles Meredith.'

'Why?' the woman asked.

'We need to speak to him, ma'am. It's a personal matter.'

'Then you'll have to come back tomorrow. He's in London till tonight.' She peered at them suspiciously. 'Why do you want to speak to him?'

'It's routine, ma'am. We have to.' Sue was quite prepared to tell a whole string of lies to get what she wanted. 'We think he may have witnessed an accident in Norwich.'

The woman took a deep breath and closed her eyes. 'When was this?'

'A week yesterday, ma'am. Friday.'

'No.' Another deep breath. 'That's quite impossible.'

After travelling fifteen miles, Sue was in no frame of mind to accept such a blank denial without probing further. 'Is it, ma'am?' she said. 'Can you possibly tell me why?'

'He was in Dublin all that week.'

'Are you sure about that, ma'am?'

The woman showed a sudden, savage flash of anger. 'I'm his wife,' she said. 'I have to be . . . Oh, for God's sake go away! Just leave me alone!'

The door slammed shut, and they heard the sound of a bolt being drawn.

Sue stared at the knocker, then she turned towards Winterton. 'Now that,' she said, 'is interesting. Wouldn't you say so, Jules?'

'Well, I suppose it could be.' Winterton gave a shrug. Miss Gradwell, he'd decided, was dangerous, devious and plainly dictatorial. The last thing she needed was encouragement from him. 'It doesn't get us much further though, does it?' he said.

3.

It didn't. All it did was to pose new questions that had no answers, and if it was the full intention of Detective Chief Inspector Michael Bruce Tench to provide some answers himself that morning, fate decreed otherwise. With every step he took, new sets of questions seemed to raise their ugly heads.

Returning from the lab, he found McKenzie waiting. 'There's a Joe Smith here to see you,' he said by way of greeting.

'And who's Joe Smith?'

'He's a painter and decorator. Has a place here in Norwich on the Aylsham road. He's the chap employed by Kingham to do up the house at Breckton.'

'Is he?' said Tench. 'Now that's a turn-up for the book. What's brought him here?'

'Lester's sent him here from Breckton. Apparently Kingham hasn't settled his bill.'

'That's not surprising . . . You've spoken to him?'

'Briefly, but I think you'd better hear what he has to say.'

'Where is he?'

'He's down in the canteen. I've given him a cup of their dirty dishwater – the stuff they call coffee.'

'Right,' said Tench. 'If he isn't dead, bring him up. I'm ready to listen to anyone who can shed some light on Mr Reginald Kingham.'

Joe Smith from the Aylsham road was a short, stocky, bald-headed man with a pendulous paunch that spoke more of an addiction to strong Norfolk ale than to canteen coffee.

'Sit down, Mr Smith,' said Tench. 'I believe you've something to tell me.'

'Aye, tha's right.' Smith lowered himself precariously on to the chair by Tench's desk. 'Tha' bugger Kingham ent paid fer what were done.'

'So Sergeant McKenzie tells me.'

'Owes nigh on sixty quid he does, an' he ent bloody paid.'

Tench was soothingly sympathetic. 'That's bad, Mr Smith.'

'It's moren' bloody bad. It's bloody well criminal.'

'Yes, it could well be.' The Chief Inspector nodded. 'What work did Mr Kingham ask you to do?'

Smith shifted himself into a more comfortable position. 'Well, it were this way like,' he said. 'He come ter me reckon it were four month aback an' said he were buyin' this ol' place at Breckton, an' there were three or four rooms as he wanted doin' over. Would I go down with him an' quote him a price?'

'And you did?'

'Aye, too bloody true I did, an' I soon wished I'd never set eyes on th'place.'

'Why was that, Mr Smith?'

'It were him an' his wife an' that bloody hall o' theirs. He says as he wants it paperin' gold, so I papers it gold an' th'stairway as well. Then along comes Mrs K. She takes one look at it an' says oh no, that'll never do, so I strips it all off an' paints it all cream just as she says, an' when he comes home an' sees it there's such a flamin' row atween 'em as never bloody was. He picks up a can o' paint an' chucks it straight at her. Gold, he says, gold. That's what I want an' that's what it's gonna be. Then he turns to me an' tells me ter do it all agen, an' when I says as that'll be double th'charge, he says never mind th'charge. It'll be paid, he says, an' paid on th'nail.'

'So you did it again?'

'Aye, that an' a lot more, an' he ent never paid.'

'And that's why you went down to Breckton this morning.'

'Aye.' The painter took a breath deep enough to shrink his paunch by a good three inches. 'Rang him every day this week an' there were no bloody answer. So I says to meself, Joe, I says, ye'd best get down there sharpish, else you ent gonna see no bloody sixty quid. An' when I gets there, there's this tape run' th'place as says CRIME SCENE, an' when I axes wha' crime, th'bloke in charge tells me I'd best get back ter Norwich an' see Inspector Tench. So what I want ter know is where's bloody Kingham an' where's my sixty quid?'

'I'm afraid Mr Kingham's missing, sir,' Tench said smoothly.

'Jus' my bloody luck!' The painter seemed more aggrieved than anything else. 'Done her in, has he, an' bunked off somewhere?'

'You mean you wouldn't be surprised if he had?'

'Well . . .' The man gave a shrug.

'Well what, Mr Smith?'

'It were plain as a bloody pritch as he'd do her in, weren' it?'

'Was it?'

'Oh, aye. He were twice her size, weren' he? An' when he'd downed a couple, she were like a red rag ter one o' they Spanish bulls, an' a filthy-tempered one an' all. They were allus at it, him an' her, hammer an' tongs, like the sight of each other were bound ter make 'em spit. It were allus on th'cards as he'd do for her one day.'

Tench was thoughtful. 'When were you last at The Woodlands, Mr Smith?'

The painter pondered the question. 'That'd be las' Friday. A week agone yesterday.'

'Are you sure about that?'

'Aye, sure as a mortal can be. Nex' day were Saturday. It blowed a bloody gale, an' then there were th'floods. I ent bin there since.'

'Why *were* you there?'

'Took Kingham another bill, didn' I? Final demand it were, all writ in red ink, an' he still ent bloody paid.'

'You saw Mr Kingham?'

'Nah.' Smith was scathing. 'Not even a bloody sniff. Rattled th'knocker, didn' I? Made enough row ter scare a bloody kitty-witch down at Blakeney Quay, but there weren' no reply. Tried the door an' all, but it were bloody well locked. On'y thing ter do were ter drop it in th'letter box an' mek off back ter Norwich.'

'What time was this?'

Smith gave a shrug. 'Mid-arternoon. Three mebbe. There-abouts like . . . Mind you,' he added, 'come ter think on it, it weren' on'y me as didn' get a sniff. There were this woman there too.'

'A woman?' Tench was quick to seize on the word.

'Aye, muffled up she were. Black coat, woolly scarf an' mit-tens, an' a red woolly hat wi' a bobble on top.'

'What was she doing?'

'Leavin'. Tha's what she were doin'. Just as I gets there, she comes a-runnin' round from th'back o' th'house. Then she sees me an' stops. "There's nobody in," she says, an' carries on past me. There's a little grey Morris that's parked on th'gravel next ter Kingham's Rolls, an' she gets in, starts it up an' off she goes down th'drive. Never says another word.'

'Did you get the car number?'

'Never give it a thought. Weren' no reason, were there? Reck-oned as she were jus' some friend o' the Kinghams.'

'And it wasn't Mrs Kingham?'

'Course it bloody weren'.' Smith was scathing again. 'Never seen her afore. God knows who she were.'

4.

'So who the devil was she?' McKenzie said, once they were alone.

'It's the old story, Mac.' Tench gave a shrug. 'Your guess is as good as mine. Could have been a friend of Mrs Kingham from Blickling. Could have been the rector's wife planning to intro-duce herself. Could even have been the jealous lover I suggested, walking coolly away after shooting her rival as she opened the door. Could have been anyone. We just don't know, Mac. But if it's nothing more than a coincidence, it's strange.'

'Coincidence?' McKenzie frowned.

'Yes. I've been down to the lab and seen Alex Carson. He says the shot that did the damage was fired from a small Beretta, a vest-pocket pistol. According to him, because it's low-powered, it's known to gunsmiths as a lady's gun. "So if there's another woman involved," he said, "it might be worthwhile to take a closer look at her."'

'And now, it seems, there is.'

'There might be,' said Tench. 'She may have been just a casual caller, not involved at all.' He paused. 'But there's another thing, too. The woman in the boat must have been Mrs Kingham. Forensics matched her fingerprints with those that Lester found all over the house and in the Rolls.'

'Then whether she was a casual caller or not, we need to know who she was . . . D'you want me to get in touch with Ransome again?'

'Yes, you'd better. Get him to add a couple of lines to his report. Ask her to come forward, whoever she is. Say we need to eliminate her from our inquiries. The usual stuff.'

McKenzie nodded. 'Right. But let's think a bit further. If she was your jealous lover, then she must have some connection with our friend Mr Meredith. His wife maybe? His girlfriend? The top and bottom of it is that we know next to nothing about the man.'

'You still rate him as a suspect?'

'I rate him as a chap who's still hiding a good deal more than he's telling. It wouldn't surprise me if part of the time he says he was in France he wasn't there at all.'

'Well, we'll know soon enough. Sue Gradwell and Winterton are doing a check on his list of hotels.'

'And of course they'll find that all the dates tally, but that's no kind of proof. If he's stayed at them before it's a pretty fair bet he's made a few contacts. I wouldn't put it past him to have done a deal with someone to provide a bit of cover.'

'Paid someone to say he was there when he wasn't? That's stretching a point, Mac.'

'Not to me it isn't. Not until I know just what he's been hiding.'

'He may not be hiding anything.'

'Oh, he's hiding something, Mike, that's for sure. I've questioned enough witnesses over the years to know when one of them isn't coming clean, and our friend Mr Meredith's got dirt all over the tip of his tongue. We need to get him back and give him a good grilling before we start assuming things that aren't true.'

Tench sat back and looked at him quizzically. 'All right, Mac,' he said, 'you go and fetch him. He'll be in his office at the Norwick Press. If he isn't, they'll be able to tell you where to find him. Ask him very politely if he'll favour us with a word. Leave Ransome to me. I'll give him a ring.'

'Fine,' McKenzie said. 'For once that's a job that's right up my street. I'll have him back here inside a quarter of an hour, but whether I'll be polite depends on Mr Meredith. If he doesn't choose to come at the first time of asking, he'll be up on the carpet for obstructing the police.'

5.

His predictions were hardly accurate. The journey to and from the Norwick Press took him twenty-five minutes, and before he returned Tench found himself besieged by yet another visitor.

He'd barely set down the phone after speaking to Ransome when he heard a heavy tread sounding on the stairs, the door was pushed open, and Lubbock stumped in. Drawing hard on his pipe and sweeping aside a couple of files, he laid his cherry wood stick on the desk and pulled up a chair. 'If the mountain won't come to Mahomet,' he said, 'then Mahomet has to struggle all the way to the mountain.'

Tench wafted away the smoke. 'The mountain's been far too busy.'

'Glad to hear it, laddie.' His old Chief dropped weightily on to the chair. 'So has Mahomet.'

'The cottage?'

'The cottage.'

'Have you managed to salvage anything?'

'Downstairs, no. It's all gone for a burton. Furniture, books, papers, absolutely everything. They're all dumped in a pile on the stretch of mud that I once called my garden. The water was six feet deep. The place stinks like a sewer. It'll have to be scoured and disinfected from top to bottom, then repainted and papered. It looks like being a hell of a long job.' He sighed . . . 'However,' he said cheerfully, 'I decided to take a morning off from my toils to track down an elusive Detective Chief Inspector. You say you've been busy, and that's a good sign. So tell me, laddie, how's this case of ours going? Do as I've done. Take a few minutes off, and brief me up to date.'

'What exactly d'you want to know?'

'Everything,' said Lubbock. 'Start at the beginning, tell me every detail, leave nothing out, and when you get to the end and I know what's what, then we can really begin to talk.'

They were still deep in conversation when McKenzie burst in.

Tench looked up. 'Well?' he said. 'Where is he?'

'He's not in his office, and the girl who types his letters doesn't know where he is. Nobody there seems to know where he is . . . He's probably legged it like Kingham to some foreign clime. And that's not all.'

'Go on,' said Tench. 'Amaze me.'

'The girl said someone else has been in this morning, inquiring about him. A policewoman in plain clothes and a constable in uniform, so it looks as if Sue Gradwell knows something we don't.'

Lubbock laid down his pipe. 'Who's this that's legged it?'

'Giles Meredith,' said Tench, 'but I'm pretty sure he hasn't.'

'You were bringing him in?'

'Yes, we were,' McKenzie said.

'What for?'

'Because we think he's hiding a good deal more than he's telling.'

'Mac does,' said Tench.

Lubbock picked up his pipe, applied a match to it, and blew out a billowing cloud of smoke. 'Waste of time,' he declared. 'Remind me. You're trying to find the chap who murdered Valerie Kingham?'

'That's the general idea,' Tench told him drily, 'though there is the possibility that it might have been a woman.'

'Woman fiddlesticks!' His old Chief dismissed the suggestion. 'And the same goes for Meredith. Believe me, laddie, you're just wasting precious time. There's only one suspect worth a second thought.'

'And who might that be?' Tench breathed heavily.

'Well, it's blindingly obvious. Kingham of course. The dead woman's husband. All the evidence points to him.'

'*All* of it?'

'All that matters,' said Lubbock. 'He's a violent drunkard, isn't he? He's attacked her before. He's done a vanishing trick. And she was shot with a Beretta. Isn't that enough?'

Tench frowned at him. 'What's the Beretta got to do with it?'

'Oh, come on, laddie.' Lubbock's face took on a pained expression. 'Do I have to spell it out? Kingham's just come back from India, hasn't he? That was what you told me. And Carson said there were thousands of Berettas floating around there. He must have brought it back with him. Why would Meredith have such a gun? How would any woman here get hold of such a gun? It's plain as a pikestaff. If Valerie Kingham was shot with a Beretta, then there's only one person in the frame for the killing. Kingham himself. It's nothing more than a domestic murder, laddie. A family affair.'

As if in confirmation, the phone on Tench's desk began to ring insistently. He snatched up the receiver. 'Tench,' he said, then 'Yes, put him through.'

He listened. 'Right,' he said. 'Where are you? . . . We'll be with you just as soon as we possibly can.'

He dropped the phone back on its hook. 'That was Randall,' he said, 'from Holt. They've found another body. He says, from our description, he thinks it could well be Kingham's.'

6.

McKenzie broke the silence. 'Where did they find it?'

'At the foot of a tower. Randall called it Prospect Tower. He says it's about four miles west of Holt on the Melton road.'

Lubbock nodded. 'He's right, but it was never built as a prospect tower, though the Home Guard did use it as an observation post during the war. It was originally a windmill, an eighteenth-century smock mill, then the mill was demolished apart from the base, and storeys were added to turn it into a residence. It's been derelict now for years. I know where it is, because I took a good look at it when I was listing all the Norfolk windmills . . . You say they found the body directly below it?'

'That's what Randall implied,' said Tench.

'Then if it does turn out to be Kingham's, it looks to me to be very much like suicide. The whole structure must be fifty feet high. The stairways are rotten, but if you take care you can get to the top.' He nodded. 'I think you'll find I'm right, laddie. It's nothing more than a purely domestic murder. The man shot his wife and then threw himself from the top of the tower. This time tomorrow you'll find you can close the case. Tie up the files in pretty red ribbon and send them down to Archives. There'll be no need to worry about Meredith any more.'

Tench, if not dismissive, was at least brusque. 'Well, we've not reached that stage yet,' he said, 'and we're not likely to if we sit here talking all day. Come on. Let's go. Mac, you drive.'

Lubbock pushed back his chair. 'Just follow me,' he said. 'I'll take you straight there.'

McKenzie wasn't happy. 'If you think I'm trailing that old three-wheeled banger for twenty-five miles, you can think again,' he said.

'If you're coming,' – Tench wasn't for wasting time – 'you can travel with us.'

'Of course I'm coming.' Lubbock was indignant. 'This is my case as much as yours. Didn't I find the first body? In my own garden?' He swept up his pipe. 'Come on. We can't afford to be standing around. You've frittered away far too much time already, chasing suspects that aren't really suspects at all.'

7.

The tower, a weathered red-brick structure, was set in a grove of oak trees and approached by a narrow lane leading off the main road. It had, as Lubbock said, clearly been derelict for a number of years, and had about it the shabby, uncared-for aspect that attends all buildings abandoned to the elements and left to slowly crumble away.

Jack Randall, a detective inspector of some experience, sturdy, square-jawed, his hair already turning grey at the temples, met them as McKenzie pulled the car to a halt. He bent down towards Tench and pointed. 'He's round the other side, sir,' he said. 'We haven't touched anything, but it's difficult to see what sort of a state he's in.'

That was true enough. The body was almost entirely covered by drifted brown leaves and part of the severed branch of an ancient oak tree felled by the storm, but enough of the face was visible for Tench, bending down, to see the heavy black moustache and a jagged white scar above the left eye.

'Well, it certainly looks like the man we're after,' he said, turning back to Randall. 'Who found him?'

'Chap called Wainright, sir. Ernest Wainright. Lives at North Walsham. Seemed genuine enough. He's a member of some society for the preservation of Norfolk's windmills. He's writing a book about them, and came here today to photograph the tower. Said it was originally built as a corn mill. We asked him a few questions and took a statement from him, but there didn't seem to be anything vital he could tell us.'

'There wouldn't be,' said Lubbock. 'Forget him. I know him. He's what he claims to be. Knows more about windmills than any man in Norfolk . . . And in any case why bother? It's suicide. He jumped. That's fairly obvious.'

'Maybe it is.' Tench turned again to Randall. 'What do *you* think happened?'

'Difficult to say, sir.' The inspector stroked his chin. 'One thing's for sure though. He wasn't killed by that bit of branch. It isn't heavy enough to do a baby much damage . . . If I had to make a guess, I'd say he was dead before that oak tree came down, but just how he died, that's another matter. Could be suicide, I suppose. He could have jumped from the top. All I can say is this, sir. If it wasn't suicide, it's a strange place to find a body. No one comes here nowadays, apart from the odd tramp seeking shelter for the night.' He paused for a moment. 'On the other hand,' he said, 'the place has been empty since the Home

Guard moved out at the end of the war, and we've never had a suicide here before, so maybe it's best to wait for the doctor to give his verdict . . . D'you want my men to shift the branch and clear away the leaves?'

'Thanks for the offer, Jack, but no,' Tench said swiftly. 'I think that's a job best left to the scene-of-crime squad. They wouldn't thank us for trampling any clues underfoot.' He turned to McKenzie. 'Mac,' he said, 'there's a phone box about a mile back at the crossroads. Get on to Lock. I want Lester and his team here in double quick time. And Ledward as well. Not that he'll thank us either. We'll probably get an abrasive lecture on the soaring rate of murder all over Norfolk.'

8.

His prediction was right, though the doctor's opening remarks were ambivalent to say the least.

By the time he arrived, Lester's men had cut away the trailing branch and swept the leaves from the body. Clothed in a black roll-necked sweater and grey flannel trousers, it lay in a peculiarly crumpled position on the bare patch of ground that had once been a path round the base of the tower.

Ledward set down his bag, removed his topcoat and gloves and handed them to Tench. 'How kind of you, Chief Inspector,' he said, 'to call me out on a Saturday afternoon instead of your usual Sunday. Is it possible, d'you think, that I might enjoy for once an undisturbed Sabbath?'

'I hope so, sir,' said Tench.

'I hope so too, but I fear it may prove otherwise. Considering the rate at which the incidence of murder in the county has increased in the past few years, my chances of passing a restful Sunday appear to be most unpromising. One killing nowadays seems to be followed in swift succession by a whole string of others, and I find myself forced to the sorry conclusion that somewhere along the line there's been a staggering decline in police efficiency. Wouldn't you say so, Chief Inspector?'

Tench drew a deep breath. 'Unfortunately, Doctor, murderers often fail to keep us informed about their intentions. The result is that you and I are left to pick up the pieces . . . Now can we please proceed? We need to know as soon as possible just what you can tell us.'

Not that there was much. Ledward, true to form, was as cautious as ever.

After a lapse of some twenty minutes, he straightened up and began to repack his bag. 'I suppose,' he said, 'you want to know the time of death.'

'It would be helpful, Doctor.' Tench was equally cautious.

'He's been dead at least a week, possibly more. That's as far as I'm prepared to go.'

'Then he died before the storm?'

'Taking the current temperatures into account, Chief Inspector, that would appear to be so.' The doctor bent down again and peered at the body. 'It's a wonder his eyes survived. The birds go for them first . . . You say there was a branch partly covering his face? Then that probably saved them.'

'And the cause of death?'

'At this stage, Chief Inspector, quite impossible to say. You really should know better than to ask such a question.'

'I'm always hoping that one day you'll confound me, Doctor.'

'Well, it won't be today.' Ledward pulled a pad of official forms from his bag, glanced at his watch, wrote something down, tore off the top sheet and handed it to Tench. 'Death was confirmed,' he said, 'at 3.58 p.m. . . . Get him down to the lab, but don't expect any results before Monday midday.'

'We need them before that, Doctor.' Tench, on this occasion, was determined to have his way. 'Until we know the cause of death our investigations are stalled. This may still be a case of murder. We can't afford the delay.'

'Then you'll have to make do with Vincent.' The doctor picked up his bag. 'I'm attending a dinner in Ipswich tonight.'

Tench frowned. 'Who's this Vincent?'

'Nick Vincent, my new assistant. It's just the sort of case to test his abilities. He'll enjoy doing it. If you're prepared to stay up late, I can guarantee you'll have a result before midnight.'

'Is he capable?'

'He's young, enthusiastic, and his qualifications are excellent.'

Tench nodded curtly. 'Then tell him I'll be waiting in my office,' he said.

9.

'There's a limit to what we can do here tonight, sir,' said Lester. 'Another hour and a half and the light'll be failing, and I wouldn't want to work by artificial light. We might well miss something really important.'

'Don't worry,' said Tench. 'Do what you can and leave the rest till morning. Just see that this area round the tower's taped off. I'll get Randall to send two men down from Holt to stand guard all night. Tell them that no one's to go up the tower till you get here tomorrow. I want the photographers and printmen to do their jobs first. If he fell from the top there may be evidence up there, and we need it recorded. And be careful. According to Mr Lubbock the stairways are rotten, and we don't want any casualties.'

'Right, sir.' Lester nodded. 'Looks like we've got a visitor.'

Tench turned to see Randall striding towards him round the base of the tower with one of his detective constables. Between them, being continually prodded in the back, was an individual of distinctly scruffy appearance, whose progression was more of a shamble than a walk. He wore an old army greatcoat minus its buttons, a battered bowler hat, a red woollen muffler flecked with the stains of long-forgotten food, and a pair of mud-spattered trousers tied up with string. Slung across his shoulder was a discarded army pack. And from it protruded the neck of a bottle. Even in the open air he was preceded by the twin fumes of whisky and sweat that hung around him like some miasmal vapour.

Tench gave him one glance that compounded both recognition and disgust. 'Not you again, Zack,' he said.

The man seemed unaware of his poisonous odour. He touched a dirty forelock. 'Art'noon, Mr Tench,' he said cheerfully enough. 'You keepin' well?' Then, catching sight of Lubbock and McKenzie who'd been deep in conversation, he greeted each of them in the same familiar manner, as if they were long-lost friends.

They were hardly that, though he knew them well enough and they knew him far too well for their comfort. Zaccheus Case was a tramp, though he was prone to reject that term with a good deal of hauteur. He was, he always insisted, a gentleman of the road.

Gentleman or not, he'd been prosecuted on innumerable occasions for vagrancy, theft and being drunk and incapable. In the course of a career that already spanned a good forty years, he'd appeared in most of the charge rooms in Norfolk and spent time in most of the county's cells, and while his claim to know every serving officer by name could only be classed as a brash exaggeration, he was certainly known to an overwhelming majority by scent as well as sight.

He was certainly known by both to Detective Chief Inspector Michael Bruce Tench. 'Stay where you are,' he said, backing off a pace. 'Don't come any closer.'

'Found him nosing around, sir,' said Randall. 'Claims he was looking for somewhere to sleep.'

Zack nodded with such force that his bowler fell off. 'An' tha's God's hones' truth, Mr Tench,' he declared.

The Chief Inspector eyed him up and down with visible distaste. 'Is it?' he asked.

'Oh, come on, Mr Tench.' Zack sounded for all the world to be mightily aggrieved. 'You know me . . . Would a be tellin' ye lies?'

'Very probably,' said Tench.

Zack wasn't merely aggrieved at that, he was deeply offended. 'Well, I ent,' he said.

'You were intending to sleep here?'

'An' what if a were? Ent no law agen kippin' in a broke-down ol' tower.'

'Have you slept here before?'

'Yes, he has,' said Randall. 'We caught him here last week.'

'Did you now?' Tench was quick to seize on the statement. 'What day was that?'

Randall frowned. 'It was before the storm broke, sir,' he said, 'and it was already blowing quite hard on the Friday morning, so it must have been Thursday.'

'Thursday.' Tench affected to be deep in thought. 'And now he's come back. That's interesting, wouldn't you say so, Inspector?'

Randall was just as quick to pick up his cue. 'Yes, sir,' he said. 'Highly suspicious.'

'Murderers always return to the scene of their crime. That's common knowledge, isn't it?'

'It is, sir, yes.'

Zack jerked his head to look at him, then back at Tench. He was visibly shaken. 'What's about murder?' he said. 'I ent done no murder.'

The Chief Inspector glared at him. 'Haven't you?' he said. 'There's a dead man here who died before the storm, and you were here before the storm. In my book that makes you a prime suspect, and with your police record . . .'

'Oh, come off it, Mr Tench.' Zack was reproachful. 'You an' Mr McKenzie know me better'n tha'. We bin pals off an' on now fer nigh on five year. Nick a can o' baked beans from time ter time mebbe, but I ent never laid a finger on no one, not ever.'

'That may be so, but there's always a first time.' Tench was dismissive. 'I think you and I should have a little talk before I charge you with murder.' He turned to McKenzie. 'Sergeant,' he said, 'take Mr Case down to the interview room at Breckton and hand him over to Detective Constable Lock.'

McKenzie blinked. 'In the car?'

'Yes, in the car.'

'But he stinks like a piggery.'

'Stick him in the back and wind down all the windows . . . And once the stench of him's cleared, come back here and collect Mr Lubbock and me.'

'I know what I'd like to do with him,' McKenzie said. 'Strip him down, burn his clothes, scrub him all over with strong carbolic soap, and then soak him in disinfectant.'

'Perhaps there'll be some at the church hall,' said Tench. 'Just get him out of here before his fleas start to jump.'

10.

The church hall at Breckton, like innumerable church and village halls in the past, had been transformed by Lock into his own conception of what an incident room should be. Half a dozen of the trestle tables stacked around the walls and normally used for whist drives, jumble sales and meetings of the parish council had been ranged in a semicircle round the room, and were furnished with filing boxes, files, typewriters and packets of paper. Facing them were two tables set end to end, which were Lock's own province, and on them, between two carved oaken book-ends of Sherlock Holmes and Dr Watson – personal treasures that had graced every one of his incident rooms – stood a row of telephone and business directories, gazetteers and guidebooks, while pin-boards on the wall behind displayed a roughly drawn sketch-map of the village of Breckton, Ordnance Survey sheets of all the surrounding areas, and blown-up photographs of Mr and Mrs Kingham, the rooms at The Woodlands, and the dinghy and the body of Valerie Kingham as they'd been found by Lubbock's cottage at Cley.

The Post Office engineers had rigged up two phones. These were positioned to left and right within easy reach of Lock as he sat at the tables, and as Tench pushed open the door, to be followed first by Lubbock and then by McKenzie, the room was already a scene of some activity. Two reserve constables drafted in from Norwich were busily coding and boxing sets of files, Rayner and Spurgeon were typing up their reports, and Lock himself, armed with a colouring pen, was marking off salient points on the maps.

'Where is he?' said Tench.

'In the stock room, sir,' said Lock. 'Couldn't have him spreading a wave of pollution here. I've opened the window and cuffed him to a couple of the heaviest chairs. He won't have moved very far.'

'He'll move fast enough,' said Tench, 'when I put my boot behind him, but that won't be just yet. Take the cuffs off him, Des, and put him as close to the window as you possibly can. I've got one or two things I want to say to Mr Case.'

Zack Case wasn't happy. He shivered in the cold breeze blowing around him, scratched his armpit and scowled at the two detectives. 'It ent fair,' he complained.

Tench was curtly unsympathetic. 'What isn't fair?'

'You lockin' me up. I ent done nothin' wrong.'

'You've offended my sense of cleanliness. That's a crime in itself. You've polluted the atmosphere. That's an offence against health regulations. You've got a record as long as Sergeant McKenzie's arm, and, added to all that, you're the prime suspect in a case of murder. Be thankful you can still breathe the fresh Norfolk air . . . Inspector Randall says you slept at the tower a week last Thursday, and I've no reason to doubt him . . . Whereabouts did you sleep?'

Zack turned mutinous. 'Never slept in no bloody tower,' he said sullenly, 'an' you ent no right ter be lockin' me up. T'ent fair, that it ent.'

'Are you calling Inspector Randall a liar?'

'Ent callin' no one, but I ent bloody slep' there an' tha's truth, Mr Tench.' Zack's voice became a whine. 'You know me long enough. Wouldn' say so an it weren'.'

'He wouldn't know the truth if it spat in his face,' McKenzie said. 'We're just wasting time. Let's take him back to Norwich and charge him.'

'With murder?'

'Why not? He's as guilty as sin.'

Tench appeared to consider the suggestion. 'I think you're right, Mac,' he said. 'He's clearly hiding something, and that's a sign of a guilty conscience . . . Put the cuffs on him again.'

Zack protested wildly. 'I ent got no guilty conscience,' he wailed. 'All I'm tellin's th'truth.'

'But not the whole of the truth,' said Tench. 'Mr Randall says you slept in the tower. You say you didn't, so you'd better explain and quick or you'll be spending tonight in a draughty cell in Norwich.'

Zack squirmed on his chair. 'I ent never slep' there, honest, Mr Tench. There weren' no bloody chance ter get a bit o' kip what wi' one thing an' t'other.'

'One thing and another? That's no explanation. What were they, these things?'

'There was ants, that were one thing.'

'Ants?'

'It's truth, Mr Tench. There were thousands o' the little bleeders a-crawlin' all ovver me an' nippin' like pincers.'

'I'm not surprised,' McKenzie said. 'There's half a dozen meals on that muffler of yours . . . Ants and what else?'

'There was folk aroun' too, a-jabberin' like mad.'

'How many of them? Thousands?'

'Nah.' Zack was scornful. 'There was nobbut two on 'em. Big chaps they was an' dark-lookin' like. Come in a car, di'n't they,

113

just as a was tekkin' a gander inside. So I hops out like, quick, an' hides in th'bushes. Jabberin' away ter one another, they was, in some furrin speak as I'd never heerd afore. Then they goes inside, an' I hears 'em clumpin' up th'stairs. They musta gone right ter th'top, fer it were a good ten minutes afore they come down, an' I'm a-shiverin' in th'bloody bushes, givin' them a good round o' swears ter keep warm. An' even then they ent fer goin'. Stands there, they does, fer another ten minutes a-yappin' an' pointin' up ter th'tower, an' even when they goes they's still yap-yap-yappin' all th' way ter th'car. An' then there were Mr Randall, an' then th'bleedin' ants, an' atween 'em I never gets a wink o' sleep all night.'

'Tragic,' McKenzie said.

'It were more'n tha', Mr McKenzie. A were chilled ter th'marrer, an' never got a bite to eat.'

'That's terrible.' The sergeant shook his head sadly. 'How could such a thing happen?'

'Dropped me can-opener, didn' I? Gawd knows where.' Zack was all but mournful. 'Couldn' even open a tin o' baked beans.'

11.

Tench sniffed the air and moved his chair back half a yard. 'So you never slept a wink and had nothing to eat.'

'S'right, Mr Tench.'

'But you stayed there all night.'

'On'y cos it were dark. I ent one fer wanderin' a lot arter dark.'

'Did you have any other visitors apart from the ants?'

'There was bats, an' a fox as come snufflin' aroun'.'

'But no more men?'

'Never heerd none, Mr Tench.'

'These two men you saw. You said they were dark-looking. What did you mean by that?'

Zack scratched his head. Flakes of dandruff descended. 'Well, they was . . . dark.'

'That means nothing.' Tench glared at him. 'What was it that was dark? Their clothes? Their hair?'

'Both o' they, Mr Tench . . . an' they looks dark an' all.'

'You mean they were black men?'

Zack screwed up his eyes in concentration. 'Coulda bin,' he said. 'They wasn' white, an' tha's a fact.'

'But you don't know whether they were black, brown or blue.'

'Well, they ent blue fer sure, but they mighta bin brown.'

'Could they have been Indians?'

Zack dismissed the suggestion with another, more forcible shake of his head. 'Not a chance, Mr Tench. They weren' red, nowhere near. I'd a known if they was red.'

Tench stared at him in disbelief. 'I didn't mean *Red* Indians.' He flung back his chair. 'Oh, what's the bloody point,' he said. 'Get rid of him, Mac. Turn him loose. Kick him out. I've seen and smelt enough of Mr Case today to last me a lifetime . . . But tell him if he ever dares to cross my path again, I'll have him scrubbed with a yard brush, fumigated twice, and then locked in the oldest and coldest cell in Norwich with a drunken Irishman who'll hammer on the door and sing "Danny Boy" all night at the top of his voice.'

12.

As he pushed open the door into the main church hall, he wasn't exactly in the sweetest of tempers.

Apart from Lubbock, enveloped in a rolling cloud of pipe smoke, and Lock, who was sorting out a batch of papers, the place was deserted. Rayner and Spurgeon had gone, and so had the constables who'd been manning the tables.

'Everyone left?' he said to Lock.

'Yes, sir, and the search team as well.' Lock shuffled the papers into a pile and laid them on the table. 'These are the reports.'

'Right.' Tench nodded. 'As soon as we've gone,' he said, 'ring Inspector Gregg and tell him to send the whole team off duty. We can't do anything more till we know where we stand. There'll be a briefing at nine o'clock tomorrow morning.'

'Right, sir.'

'Tell him to collect all the reports and leave them on my desk. After that you can shut up shop. Take those reports with you and drop them into my office. I'm likely to be there until late tonight.'

Lubbock blew out more smoke. 'I gather,' he said, 'that you didn't get much from our friend Mr Case.'

'He's no friend of mine.' Tench was dismissive. 'Never was. Never will be. The man's a peripatetic plague, and that's putting it mildly . . . No, we didn't get much. Little that made sense apart from one thing that just might be vital.'

'Well, that'll be something new.' Lubbock laid down his pipe. 'I've never known Zack Case come up with a vital clue in the whole of his life. What was this piece of nonsense that might be so vital? Hosts of angels flying round the tower?'

'Not exactly.' Tench explained.

His old Chief suppressed a yawn. 'Is that all?'

'It could be important.'

'What, two coloured men exploring a tower? It's not exactly a cataclysmic piece of information, is it? They were probably nothing more than a couple of foreign visitors who'd stumbled on the place and wondered what it was.'

'They could have been, yes. On the other hand they could have been something more sinister.'

Lubbock raised a couple of bushy grey eyebrows. 'Could they? Such as what?'

'Indians,' said Tench, 'and the Kinghams came from India. There could be some connection.'

'That's stretching a point, isn't it?'

'Maybe, but it's possible.'

Lubbock studied him intently for a moment and frowned. 'Am I right in thinking you've some outlandish notion that these two men travelled six thousand miles with murder on their minds?'

'Why not?'

'Because if you have, laddie, you're committing the cardinal sin that every good detective ought to shun like the plague. You're twisting the evidence to fit your own theory. Never do that. It's far too dangerous. You'll find yourself chasing flights of wild geese to the edge of oblivion. What you should be doing is letting the evidence dictate the theory.'

'And that's what you've done?'

'Of course it is.'

'And you still think it's a purely domestic murder and Kingham was the killer?'

'I do, and I've seen nothing today to make me change my mind. Look at the evidence, laddie. Kingham was a drunkard, and violent with it. He'd attacked his wife before. Her bedroom was wrecked, but his was left untouched. He used a Beretta. He fled the scene of the shooting, and now a body that strongly resembles his has been found at the foot of a long-deserted tower. The evidence all points in one direction, straight at Kingham. He killed his wife in a drunken temper, savaged her bedroom, hid her body in a boat, and then, in a fit of remorse, jumped to his death from the top of a tower . . . Murder and suicide, end of case, close the file.'

'You're very sure, aren't you?'

'At the moment, laddie, positive. Why deny the evidence?'

'Point One,' said Tench: 'the evidence is incomplete. We don't yet know what the members of the team have discovered today. There's a sheaf of reports that are still to be read. What they have to say may change the whole complexion of the case.'

'I doubt it,' Lubbock said.

Tench ignored the interruption. 'Point Two,' he continued: 'the body at the tower hasn't yet been identified. We don't know for certain that it is that of Kingham.'

'Of course it is. It must be.'

'Point Three: from what I've heard of him, he wasn't the sort of man to feel any remorse, let alone throw himself from the top of a tower. Such an act would be out of character. Point Four: like Sergeant McKenzie, I'm still not happy about the part that Giles Meredith has played in all this. There's a lingering suspicion that he hasn't told us the whole truth, and his association with Mrs Kingham seems far too close for comfort. Point Five: we've evidence that a woman was seen at The Woodlands on the day before the storm, and now, Point Six, we have two men, possibly Indians, inspecting the tower on the previous afternoon, and we've no idea as yet who any of them were.'

'Casual visitors, all of them.' Lubbock seemed determined not to yield an inch.

'They could have been, granted,' – Tench, for his part, was equally determined – 'but I'm not prepared to close the case till I've read the reports and heard what young Vincent has to say tonight.'

'Take my advice, laddie, get off to bed. You know what young Shakespeare had to say about sleep. It knits up the ravelled sleeve of care. Have a good night's rest and let it do some knitting. You'll wake up tomorrow morning bright and early and find that I'm right.'

'And I might wake up and find that you're wrong,' said Tench, 'and if you are, then I'd sooner know tonight than tomorrow. I've a briefing at nine o'clock, and I need to know just how many murders I'm facing.'

Lubbock pushed back his chair and stretched. 'Take my word for it, laddie,' he said. 'It'll still be just one, even if you sit up till three in the morning.'

13.

As events turned out, Tench had no cause to sit up till three in the morning.

He drove back home to Cringleford, made himself a flask of coffee and was back in his office by half past seven. Sorting out the pile of reports on his desk, he read them carefully from end to end, and then read them a second time, making notes as he progressed.

After that he sat for a long time deep in thought, staring at his notes, trying to work them into some kind of credible pattern, but there were too many facts that still needed checking, too many questions still to be answered.

At some point he must have dozed off in his chair, because he woke with a start to the sound of the phone bell shattering the silence. Glancing at his watch, he saw that the hands showed a quarter to midnight. He snatched up the receiver.

'Chief Inspector Tench?'

'Correct.'

'Ah, good evening, Chief Inspector.' The voice was young, smooth and confident. 'Nick Vincent from the lab. Dr Ledward said to ring you once I was through.'

'And you are?'

'Yes, just about.'

'So what can you tell me?'

Vincent seemed to hesitate. 'First of all, Chief Inspector,' he said, 'I'd like you to tell me something. Precisely whereabouts was this man's body found?'

'At the foot of an abandoned tower a few miles from Holt.'

There was a pause. 'And how high's the tower?'

'Roughly fifty feet.'

Another pause. 'Yes, that was what I thought.'

Tench showed some impatience. 'You mean the cause of death was a fall from the tower?'

'Oh, yes, Chief Inspector. There's no doubt about that. The body shows injuries fully consistent with a fall from such a height, and they were the cause of death . . .'

'But you've doubts about something else?'

'Yes, I have.' Tench could almost see him nodding.

'Go on.'

'Well . . .' Vincent paused again. 'Dr Ledward inferred that it was probably suicide.'

'But you don't think it was?'

'There's no means of telling for sure, Chief Inspector, but if I had to make a guess I'd say no, it wasn't.'

'What makes you say that?'

'There were other injuries too, ones that wouldn't be apparent from a casual inspection, especially since the man was fully clothed and wearing a long-sleeved sweater.'

'Tell me more,' said Tench. 'What were these injuries?'

'Distinct abrasions on the wrists, the ankles, the corners of the mouth, and some faint contusions inside the cheeks.'

'Which mean what?'

'My reading of them would be that for some little time prior to his death this man was bound by his hands and feet and gagged.'

'So you'd say it was murder rather than suicide.'

'As to that, Chief Inspector,' – Vincent was cautious – 'it would be rash of me to make a definitive statement. All I'm prepared to

119

say is that, for some short time not long before he died, this man was not a free agent.'

Tench took a deep breath. 'Thank you very much, Dr Vincent,' he said.

'You're happy with the findings?'

'More than that, Doctor. A good deal more than that. It'll give me great pleasure to tell a colleague of mine that for the first time in our long acquaintance I'm right and he's wrong.'

'You'll sleep soundly?'

'I will.'

'Then I'll say goodnight, Chief Inspector. You'll have my full report by lunchtime tomorrow.'

'I look forward to it,' said Tench. 'And once again, thank you.'

He dropped the receiver on its hook, and, strangely for an undemonstrative man, thumped the desk so hard that his coffee cup danced and fell back with a clatter sideways in its saucer.

VI

INTO THE DEPTHS

Truth lies at the bottom of a well.
English proverb

1.

Promptly at nine o'clock the following morning, he rapped on a table in the CID room and the chatter subsided.

'Thank you,' he said. 'Save the chatter for later on. It's my turn now, and I've a good deal to say.' He glanced down at his notes. 'Since yesterday morning the whole complexion of the Kingham case has changed, and it's vital that you should be brought up to date. As all of you must know, at midday yesterday Detective Inspector Randall rang up from Holt to say that the body of a man had been found at the foot of the Prospect Tower at Sunningham on the road to Melton Constable. The body, he said, seemed to fit our description of Reginald Kingham, and a cursory inspection revealed this to be true. According to Dr Ledward, the man had been dead for at least a week and possibly longer, which meant that he could have died at roughly the same time as Valerie Kingham was shot.'

He paused and looked round the team. 'The position of the body, at the foot of a derelict tower some fifty feet high, created a first impression that the man could well have committed suicide by jumping from the top, but last night Dr Vincent, Ledward's young assistant, performed an autopsy, and this told a very different tale. The body, he said, showed injuries consistent with such a fall, but there were others which suggested that for some little time not long before his death the man had been bound hand and foot and gagged. If, therefore, the body proves to be that of Kingham, we need to rethink our whole approach to the case.

'Identification of Mrs Kingham's body has been difficult to achieve. She was an only child, both her parents are dead, and despite an intensive investigation by Detective Inspector Gregg, we've failed to trace any other living relative. To identify the body, we've therefore had to rely on someone who claimed to have known her well and fingerprints taken by the scene-of-crime squad.

'The same problem occurs in Mr Kingham's case. He, too, was an only child. He, too, has lost both his parents, and here again

123

there appear to be no living relatives we can call on to help, which means that we have to rely on the same apparently compelling but inconclusive evidence. I say inconclusive because Mrs Kingham's body was identified by Giles Meredith, the publisher from Blickling, and he's the one we'll have to call upon again to do the same for the body found by the tower. And as I'll explain later on, we've an equally compelling reason to doubt Mr Meredith's integrity as a witness.'

Another long pause. 'I said yesterday that, apart from Kingham, there were two other men that we couldn't entirely rule out as suspects for Mrs Kingham's murder. They were the ex-naval officer from Shotton Corner, Anthony Bridgeland, and Meredith himself. Since we weren't completely happy about Bridgeland's statement, Bob Ellison went to check the details with him, but first he paid a visit to Isaac Jacks, the boatman at Blakeney. Jacks gave him a very interesting piece of information. Bridgeland's statement about the dinghy, he said, was wrong. It wasn't moored at Blakeney at the time of the storm, but already laid up for the winter at Morston. When taxed about this, Bridgeland admitted that Jacks was right, but insisted that he'd never said it was moored at Blakeney, and we must have misread his statement. He was very curt with Bob Ellison and cut the interview short by driving off to Cawston, where he said he had an appointment to keep.'

He turned towards Ellison. 'Perhaps, Bob,' he said, 'you'll tell the team exactly what happened after that.'

'Well, sir,' said Ellison, 'I followed him to Cawston. He drove through the village and stopped at a large house about a mile the other side, where he picked up a young woman, smart, dark-haired and very attractive. They drove from there to Salle, parked by the church and went inside. I waited a few moments, then followed them in. They were talking to a man I assumed to be the rector, so I sat down in a pew as close as I dared, pretended to be deep in prayer, and tried to catch what they were saying.'

'And did you?'

'Just about enough, sir. It seems that the young woman's Mr Bridgeland's fiancée, and they were discussing a date for their wedding at the church. They both signed the visitors' book before they left. She's a Miss Angela Fleetwood, and her address is The Larches, Eastwood, near Cawston. They lingered about twenty minutes, looking round the church, then he drove her home and went back to Shotton Corner, but I made a few discreet inquiries in Cawston. Apparently the Fleetwoods are well known and respected. Her father owns two large hotels in Cromer and another in Yarmouth, and he and Bridgeland have been good friends for years.'

'And you checked the statement he made to Sergeant McKenzie?'

'Yes, sir. He's right. There's no mention of the dinghy. Simply that the yacht was moored at Blakeney Quay. I think we must have assumed that the dinghy was with it.'

'Then you think we can rule him out as a suspect?'

Ellison was cautious. 'Perhaps not entirely, sir, but I think we can drop him to the bottom of the list.'

'Right. Thank you, Bob.' Tench nodded slowly. He turned to the team again. 'I agree with that,' he said. 'I think for the moment we can afford to disregard Mr Bridgeland in spite of his somewhat uncooperative attitude, but unfortunately the same can't be said of Mr Meredith. The doubts about him seem merely to multiply.'

2.

He shuffled his notes. 'I said yesterday morning that we weren't entirely happy about him. We felt he was telling only part of the truth, and suspected his relationship with Mrs Kingham was a good deal closer than he claimed it to be. Because of that, Sue Gradwell and Constable Jules Winterton were given the job of checking his movements while he was in France, and what they discovered confirmed our suspicions. He told us he went to France for two separate reasons: first, to negotiate a contract with a Paris publisher, and second, to conclude the purchase of a cottage at Coursac, down in the Dordogne. For these reasons, he said, he spent three nights in Paris, Wednesday the 28th, Thursday the 29th, and Friday the 30th of January. Next day, the 31st, he drove to Châteauroux, where he spent a further night before arriving at Périgueux in the Dordogne on Sunday the 1st of February.

'The checks made on these movements have revealed something different. On Wednesday the 28th he certainly booked into the Hôtel Martinique in Paris for a stay of three nights, but he didn't stay for three nights. He left on the Friday morning, the day before the storm, and the next thing we know is that late on the Saturday he arrived at Châteauroux. We have therefore no idea just how he spent the Friday or where he slept that night.

'However, once they'd uncovered this peculiar discrepancy, Sue and Constable Winterton decided to question Meredith about it, and, failing to find him at his office here in Norwich, they drove out to Blickling, and what they found there merely added to the mystery. They were confronted by a woman who claimed to be his wife. Her husband, she said, was in London for the day and wouldn't be home until late that evening, but when asked where he'd been on the Friday in question, she replied that he'd been in Dublin, had been there all that week.'

He looked across at Sue Gradwell. 'Sue,' he said, 'what was your impression of this woman?'

'She was very nervous, sir. She seemed to be under considerable strain. Didn't want to talk to us. Told us to go away and leave her alone.'

'D'you think the strain was connected with her marriage?'

'Yes, sir, I do.' Sue Gradwell nodded swiftly two or three times. 'She didn't seem to trust what Mr Meredith told her. I had the feeling she suspected him of lying.'

'Lying about his movements and what he'd been doing?'

'Yes, sir. When I asked her was she sure he was in Dublin that week, she said, "I'm his wife, I have to believe him," but it was pretty clear she didn't.'

'And that poses more questions. Why did he lie to her? What did he have to hide about his visit to France?'

'And,' McKenzie said, 'had it some connection with Valerie Kingham?'

'That too,' Tench agreed. 'It seems in fact that our friend Mr Meredith has much explaining to do, and perhaps his wife as well, since we know that a woman was seen at The Woodlands on that same Friday. We've no idea who she was, but she was wearing a black coat, a woollen scarf and mittens, and a red woollen hat with a bobble on top, and she drove away in a small grey Morris, almost certainly a Morris Minor. This was about three o'clock on the Friday afternoon, the very time at which we can't account for Mr Meredith.'

He paused yet again. 'There are, as you can see, a whole host of questions to which we need answers, but since this time yesterday we have made some progress, not least with regard to Mrs Kingham's murder.

'First, to Dr Ledward's autopsy report. Her body, he said, showed no signs of sexual interference or of any recent sexual activity, but she was already three months pregnant. Apart from the wound made by the bullet that killed her, there were no signs of physical injury, nor any to indicate involvement in a struggle, and no blood, skin or fibres had been found beneath her finger-nails, but he had found some fibres adhering to the body. He'd passed these to Ted Merrick at the lab for further inspection. These fibres proved to be particularly significant, as did the stomach contents, which revealed that she'd taken a meal of orange juice, white toast, marmalade and coffee some two hours before her death.

'According to Merrick, the fibres were fragments of a cotton fabric known as candlewick. They were pink in colour, probably from a bedspread, and traces of them were also found in the dinghy. His belief was, he said, that Mrs Kingham, once shot, had been stripped of her clothes, wrapped in such a bedspread and taken down to the dinghy. Whoever did it had then dumped her body in the boat and pulled the bedspread roughly from beneath her, dragging it across the planking. The absence of a bedspread on Mrs Kingham's bed appears to lend credence to this belief, and, unless she was a woman of eccentric eating habits, the contents of the stomach suggest that she was murdered sometime in the morning, but which day this was we've as yet no means of telling. As far as we know, the last time anyone saw her or spoke to her was on the evening of Tuesday, the 27th of January, four days before the storm, and for this we have to rely once again on the doubtful evidence of Mr Giles Meredith.'

Tench looked down and reshuffled his notes. 'The weapon that fired the bullet that killed Mrs Kingham hasn't yet been found, but Mr Carson, the ballistics expert at the lab, believes it to have been a small calibre Italian Beretta, a vest-pocket pistol, and in view of the point of entry, the track of the bullet and its position of lodgement inside the brain, he concludes that it must have been fired from a distance of two or three yards.

'He also mentioned, in the course of conversation, that there were thousands of such Berettas to be found nowadays in India as a legacy of the war, and they were easy to obtain by anyone who lived there.

'Which brings us,' he said, 'to Mr Reginald Kingham.'

3.

He pushed aside his notes. 'There are mysteries about Kingham that need to be resolved. We believe that he and his wife arrived in England from India some twelve months ago, rented the lodge on Meredith's estate at Blickling, and remained there until October last year when they bought The Woodlands at Breckton. Up to yesterday morning we knew little about what he'd been doing in India, save for what we were told by Meredith: that he worked for a jute firm, lived in Calcutta, and married his wife there.

'To find out more about him, we asked Inspector Gregg to make further inquiries. He therefore rang the London office of the firm, and spoke to a Mr Dauncey. What he discovered was very strange indeed. Kingham, it seems, was employed by a firm called Mitchison and Blake. He worked with them for nine months, from February to November 1951, training to be a clerk in charge of the office at one of their mills, and during this period he lived with other trainees in a company house in Calcutta known as the Battery.

'According to Dauncey, Kingham's period of training was supposed to last for twelve months, but since he left after nine he never completed the course, and when Gregg inquired why this was so, he was met with a blank refusal to answer. Dauncey wouldn't say just why Kingham left. The company had rules, he said, that forbade him to divulge any such information. It could only be obtained by contacting Calcutta, and if the inspector needed to know anything more, that was what he should do. And at that point Dauncey abruptly rang off.'

He looked towards Gregg. 'Correct?' he said.

Gregg nodded. 'Absolutely correct, sir, yes.'

'So what did you think?'

'I had a feeling that this wasn't just a matter of company rules. There was something more suspicious that lay behind Dauncey's reluctance to talk, something perhaps about Kingham's early departure that was far too sensitive for the firm to admit, and if that was the case then we needed to know exactly what it was. I rang back and asked to be connected to Dauncey, but the girl on the switchboard had clearly had her instructions and told me that Dauncey was unavailable.'

'But you didn't ring Calcutta.'

'No, sir. There didn't seem to be a great deal of point. It was already late Saturday afternoon in India, and even if I'd managed to get through quickly, the chances of finding anyone there who could answer my questions seemed to be remote.'

'But you didn't leave it at that.'

Gregg shook his head. 'No,' he said, 'I couldn't. I knew that the London office would probably close at lunchtime and wouldn't open again until Monday morning, so I rang Lock at the incident room in Breckton and asked him to check on his business directories and let me know who was in charge of the London branch. It took him some time, but he rang me back and said that the managing director was a man called Maurice Cracknell.'

Tench nodded. 'Go on. Did you get through to Cracknell?'

'Eventually, sir, yes, by a devious route and only by pretending I was someone I wasn't. But I got the name I wanted. The king-pin of the firm in 1951 was Alan Devereux. He retired the following year, 1952, and received a knighthood for his services to industry. He's now Sir Alan Devereux. He lives on the Helford River in Cornwall. His address is Porthallack, Toll Point, Mawnan, and his phone number's Mawnan Smith 247. He seems to me to be the person most likely to know the truth about Kingham.'

'Did you try to get in touch with him?'

'No, sir. In view of the man's status, I felt that any request for an interview – and we really need to speak to him face to face – would be better if it came from either you or the Chief Super.'

'Yes, you're probably right.' Tench nodded again and turned back to the team. 'It's possible,' he said, 'that another piece of evidence we received yesterday may have a connection with this business of Kingham's unexplained departure, though here we're entering the realm of speculation. Late on the Thursday, two days before the storm, a pair of coloured men speaking a foreign language were seen inspecting the tower near Holt where Kingham's body was found, and it seems they showed a particular interest in one of the upper floors. There's nothing to indicate whether or not these men were Indians, but if they were their appearance at that time could prove to be significant, since the last positive sighting we have of Kingham was on that same evening when he was seen drinking at the Bottle and Glass, a public house some two miles from Breckton, and both he and Mrs Kingham were certainly dead before the storm broke in all its fury on the Saturday.'

He took a deep breath. 'Now you'll realize,' he said, 'that we've learnt quite a lot since yesterday morning, but you'll also be aware that we're left with a host of unanswered questions: questions to which we need to find the answers before we can decide which way to go from here. As you're also no doubt aware, the Chief Super's away this weekend attending a conference down in Brighton. He's due back this evening, and if he isn't to have the Chief Constable on his back threatening us with intervention by the Met, we need to be able to show him some visible signs of progress. So let's look at the questions and the steps we need to take.'

4.

Another pause, but a short one. 'The questions form a collection as long as both my arms. Is the body found at the foot of the tower that of Mr Kingham? Why did he leave his job in Calcutta, and what is it about his leaving that the firm wants to hide? Why did Giles Meredith lie about his movements, both to us and his wife? Where was he and what did he do on that Friday, the day before the storm? Where did he sleep that night, if not at his Paris hotel? Was the woman who spoke to Sue Gradwell at Blickling really his wife, and if she was, what was the state of her marriage? Was she jealous of her husband's association with Mrs Kingham? Did she know that Mrs Kingham was pregnant, and suspect that her husband was the father of the child? Was she the woman who was seen at The Woodlands that Friday afternoon? If she wasn't, then who was this woman, and why was she paying a visit to the house? Who owns the small grey Morris car in which she drove away? Where is the Beretta pistol used to kill Mrs Kingham? Where are her clothes and the candlewick bed-spread, fibres of which were found on her body? Who were the coloured men inspecting the tower, and did anyone see them hanging around The Woodlands? Did anyone at Morston see a strange car parked somewhere close to Bridgeland's dinghy on the Thursday or Friday nights before the storm? And when exactly did Mr and Mrs Kingham die?

'So many questions. Too many for comfort. Too many to solve in a single day, especially when that day, like today, is a Sunday. Sundays tend to be difficult. People may not be where we expect them to be. We may find it impossible to contact them at all. But we have to do what we can. We have to concentrate on those questions that seem to be of immediate importance: those that we need to solve before we can clearly see the road that lies ahead.

'I've already spoken this morning to Inspector Gregg and to Sergeant McKenzie, and we've decided that there's only one way to proceed. I'll arrange for Inspector Gregg to see Sir Alan Devereux, and he'll travel down to Truro by the first available train. I also intend to speak to the head of the CID in Truro, Detective Chief Superintendent Tremayne, and I'm sure he'll provide all the help that he can.

'The rest of us have other, very different priorities. First of all, Meredith . . .'

131

5.

At quarter to twelve on that same Sunday morning, yet another lab assistant drew back the sheet from yet another body.

'Mr Meredith,' said Tench, 'to the best of your knowledge is this Reginald Kingham?'

Meredith looked at the face. 'Oh yes,' he said, 'it's Kingham all right.'

'Are you sure?'

'More than sure, Chief Inspector. I'm positive.'

'Take another look,' McKenzie told him. 'We need to be just as positive as you.'

Meredith bent down and peered at the body. 'It's Kingham,' he said. 'I've seen him too many times to be mistaken. And I'll tell you this, Sergeant. I'm shedding no tears. He's no loss to the world.'

'Well, thank you, sir.' Tench was nothing if not courteous. 'Perhaps you'll come back to the office and make a statement.'

'Of course, Chief Inspector.' Meredith was prepared, so it seemed, to be equally courteous. 'If there's anything I can do to help . . .'

McKenzie was not inclined to be either courteous or cautious.

He sat facing Meredith behind Tench's desk, the Chief Inspector to his right. 'You offered to be of help, Mr Meredith,' he said. 'I can only hope that this time you stay true to your word.'

Meredith frowned. 'True to my word?'

McKenzie gave a nod. 'That's exactly what I said.'

'Then tell me, Sergeant. Exactly what are you implying?'

'I'm not implying, sir. I'm stating. Your word isn't one that I'm ready to trust. You're a liar, Mr Meredith.'

The man was on his feet in a flash. He kicked back his chair and turned towards Tench. 'I didn't come here to be maligned, Chief Inspector,' he said. 'Will you kindly explain what this is all about?'

'Please sit down, Mr Meredith.'

'Not if I'm going to be subjected to insults. I resent being characterized as a liar . . .'

'Sit down!' The voice was weary, but firm and authoritative.

Meredith hesitated a moment, and then, glaring at McKenzie, resumed his seat.

'Now,' said Tench, 'Please listen, Mr Meredith, and listen very carefully. You may find the sergeant's approach distasteful, but he has every right to say what he did, so just answer his questions.'

'Am I under arrest?'

'No, sir, you're not, nor are you under oath, but for your sake as well as ours we need to clear up certain discrepancies in your statement, so please be patient . . . Carry on, Sergeant.'

'Very well.' There was a shrug from Meredith. 'But I still think the sergeant should offer an apology.'

'If he proves to be wrong,' said Tench, 'then no doubt he will.' He nodded at McKenzie.

The sergeant turned a sheet in the file that lay before him. 'Are you married, Mr Meredith?' he asked very blandly.

'Yes, I am. Does it matter?'

McKenzie ignored the question. 'Your wife. Does she live with you at Blickling?'

'Where else would she live?'

'I don't know, Mr Meredith. I'm asking you to tell me.'

'She lives with me at Blickling. Satisfied?'

'Partly,' McKenzie said. 'How long have you been married?'

'I've been married four years.'

'Happily married?'

'I believe so.'

'You trust her?'

Meredith turned again to Tench. 'What is all this?' he said.

'Just answer the sergeant's question, sir.'

There was a pause, then Meredith took a deep breath. 'Yes,' he said, 'I trust her. I trust her implicitly.'

'And *she* trusts *you*?'

'Of course.'

McKenzie leaned forward. 'Then why,' he said, 'when you were going to France, did you tell her you were spending a week in Dublin?'

133

6.

Meredith looked astounded. 'Why on earth would I do that?'

'You mean that you didn't?'

'Of course I didn't.'

'But we have it on very good authority that you did.'

'Then your authority must be wrong.'

'I very much doubt it.'

'Who was this authority?'

'The authority,' McKenzie said, 'was one that you trust implicitly. Your wife, Mr Meredith.'

'Then she must have misheard me. I said no such thing.'

'You were in France?'

'Of course I was in France. I told you I was. I gave you a list of the places where I stayed.'

'So you did,' McKenzie said. 'Thank you for reminding me.' He turned to another page in the file, and ran his finger down the sheet. 'You stayed three nights in Paris at the Hôtel Martinique on the Rue Vermet.'

'That's correct. I did.'

'Wednesday, Thursday and Friday, the 28th to the 30th of January.'

'Yes, that's right.'

McKenzie frowned. 'Are you absolutely sure?'

'Yes, I am. How many more times do I have to repeat myself?' He glowered at McKenzie. 'I'm warning you, Sergeant, I'm beginning to lose patience. Are you trying to accuse me of lying again?'

'Not exactly, sir, no.' The sergeant's tone was almost apologetic.

'But you're doubting my word?'

'I thought perhaps we'd misheard what you said.'

'You couldn't have done, Sergeant. My statement's perfectly clear. I read it through myself. I stayed in Paris from the Wednesday evening till the Saturday morning, and then drove to Châteauroux.'

'You slept at the Martinique on the Friday night?'

'For the last time, yes.'

McKenzie frowned again and scratched his head. 'Then we're facing a bit of a problem, Mr Meredith,' he said. 'Can you explain why the manager of the Martinique is so sure that you didn't?'

'No, I can't. He knows perfectly well that I did.'

'You mean we must have misheard what he said?'

'Since I know very well that I slept there, Sergeant, there seems to be no other explanation, does there?'

McKenzie pushed aside the file and leaned back in his chair. 'I can think of one,' he said.

'Then perhaps you'll be inclined to enlighten me, Sergeant, since I've no idea what it can possibly be.'

'You haven't? Then I'll tell you, Mr Meredith.' McKenzie's voice suddenly hardened. 'Everything you've told us so far is nothing more than a tissue of lies. You've spun us a web of falsehoods, and now you're trapped inside it. Isn't it about time you started telling us the truth?'

'I've told you the truth.' Meredith was on his feet again. 'If you're not prepared to accept it, there's nothing more I can do. Kingham's dead, I've seen him, and as far as I'm concerned the case is now closed.' He looked down at Tench. 'I take it I'm free to leave?'

Tench gave a nod. 'Whenever you wish to do so.'

'Then I'll say good morning, gentlemen.' He turned on his heel swiftly and made for the door.

'Before you go,' said Tench, 'just answer me one question.'

Meredith halted and turned back to face him. 'What question is that?'

The Chief Inspector took his time. 'Were you aware, sir,' he said, 'that Mrs Kingham was pregnant?'

7.

Meredith seemed to hesitate. 'Yes,' he said, 'I was. What of it?'

'Did she tell you the child was yours?'

'That's a completely unnecessary question, Chief Inspector. How could it possibly be mine? I was a friend, nothing more. I told you so.'

'Does your wife own a car?'

'Yes, she has one.'

'What type of car?'

'It's a Morris Minor.'

'What colour?'

'Grey. What the devil does it matter?'

Tench ignored the question. 'Then can you explain why she paid a visit to Mrs Kingham on the Friday afternoon when you claim you were in Paris?'

'No, I can't. I was hundreds of miles away. How the hell can I possibly know what she did?'

'Please sit down again, Mr Meredith.'

'Why should I?'

'For one very simple reason, sir,' said Tench. 'I don't think you realize the danger you're in. I could detain you here and now in connection with the murder of Valerie Kingham, and if you don't sit down I'll be forced to do just that. So sit down, sir, and listen.'

Meredith walked reluctantly back to the chair and lowered himself on to it. 'This is intolerable,' he said. 'You've no reason to detain me.'

'I've every reason, Mr Meredith.' Tench was slow and deliberate. 'It's clear that you've misled us, purposely misled us, and that can only mean that you've something to hide. Unfortunately for you, a very different interpretation can be placed on what you say . . . Explain to him, Sergeant.'

McKenzie wasn't one for circumlocutions. He came straight to the point. 'You've lied to us on two counts, Meredith,' he said. 'You deny that you told your wife you were spending the week in Dublin, but we know you did. You deny that you left your Paris hotel on the Friday morning. Once again we know you did. That being so, there's only one interpretation we can place on your words. Your relationship with Mrs Kingham was more than just friendship. You seduced her, didn't you, and when she told you she was pregnant and the child was yours, you had to get rid of her. You told your wife you were going to Dublin, and to provide yourself with an alibi you thought up some tale about business in Paris and a cottage you were buying down in the Dordogne. You left the hotel in Paris early on the Friday morning, drove to Calais, crossed to Dover on the ferry, and made your way to Breckton. You waited till dark, till Kingham was out drinking, then you murdered Mrs Kingham, hid her body in a boat, and laid waste to a couple of rooms at the house to make it appear that Kingham had yielded to a fit of violent temper. You then made for Dover, crossed back to France on the early morning ferry, and drove straight down to Châteauroux, arriving there late on the Saturday night. And that' – the sergeant's tone was decisive – 'makes you the prime suspect for Mrs Kingham's murder, so unless you want to spend the night banged up in a cell, you'd better start telling us the truth, and make it quick.'

There was silence for a moment.

'Well, sir?' said Tench.

Meredith seemed to be struggling with himself. 'You're wrong,' he said, 'so very, very wrong.'

'Then perhaps you'll correct us.' Tench was patient, persuasive, and yet at the same time firm and insistent.

Meredith looked first at him, and then at McKenzie. He drew a deep sigh, all the way it seemed from the soles of his feet. 'I haven't much option, have I?' he said.

8.

'Not a lot.' McKenzie showed nothing in the way of sympathy. 'So get on with it, and this time make it the truth.'

For one brief second a flicker of defiance seemed to cross the man's face, then it yielded to one of weary resignation. He gave a little shrug. 'It's difficult to know,' he said, 'just where to begin.'

Tench intervened. 'Suppose you begin by answering a very simple question.'

'What question's that?'

'You told Sergeant McKenzie that you'd been married four years. Am I right?'

There was another sigh from Meredith. 'Yes, four years.'

'And that you trusted her implicitly and she trusted you?'

Meredith nodded. 'Yes.'

'Then I'm forced to repeat his question. Why did you tell her you were going to Dublin, when you knew all the time that you were going to France?'

Meredith sighed yet again. 'Simply because we trusted one another.'

Tench raised his eyebrows. 'What d'you mean by that?'

'Exactly what I said.'

The Chief Inspector frowned at him. 'If this is your attempt to explain things, Mr Meredith, I find it even more confusing than your lies.'

'Charge him,' McKenzie said. 'He's just wasting our time.'

'Well, Mr Meredith?' Tench was tight-lipped.

'It's a long story.'

'Then the sooner you make it clear to us, the better.'

Meredith drew another deep breath. 'It all began,' he said, 'when I left university after the war. I wanted to go into publishing, and my tutor at Cambridge was a very good friend of Henry Millward, the founder and head of the Norwick Press. He got me a job with the firm, and it was there that I met my wife, Millward's daughter, Josephine. She was attracted to me – I don't quite know why – and though I wasn't in love with her, I found her pretty enough in a pallid sort of way. Her father encouraged the friendship between us, and I let it run on because it offered me a chance to improve my prospects inside the firm. Josie was an only child, a late arrival in the family, and the apple of her father's eye. The old man was a widower and close to retiring age, and he made it fairly clear that if Josie and I should marry, he'd make me a partner with him in the firm . . .'

'So you married her.' McKenzie's comment was scathing.

'Yes, I married her. Perhaps I shouldn't have done, but I was young and ambitious, and it seemed an opportunity too good to be missed.'

'How very commendable!' McKenzie said.

Meredith ignored him. He continued to speak directly to Tench. 'Three months after we were married, the old man died from a heart attack. He left the house at Blickling to Josie and the Norwick Press jointly to her and me.'

'Oh, happy day!' This time the sergeant was even more sarcastic.

Meredith nodded. 'I thought it was, yes, though I was fond of the old chap. I had control of the Press and that was what I'd wanted, but I didn't know then what a heavy price I'd paid.'

'And what price was that?' Tench inquired smoothly.

'It didn't take me long to find out,' Meredith said. 'Less than a year, to be precise. By the end of that time I'd discovered to my cost just what kind of woman it was that I'd married.'

'And what kind was that?'

'One who was almost insanely possessive.'

'Clipped your wings, did she?' McKenzie said.

'More than that. She killed off any affection I might have felt for her.'

Tench frowned at him again. 'Then, contrary to what you told us, it wasn't a happy marriage?'

'No, Chief Inspector, it wasn't. Far from it.'

'Then why did you say it was?'

Meredith, all at once, seemed unutterably weary. 'When I heard that Val was dead,' he said, 'it didn't seem to matter very much any more.'

McKenzie, for all his long years of service, had never found patience to be much of an asset. 'Come to the point,' he growled. 'If you didn't spend that Friday night back in England, then where did you spend it?'

Meredith raised his eyes and looked straight at him. 'I spent it,' he said, 'at a tavern to the east of Paris in a village called Chaumes-en-Brie.'

9.

'And what the devil were you doing there that you didn't want your wife to know about?'

'It was a private business matter.'

'So private that you told us a string of lies?'

'If I'd told you it would have got back to her, and once Val was dead there was no cause for her to know anything about it.'

'Then this private business had some connection with Valerie Kingham?'

'Yes, it had.'

'Are you telling us,' said Tench, 'that you lied to your wife because she was jealous of your association with Mrs Kingham?'

'Partly.'

'But not wholly?'

'No, not wholly. There was more to it than that.'

Tench showed a sudden flash of exasperation. 'Mr Meredith,' he said, 'we haven't got all day to listen to a lot of convoluted nonsense that's getting us nowhere. Sergeant McKenzie was right to say what he did. Come to the point.'

There was another deep sigh. 'When you asked me, Chief Inspector, whether my wife and I trusted one another, I said yes, we did, and that was the truth, though not perhaps in the way that you meant. She always trusted me never to tell the truth, and I always trusted her never to believe a word that I said.'

'So you told her you were going to Dublin. Why there in particular?'

'We had connections there with an Irish publishing firm, and even before I was married I'd had to make frequent trips to Ireland. In the course of them I'd had a brief affair with a girl, one of the firm's secretaries, and Josie found out about it, don't ask me how. She never trusted me after that. If I said I was going to Dublin, I knew the first thing she'd do would be to ring up the firm and check that I was there. She was still a good friend, this Irish girl, and I briefed her in advance to say that I'd arrived.'

'When all the time you were in France.'

Meredith nodded. 'When all the time I was in France.'

'Lies, lies, lies!' McKenzie said. 'Don't you ever tell the truth?'

'I'm telling it now.' Meredith spat the words at him.

'Then this visit to France. What connection did it have with Valerie Kingham?'

'I was preparing a refuge for her.'

'A refuge? You'd persuaded her to leave her husband?'

'Yes, I had.'

'Were you the father of this child of hers?'

'She told me I was. I believed her.'

'So,' said Tench, 'your relationship with her was closer than you've admitted.'

'It didn't start off that way. In the beginning it was mere compassion, but by that time all I felt for Josie was indifference, nothing more, and compassion grew slowly into something more intense.'

'You fell in love with her?'

'Yes.'

'Were you planning to leave your wife?'

Meredith nodded. 'I was planning to leave both her and the Press.'

'And live with Mrs Kingham?'

'That was what I planned.'

'In France?'

'Yes, in France.'

'At this refuge?'

'No.'

'Then what were your plans?'

'The tavern at Chaumes was to be a temporary refuge. We intended to live at the cottage I was buying down in the Dordogne. I was setting up my own firm in Bordeaux.'

'And this was a secret between you and her?'

'Of course. It had to be until we were both in France. Once I'd made the arrangements I was coming back here. Kingham went out drinking every night – he never failed – so Val and I were to fix a night between us. I'd work late at the office, and once he'd left the house Val would ring me there. I'd drive to Breckton, pick her up and take her to Chaumes, and she'd stay there until I was ready to join her. The tavern was a pleasant place down by the river. I'd used it on one or two occasions before on my way down to Coursac, and there wasn't any reason why anyone else should know where she was. Once I'd told the staff at the Press that I was quitting the firm, I'd leave a letter for Josie telling her the marriage was over, and join Val at Chaumes.'

'How very gallant!' McKenzie said sourly.

'Ungallant maybe,' Meredith acknowledged, 'but the links had to be cut at a stroke without warning, and I couldn't afford to be leaving a trail. By the time that anyone really knew what was happening, Val and I would be driving down to the Dordogne.'

'And then it all went wrong.'

'Tragically wrong. The whole plan was shattered. Kingham, the bastard, did what I'd always been afraid that he'd do. He came home drunk, picked one of his quarrels, and killed her before I had any chance to save her. It's a good job he went on to kill himself. In my frame of mind I might well have done it for him.'

McKenzie sat back and fixed him with eyes like a couple of

gimlets. 'All very plausible,' he said. 'Quite ingenious. And you expect us to believe it, after all the lies you've churned out to deceive us?'

'It's the truth.'

'Is it? Is it true that you still believe Kingham killed his wife?'

'Yes, of course he killed her.'

'Then tell us,' McKenzie said. 'Who killed Kingham?'

10.

Meredith stared at him in what appeared to be blank amazement. 'Killed him?'

'Yes, that's what I said. Who was it killed Kingham?'

'Nobody *killed* him. He killed himself.'

'How did he do that?'

'You know as well as I do. He threw himself from the top of that tower.'

'Then he must have been a man of truly magical powers.'

'What d'you mean by that?'

'Well, he must have gagged himself, tied his feet and hands together, and then somehow transported himself through the air.'

Meredith scowled at him. He turned towards Tench. 'What's he talking about?'

'What Sergeant McKenzie means is that Kingham didn't commit suicide, he was murdered. He was gagged, bound hand and foot, and then thrown or pushed from the top of the tower.'

'So, since you're so good at thinking up fanciful explanations,' McKenzie said, 'just explain to us who murdered him.'

Meredith seemed stunned. 'Are you seriously telling me Kingham didn't take his own life?'

'Correct. To the letter. And that opens up a host of new possibilities . . . You could have killed them both.'

'That's ridiculous.'

'Is it? You had it in for Kingham. His wife was carrying a child you didn't want . . .'

'I didn't kill either of them. You know that. I couldn't have done. I was miles away, in France.'

'So you say.'

'It's the truth. How many more times do I have to repeat it?'

'Then I come back,' McKenzie said, 'to my original question. If you didn't kill Reg Kingham, who did?'

Meredith gave a weary shrug of his shoulders. 'I've no damned idea.'

'There are other possibilities,' Tench interposed gently. 'Perhaps Kingham didn't kill his wife after all.'

'Of course he killed her.' The words were dismissive.

'Perhaps he did, perhaps he didn't. We've no proof yet either way. But we're facing a new situation, Mr Meredith. You must appreciate that. Yesterday we had one murder, now we have two, and as Sergeant McKenzie said that raises the possibility that both Kingham and his wife were killed by the same person.'

'Well, it wasn't me, that's for sure,' Meredith said savagely.

'No, I don't think it was' – Tench was quiet, restrained – 'and I don't believe for a moment that Sergeant McKenzie thinks so either. Kingham was not merely tall, but broad and strong. It would have needed a man of exceptional strength to have overpowered him, bound him, and dragged him up to the top of that tower, though two men could have done it. All we're asking from you at the moment, Mr Meredith, is the help you so readily promised to give us. You say you didn't kill either Mr or Mrs Kingham. If you didn't, then we need to discover who did. Are you still willing to offer that help?'

Meredith threw out his hands. 'Yes, of course I am, but I don't see what possible help I can be.'

'Just think back,' said Tench, 'and think very hard. You admit you were on very close terms with Mrs Kingham.'

'We loved one another.'

'Then she must have confided in you a great deal.'

'Yes, she did.'

'Did she speak of her life with Kingham in India?'

'Yes, from time to time.'

'Did she tell you why he left his job with the jute firm?'

'Not in so many words. I think there was some trouble. He had to leave.'

'What kind of trouble?'

'That she didn't say. I thought at first that it might have been to do with his drinking.'

'At first?'

'Yes, but later on I changed my mind.'

'Why was that?'

'It was an odd remark she made. She said they had to get out of the country. It was dangerous for them to stay there any longer.'

'She actually used the word "dangerous"?'

Meredith nodded. 'Yes, she did.'

'What d'you think she meant by that?'

'I don't know. She wouldn't say any more, but whatever the trouble was, it was clearly something more serious than Kingham's drinking.'

'And that's all you can tell us?'

'Yes, I'm afraid it is. I didn't press her just then. The time wasn't right.'

Tench was thoughtful. He seemed to be studying the man. Then he made up his mind. 'Mr Meredith,' he said, 'you've offered false testimony not once, but twice, and wilfully misled us in the course of a vital murder investigation, and you still expect us to believe what you say. I could charge you here and now with wasting police time, and detain you for further questioning . . .'

'This time it's the truth. I swear it's the truth.'

'However,' the Chief Inspector continued, 'I'm prepared to release you pending further investigations, but only on three conditions. Since I may need to question you again, you will not go further than Blickling without first informing me, you will not on any account go anywhere near Breckton, and you will surrender your passport to me within the next two hours . . . You agree?'

A shrug. 'I can do nothing else.'

'Then you're free to leave, Mr Meredith.' Tench was curt. 'But remember. Any breach of your word and you'll be under arrest.'

Meredith made no reply. He pushed back his chair and made for the door. Once there, he seemed to hesitate for a moment as if he were going to speak. Then he changed his mind and, leaving the room, closed the door very gently behind him.

11.

McKenzie narrowed his eyes and looked down his nose.

'Don't say it,' said Tench. 'You wouldn't have let him go.'

'Too damned true I wouldn't.'

'We've no cause to hold him unless we find evidence that links him to the murders.'

'We could hold him on suspicion. He's lied to us twice.'

'We can't lock him up for any length of time on mere suspicion. We'd have to charge him, you know that. And I'm inclined to believe that this time he may very well be telling the truth.'

'Well, I'm not. The man's an inveterate liar. He wouldn't know the truth if it hit him in the face.'

McKenzie was blunt, but Tench, on occasion, could be equally so. 'That may be your view of things, Mac,' he said, 'but as far as we know Mr Meredith was in France from three days before the storm until five days after it. Before we can charge him, we need some solid evidence to prove that he wasn't.'

'And finding it won't be easy,' McKenzie said. 'If he was the one who dumped that body in the dinghy, we might well have found something vital at Morston – tyre marks or footprints – but the floods have washed away any chance we might have had.'

Tench thought for a moment. 'That's true enough,' he said. 'Not that I think Meredith was anywhere near Morston, but it does mean we need to look further afield.'

'You mean closer to home?'

'Much closer to home.'

'His nearest and dearest? The fragile Josephine?'

'Right first time.'

'Is she here yet?'

'She should be, unless Sue Gradwell's been having some trouble.'

'Fine. Let's have her in then. It's high time we had a little chat with this woman. If *she* can't shine a light on the dark side of Meredith, then nobody can.'

Tench dragged the phone towards him and lifted the receiver. 'Put me through to the CID room,' he said.

There was a pause, then he heard Lock's voice. 'Des,' he said, 'is Sue Gradwell back yet?'

'Yes, sir. She's with me.'

'Put her on then, will you?'

Another pause . . . 'Sir?'

'You managed it, Sue?'

'Yes, sir.'

'No trouble?'

'No, sir, none at all. She came like a lamb.'

'Where is she now?'

'Down in the canteen, sir, with Jules.'

'How does she seem?'

'Frighteningly normal, sir. An utterly different woman from the one we saw yesterday. She seemed to be expecting us. Just put on her coat and came without a murmur.'

'That's strange.'

'Yes. I thought so myself, sir.'

Tench gave a shrug. 'Well, bring her up, Sue,' he said, 'and bring Jules with you. I'll be interested to meet this female chameleon. I'm beginning to wonder which is the bigger dissembler, she or her husband.'

12.

Sue Gradwell showed her in, a pallid, slim, frail-looking woman, but one who carried herself erect and, facing the two detectives, seemed strangely undeterred.

Tench was already on his feet. 'Mrs Meredith?' he said.

'Yes.' Her voice was firm, the word crisp and clean.

'Thank you for coming.' He pulled out a chair. 'Please sit down.'

He saw that she was settled, and then resumed his seat with McKenzie behind the desk. 'This, ma'am,' he said, 'is Detective

Sergeant McKenzie and my name is Tench. Detective Chief Inspector Tench.'

She nodded and clasped her hands on her lap.

'Let me make things clear to you, ma'am,' he went on. 'You're not under arrest and you're not under oath. You're perfectly free to leave this room whenever you wish to do so. We've asked you to come here simply because we think you can help us. You understand that?'

She nodded again.

'There are certain formalities, ma'am, that we have to go through first. You are Josephine Meredith?'

'Yes.'

'You live at Green Park, Blickling?'

'Yes, I do.'

'And you're married to Giles Meredith, who lives at the same address?'

'Yes, that's right.'

'Thank you, ma'am,' said Tench. 'Now, as you may have heard, there has been a double tragedy at a house called The Woodlands in the village of Breckton. The owners of the house, a Mr and Mrs Kingham, have both been found dead in circumstances that we have to treat as suspicious.'

'Yes, I heard.' The admission sounded lazy, all but indifferent.

'That being so,' Tench continued, 'we need to check any movements seen around the house . . . You own a car, Mrs Meredith?'

'Yes.' Another nod.

'What make is it?'

'A Morris Minor.'

'What colour?'

She shrugged. 'It's a kind of gunmetal grey.'

'And the registration number?'

'CL4287.'

Tench glanced at McKenzie, and then resumed his questioning. 'I'd like you to think back, ma'am, to a week last Friday, the day before the storm. On the afternoon of that day you were seen at The Woodlands. What were you doing there?'

She gave a little laugh that transformed her face, making her appear for a moment almost beautiful. 'Are you really sure you want to know?' she said.

'If I didn't,' said Tench drily, 'I wouldn't have asked the question.'

'Very well.' She paused. 'I'll give you a straightforward answer, Chief Inspector. I went to The Woodlands with one intention, to kill Valerie Kingham.'

'And did you kill her?' This from McKenzie.

'No, I didn't.'

'Why not?'

'For the simple reason that I couldn't get in. The house was locked up. There was nobody there.'

'Are you sure about that?' said Tench. 'Did you look through the windows?'

'Those at the front, yes. You can't see through the back. The ground falls away, and the windows are too high. That's why the only other doors are on the sides.'

'Did you try them?'

'Yes. Both of them were locked.'

'Did you see anyone else while you were there?'

'Yes,' she said. 'There was a man in a van. I don't know who he was. He drove up just as I was leaving. I told him it was no use knocking, there was nobody in.'

Tench frowned. 'You say you intended to kill Mrs Kingham. Why on earth should you want to do that?'

'I wanted her out of our lives.'

'You mean yours and your husband's?'

'Yes.'

'But why?'

'She was stealing Giles away from me. I couldn't let her do that.'

'You're fond of your husband?'

'I love him,' she said. 'I've loved him ever since I first laid eyes on him. And apart from that . . .' She paused.

'Yes, Mrs Meredith?'

'He's mine,' she said fiercely. 'I married him, he's mine, and nobody, *nobody*, Chief Inspector, is ever going to steal what's rightfully mine.'

13.

McKenzie leaned back in his chair and stared at her. 'You expect us to believe all this rubbish?' he said.

'Rubbish?'

'Well, that's all it is, isn't it? If you find the word distasteful, let's call it a fabrication.'

'It isn't a fabrication.'

'You expect us to believe that, intending to kill Mrs Kingham, you drove to The Woodlands in your own car, a car that could be easily traced back to you? No sane person would ever do such a thing.'

She gave a little shrug. 'Perhaps at that time I wasn't exactly sane.'

'And just what d'you mean by that?'

'I was desperate. I knew she and Giles were planning something between them, and I'd no idea where either of them were.'

'But your husband was in Dublin. He told you so.'

'He was lying. I knew very well he was lying.'

'How did you know?'

'I can always tell.'

'Then why didn't you ring up Dublin, and check if he was there?'

'I did, and Paris. They both said he was with them, but attending a meeting. A man can't be in two places hundreds of miles apart at one and the same time.'

'But you must have thought Mrs Kingham was still at The Woodlands. You went there to kill her.'

'I didn't know where she was. I'd rung her up twice, and there'd been no reply.'

Tench intervened swiftly. 'When did you ring her up?'

'On the Friday morning.'

'Exactly when?'

'Once about eleven and then again at half past twelve.'

'And both times there was no reply?'

'That's right. I could hear the bell ringing, but nobody answered.'

'Then if it was clear she wasn't there,' McKenzie said, 'why did you go to the house intending to kill her?'

'I didn't know *where* she was, but it made no difference. If she *had* been there when I called, I'd have killed her.'

'You say you were desperate.'

'Yes.'

'Were you still desperate when WDC Gradwell and Constable Winterton called on you yesterday morning?'

'Of course I was.'

'Why? Your husband was already back from his travels. You must have known he wasn't with Mrs Kingham.'

She shook her head forcefully. 'That's just the point. I didn't.'

McKenzie glared at her. 'Why not?'

'I hadn't seen him.'

'But your husband arrived back on Thursday night. It was Saturday morning when Constable Gradwell called to see you. Are you telling us you still hadn't seen him by then?'

'Yes, that's exactly what I'm telling you.'

'He'd been back for thirty-six hours and you hadn't seen him?'

'No, I hadn't.'

McKenzie threw out his hands and looked towards Tench.

'I think, Mrs Meredith,' the Chief Inspector said, 'that we need to get things a little bit clearer. You say that on the Friday before the storm you were desperate to know where Mrs Kingham was, because you feared that she'd gone away with your husband?'

'Yes.'

'And when you left The Woodlands you still didn't know.'

'That's right.'

'Then once the storm was over, did you go back to the house?'

'No.'

'Why not?'

'Because I knew she wasn't there.'

'How did you know that?'

'I rang up every morning. There was still no reply.'

Tench gave a little nod. 'Now, Mrs Meredith, we know that your husband returned on the Thursday night, but you say that by the Saturday, when Constable Gradwell paid you a visit, you still hadn't seen him. Why was that?'

'He never came to Green Park that Thursday night, or if he did

150

I was asleep. There was certainly no sign of him on Friday morning and he didn't turn up all day, but when I got up on Saturday I found a note pushed through the door saying that he'd gone to London.'

'And that made you even more desperate.'

'Of course it did. I could only conclude that he'd taken her somewhere and was going to join her.'

Tench frowned. 'That was yesterday morning, Mrs Meredith, not much more than twenty-four hours ago, and yet you don't seem to me to be desperate now.'

'No, I'm not.'

'Then something must have happened to make you feel so different.'

'Yes, it did.'

'Then I'd very much like to know, ma'am, exactly what it was.'

'Quite simply,' she said, 'Giles came home last night and told me that Valerie was dead, and that Reg had killed her.'

'That must have been a great relief to you.'

She nodded. 'Yes, it was.'

'He said nothing about Reg also being dead?'

'No, he just said he was missing, and that you were trying to find him.'

'Then you didn't know he was dead till you came here this morning?'

'Not until Constable Gradwell told me.'

'Were you surprised?'

'No, not really. I just assumed he'd killed himself.'

'In a fit of remorse?'

'Oh, no, he wasn't the kind of man to feel any remorse. He must have known that with his record you'd be on to him pretty quickly.'

'His record? You mean because he was a drunkard who'd assaulted her before?'

'Yes, that of course, and what happened out in India.'

It was now Tench's turn to narrow his eyes. 'And what *did* happen in India, Mrs Meredith?'

'Surely you know.'

'Yes, but I'd still like to hear it again from you.'

She made a little helpless gesture with her hands. 'Well, I don't know very much, but Reg got into some kind of trouble out there.'

'What sort of trouble?'

'I don't know exactly. Val didn't say, but I think he got himself mixed up in a court case. Whatever it was, it must have been quite serious, because she said that was why they'd had to come back to England.'

'When did she say this?'

'Oh, very early on. Soon after they rented the lodge at Blickling.'

'Did you tell your husband?'

'No, I don't think I did.'

'Why not?'

'I can't really remember. I must have assumed that he already knew.'

Tench nodded again thoughtfully. 'Well, thank you, ma'am,' he said. He turned towards McKenzie. 'Are there any more questions you'd like to ask Mrs Meredith?'

The sergeant breathed deeply. 'No, sir,' he said. 'Not at the moment.'

'Constable Gradwell?'

Sue shook her head.

'Then that's all, Mrs Meredith.' Tench spoke smoothly. 'Thank you for your assistance and for being so patient.'

'I take it your sergeant's satisfied?'

'I'm sure he's been most impressed by your candour, ma'am. We may of course need to ask for your help again later, but in the meantime you're perfectly free to leave. Constable Gradwell will drive you back to Blickling.'

'Then I'll say good afternoon to you, Chief Inspector.' She pushed back her chair, and with one last withering glance at McKenzie turned on her heel and walked out of the room.

14.

Sue Gradwell and Winterton followed her out, and the door closed behind them.

'Well?' said Tench.

McKenzie gave a hollow kind of laugh. 'Don't ask me,' he said. 'Between the pair of them they've got me completely confused. There's only one thing I'm sure of. They're both of them lying. It wouldn't surprise me to find that they'd hatched some plan between them to get rid of both the Kinghams.'

'What she said was plausible.'

McKenzie gave another laugh. 'In my long experience that's a word people use when they're trying to convince themselves against all the odds. You're reluctant to think they're guilty.'

'I need some solid evidence to prove that they are, and so far we haven't got any.'

'It must be somewhere around. I've questioned enough suspects to know when someone's lying. They're mixed up in these murders somehow, but don't ask me how.'

Tench was silent for a moment. 'They're mixed up in them, yes. They were both too closely connected to the Kinghams not to be involved, but that may simply be due to a coincidence of timing: the fact that Kingham and his wife were both of them murdered at precisely the time when Meredith was planning to leave his own wife and make off with Valerie to some place in France.'

'And that's a recipe for murder if ever there was one. It's the old eternal triangle, Mike. It has to be.'

'Possibly, but from what I've seen of Meredith I doubt very much if he's capable of murder, and the same goes for Mrs Meredith too.'

'Crippen seemed to be the last sort of chap who'd commit a murder, but he chopped up his wife and made off with his mistress on a ship to New York.'

'Yes, that's true.'

'And sweet Josephine, in this very room less than half an hour ago, said she went to Breckton to kill Mrs Kingham.'

Tench nodded. 'That's also true, but when it came to the pinch I don't think she'd have done it.' He paused. 'Look, Mac,' he said, 'my point is this. We've got two unsolved murders on our hands. It's ten days ago since either of the victims was last seen alive, and apart from Kingham himself, who's one of the victims, and Mr and Mrs Meredith, who seem to me to be unlikely killers with no scrap of solid evidence against them, we've only two other possible suspects.'

153

'You mean Zack's two little pals at the tower?'

'The coloured men, yes.'

'You're still trying to make a connection with this Indian business?'

'Why not?' Tench looked at him sharply.

'Well, it seems a very long shot to me. India's thousands of miles away, and these men may not be Indians at all.'

'But they could be, and if they are they may hold the key to this case. It seems to me, Mac, that, just at the moment, we're wasting far too much time on the Merediths. I think we should set them aside, at least for a while, and look a bit closer at these two men who showed such an unexplained interest in the tower. I want to know more about this Indian business. What was this court case that Kingham was involved in that made it too dangerous for him and his wife to stay in the country? If he was in danger when he left, he might still have been in danger once he got back here.'

McKenzie shook his head. 'Well, he might, I suppose. It's a remote possibility, but I can't imagine two Indians travelling six thousand miles just to throw Kingham from the top of a tower.'

'India's a strange country, Mac.'

'Maybe it is, but it'll take more than an Indian rope trick to persuade me there's a link.'

Tench was stubborn. 'I still want to hear what Gregg has to say.'

McKenzie gave a shrug. 'Well, fair enough,' he said. 'Devereux's the man to know all the facts. When's Gregg seeing him?'

'Not till late tonight. I've arranged with Tremayne for a car to be waiting at Truro station. He'll be driven from there down to Porthallack. It has to be tonight, because Devereux's sailing from Southampton tomorrow. He's off to a lecture tour in the States.'

'That means Gregg won't be back until late tomorrow. So what do we do? Wait?'

'We wait. Unless the team's turned up something else in the meantime, it's all we *can* do. There'll be an appeal in the press tomorrow morning for the two coloured men to make themselves known.'

'You've not forgotten the Chief Super's due back this evening?'

'No, but I'll not be seeing him until tomorrow morning, and I've told Gregg to ring me as soon as he gets back to Truro. It'll mean a late night, but I'm hoping he'll tell me enough to be able to prove to Hastings that we're making some progress. Enough at least for him to stave off the Met.'

McKenzie yawned and stretched. 'Well, the best of British luck,' he said. 'I think you're going to need it. When you say your prayers tonight, just take care to add a couple of other requests.'

'What are they?'

'That you're right and I'm wrong, and that we don't find ourselves stuck up an Indian gum tree without a rope ladder.'

VII

THE CASE OF SOURAV SINGH

Revenge is a kind of wild justice.
Francis Bacon: *Of Revenge*

1.

It was late in the evening when Andrew Gregg stepped from the train at Truro station and into the car that was waiting to take him down to Porthallack. The air was cold and still, a pleasant change from the cutting Arctic winds that had swept across Norfolk, and having slept at least half the way from Paddington, he was wide awake and ready to face the world with more than a little optimism.

This was the kind of assignment he always enjoyed: to hop on a train, sit back and relax, think about a way to tackle the task ahead, drift off to sleep, and once at his destination ask the questions he'd prepared to get the answers he needed. Then back on the train to Norwich to make his report, happy in the knowledge of a job well done.

It was, of course, never as simple as that. More often than not he'd have to pit his wits against people reluctant to reveal the facts he needed, but this he regarded as a challenge to be faced, a chessboard battle to be fought with ruthless persistence and won. He'd fought such battles before, against tight-lipped mandarins in Whitehall offices intent on preserving War Office secrets, against crusty old colonels jealously clinging to regimental loyalties, and grief-stricken mothers determined to protect their sons' reputations, and he was quite prepared to fight one against Sir Alan Devereux should he prove to be awkward.

The trouble was that he knew nothing at all about him except that he must have been a very successful man of business, and such men were usually not just astute, but ruthless and secretive into the bargain.

So just how secretive was he likely to be about Reginald Kingham? That was the vital question, and one to which Gregg would have given much to find an answer before he came face to face with the man.

He turned to the driver, a young constable from Truro. 'D'you know anything about Sir Alan Devereux?' he asked.

The young man gave a laugh. 'Sorry, sir,' he said. 'Can't help you, I'm afraid. Never heard of him myself till a couple of hours ago. What does he do for a living?'

'He's retired now,' said Gregg. 'Spent most of his life in India. Ran a company out there.'

'Don't know much about India.' The young man kept his eyes on the ribbon of road ahead. 'Met a brigadier once though who'd made a career there. Riding a bike, he was, in Helston. Put up a hand and stopped me. Said I was driving too fast. Bit my head off, he did. Threatened to report me to the Chief Constable. Red-faced bloke, moustache, proper short-tempered. Reckon it was living out there too long had made him like that. They say it's the sun, sir, don't they? Dries 'em up inside.'

Gregg nodded and smiled. 'Yes, Constable, I believe they do, but let's hope it doesn't apply to Sir Alan. I'd rather not go back to Norwich without a head.'

He drew a deep breath, and resigned himself to watching the road unwind in the headlights as the car sped on through the night towards the Helford River.

2.

Devereux's house at Porthallack was set transversely across the point at the mouth of the river, commanding unrivalled views of both the coast and the river itself as it wound upstream to Helford, but all Gregg could glimpse before he rang the bell on that moonless night was the bulk of the house, even darker than the night, and a white-pillared porch enclosing what appeared to be a heavy oaken door.

As it opened, light flooded out to reveal a thin young man wearing rimless spectacles, who announced himself as Devereux's private secretary. 'Sir Alan's expecting you, Inspector,' he said. 'He's waiting in the library. If you'll please follow me . . .'

The library was a spacious oak-panelled room, two walls of which were lined with floor-to-ceiling bookshelves. The third was covered by rich green velvet curtains, while the fourth contained a wide-spreading hearth with a log fire that threw flickering shadows across the shelves.

The lighting was soft and warm from a single standard lamp set beside an armchair close to the hearth, and the whole effect was one of a peaceful retreat where a man could relax and smoke a pipe with an after-dinner drink.

The figure that rose from the chair to greet him was as far removed from that of a choleric brigadier as it was possible to imagine. Sir Alan was short of stature, five foot four at the most, clean-shaven and wearing an open-necked shirt, black sweater and flannels. His voice, when he spoke, was quiet, almost gentle, but it carried with it a hint of that confidence that always accompanies success.

'Inspector Gregg?' He offered his hand. 'Glad to meet you. Do please sit down.' He gestured to a second armchair on the opposite side of the hearth. 'You've had a long journey.'

'Yes, quite long, sir,' said Gregg, 'but I managed to sleep for most of the way.'

'Very sensible.' Sir Alan nodded. 'I'm sorry our meeting has to be late at night, but, as you know, I'm off across the pond tomorrow, and your chief inspector – Tench is his name? – made it clear that he was dealing with a case of murder and that time was of the essence . . . Can I offer you a coffee?'

'Oh, please, sir,' said Gregg. 'At the risk of mixing metaphors, railway coffee isn't my cup of tea.'

Devereux smiled. 'Nor mine.' He crossed to a percolator simmering on a stand in the corner of the room. 'Black or white?'

'Black, please.'

'Sugar?'

'No, sir. Never take it.'

Devereux poured a cup, set it on a small table beside Gregg's elbow, and repeated the process for himself. 'Now,' he said, settling down in the chair, 'let's get down to business. I gather that this case concerns one of my ex-employees.'

Gregg nodded. 'That's right, sir.'

'Is he a suspect?'

'No, sir, the victim.'

'I see.' Sir Alan took a sip of his coffee. 'And his name?'

'Kingham, sir. Reginald Kingham.'

'Of course.' Sir Alan nodded twice slowly.

'You don't sound surprised, sir.'

'No, Inspector, I'm not. It had to be Kingham . . . So what is it you need to know?'

'Whatever you can tell us about him, sir. As you'll realize, in a case of murder the best hope we have of tracing the killer is to find out everything we can about the victim, and what we know about Kingham is little enough. We've been told that he was employed by your firm in Calcutta as a trainee manager for one of your jute mills, but that he left before completing the course.'

'Yes, that's correct.'

'And also that he left because he was mixed up in some court case that made it too dangerous for him to stay in the country. Is that correct as well?'

'Yes, absolutely.'

'Then it must have been something particularly serious.'

'It was. It was indeed.'

'Can you tell us precisely what?'

Sir Alan took a long, deep draught of his coffee. 'Oh, yes, I can tell you, Inspector. There's no secret about it. It's all in the records.'

He paused for a moment.

'Kingham,' he said, 'was tried on a charge of murder.'

3.

'Was he?' Gregg's eyes revealed more than a flicker of interest. 'Now why is it my turn not to be surprised?'

'Perhaps,' said Devereux, 'because all you've heard about the man is unfortunately true. Kingham was the type who, sooner or later, was bound to be charged with murder.'

'Who was he accused of killing?'

Sir Alan drained his cup. 'Before we get on to that,' he said, 'since you seem to know nothing at all about the case, I think it'd be better to start at the beginning. Are you a good listener?'

'In my job, sir, I have to be.'

'Good,' – Sir Alan nodded approvingly – 'because we need to go back a considerable way, two generations to be precise, to Kingham's grandfather. His name was Mitchison, Oliver

162

Mitchison, and he was the man who founded the firm and built it up into a profitable and well-respected trading concern. He'd hoped to have a son to succeed him in the business, but unfortunately all he had was a daughter, Angeline. She married an army officer, a colonel in the Gurkhas, John Kingham by name, and their son, the only child of the union, was christened Reginald . . . Clear so far?'

'Yes, sir. Perfectly clear.'

'Right. Let's move on. Old Oliver left everything he possessed to his daughter, so Angeline, when she married John Kingham, was, in her own right, a very wealthy woman who retained a controlling interest in the firm. However, there was some disagreement between her and her husband over Reginald's future. John Kingham, perhaps naturally, wanted his son to make a career in the army, but Angeline had very different ideas. She wanted him to join the firm and hoped that he'd eventually take his grandfather's place. She had her father's strength of character. Her views prevailed over those of her husband, and so, when he was old enough, she sent him to England to stay with her only living relative, an elderly aunt who was living in London, and paid for him to receive the best education she could possibly buy. He went first to Eton and then to Trinity College, Cambridge, but even so early he betrayed both his mother's trust and her ambitions. At the end of his second year at Trinity he was sent down for gambling, drinking and breaking a fellow undergraduate's jaw. At that point, it seems, the aunt had had enough of him. She packed him off back to his mother in Calcutta with the stricture that he needed a father's discipline . . . Are you still with me?'

'Every inch of the way, sir,' said Gregg. 'Please carry on.'

'Well,' – Sir Alan poured himself more coffee – 'this was 1944, a time when the Japs were threatening to break through the Allied defences into India. Travelling was difficult. He had to join a convoy of British troops bound for Bombay, and the journey, halfway across the Atlantic and then round the Cape, took him two months. During that time his father was killed in the fighting around Imphal and Kohima, and he landed back home to find his father dead and his mother distraught. For a short while this seemed to sober him down, but he was adamant he wasn't going to join the firm. Pushing a pen in an office, he said, wasn't his type of work. His mother found him a post with the river authority, training to be a pilot, but he didn't hold it for long. After a night's hard drinking he ran a boat aground on some mud flats in the Hooghly, and the authority dismissed him.

'For the next five years he had a succession of jobs in and around Calcutta, but wherever he went and whatever he did his addiction to drink and his violent temper led in the end to abrupt dismissal. At last even his mother lost patience. She issued him with an ultimatum. He would either join the firm and buckle down to some serious work, or she'd alter her will and cut him off without a penny to his name. At first he was mutinous, but she too was adamant, and after a while he sullenly acquiesced, and two years ago, almost to the very day, she came to me and asked me to take him on as a trainee manager.'

Sir Alan gave a sigh. 'I was reluctant to do it, and told her so. I'd heard quite a bit about Reginald Kingham, and the idea that he'd make a successful manager seemed to me to be grotesque, but she simply wouldn't take no for an answer. "He's been wild," she said, "yes, but he's a good boy at heart, and I'm sure he's learnt his lesson."

'I still argued against it, but in the end, her interest in the firm being what it was, I couldn't refuse, and a few days later he came to see me and commenced his course of training.'

Sir Alan sighed again. 'I should never have agreed. He cost his mother her life, placed his own in jeopardy, and caused the firm intense embarrassment. He proved, in fact, to be what I'd always feared he would be. A total disaster.'

4.

'We assumed that much, sir,' said Gregg, 'from the few facts we were able to piece together, but we've still no idea what he actually did. You say he was tried for murder?'

'Yes, he was, with all the publicity attendant on such a trial, and a lot more besides.'

'Who was he accused of killing?'

'An Indian unfortunately, and worse still, a Hindu.'

'Ah,' said Gregg, 'I see.'

Sir Alan shook his head. 'No, Inspector, I don't think you do. You can't possibly see until you have all the facts laid out before you, so let me explain. Mitchison and Blake was a British company. We owned half a dozen mills on the banks of the Hooghly, processing the jute that was grown in the Ganges delta, spinning and weaving it into coarse cloths such as canvas and hessian, and making such articles as tents and gunny bags. We were also a trading concern, exporting raw jute to places like Dundee, the jutopolis of Scotland as it used to be called, where it was processed in mills on the side of the Tay.

'We'd operated for years in British India, and built up a reputation for honesty and respectability, but this was 1951 and the land was no longer British. It wasn't the Raj. It was an independent India, a Hindu state four years into its life. We were, in effect, a foreign concern, dependent for our survival on steering clear of controversy and doing nothing to offend Hindu susceptibilities. We were also, and this was equally important, in a country where the Muslims who'd chosen to remain were viewed with suspicion, especially in Calcutta, which had always been a predominantly Hindu city . . . D'you follow me?'

'Yes, sir.'

'It's a long tale, Inspector . . . How about more coffee?'

'Thank you, sir,' said Gregg. 'I think perhaps I will.'

Sir Alan poured him another cup and set it down on the table. 'We gave our trainee managers a twelve-month course,' he said. 'For the first six months they worked in the office at one of the mills, learning about the business in all its different aspects, and then a further six months side by side with a manager. During the whole of this time they were lodged in a three-storey building in one of the Calcutta suburbs. Known as the Battery, it had been the firm's headquarters till we moved to new offices closer to both the river and the mills. It had then been converted into flats, each of which was shared by two trainees, and Kingham was allotted a top-floor flat, which he shared with a young man fresh out from England, Patrick Beresford.

'The trainees worked a long day, from ten to twelve hours, the heat in the city was oppressive, and once the day's work was over, it was their custom to gather together in the Gymkhana

Club for a drink and a chat before dinner, and Kingham, of course, was prone to drink more than most of his friends.

'Each pair of trainees had a servant who lived in the Battery grounds, and Kingham and Beresford took on as theirs a young Hindu called Sourav Singh. He had a wife, Lakshmi, and a small son not more than nine months old, both of whom lived with him in the compound.'

Sir Alan paused. 'All might have been well,' he said, 'if Kingham had not been the type of man he was, and Sourav Singh had been a different kind of servant, but Kingham was a drinker with a violent temper, and Sourav Singh . . . well, who knows what he was?

'Whatever he may have been, their close association provided a mixture that was potentially explosive. It blew up in their faces. The results were catastrophic.'

5.

'For several months,' Sir Alan went on, 'Singh proved to be a more than competent servant, but then his work began to deteriorate, and it was during the steamy heat of the monsoon season that the incident occurred which led to all the trouble.

'For some little time Kingham and Beresford had been missing things from the flat. Kingham had lost a couple of shirts, Beresford a suit, and other small articles of clothing such as socks and ties unaccountably disappeared. The obvious suspect was Singh, but when taxed with the thefts he roundly denied any knowledge of what had happened.

'Then, both on the same day, Beresford lost a pair of gold cufflinks and Kingham a signet ring that had, for him, great sentimental value. The thief, they decided, had to be Singh, and they determined to search his quarters in the compound, and taking with them as a witness a trustworthy Indian called Ram Gopal, the head waiter from the company's communal dining room, they entered the place and, as Singh and his wife stood by, conducted their search.

'They turned out all his boxes, but despite going through them a second time just to make sure, could find no trace of the missing articles. It would have been a frustrating hour if they hadn't made two other significant discoveries. In one of the boxes Kingham found a number of pawn tickets that seemed to refer to items of clothing, and Beresford uncovered a small tin containing a soft black substance which had a peculiar smell. He handed it to Ram Gopal. "What's that?" he asked. The Indian sniffed at it. "Opium, sahib," he said. "Are you sure?" Kingham asked him. Ram Gopal gave a sad little smile. "Oh, yes, sahib," he said. "I am seeing it and smelling it too many times not to be sure."

'The two men looked at one another, and then at Sourav Singh. They said nothing more. Picking up the tin and the tickets, they left, taking Ram Gopal with them, but as far as both were concerned Singh's guilt had been proved. The company servants were forbidden to smoke opium, and if Singh was an addict he was going to need money to fund his addiction. Opium was expensive. It cost far more than his wages would provide, and what better way was there of finding the money than by stealing from his masters and pawning or selling the stolen articles down in the bazaar?

'That night they gave the tickets to Ram Gopal, and provided him with enough money to visit the pawnshops the following morning and redeem what was listed. "And if my ring and your cufflinks aren't among them," Kingham said, "we'll have Singh up here in the Battery tomorrow night, and make him tell us where they are."'

Sir Alan gave a shrug and made a helpless gesture with his hands. 'What happened after that,' he said, 'was totally predictable.'

6.

Gregg nodded. 'I think I can guess, sir,' he said.

'You do?' Sir Alan seemed amused. 'If you did make a guess, I'm quite sure you'd be wrong. You see, Inspector, though what happened was in one sense totally predictable, in another it was utterly unexpected. Not even those who knew Kingham as we did could have foreseen the pattern events were to take . . . Let me explain.

'The following day was particularly hot and sultry. The temperature was close on a hundred degrees, and when at last the two men repaired to the Gymkhana Club, they probably drank a good deal more than usual. Ram Gopal had managed to redeem most of the stolen items of clothing, but he'd found no trace of either the ring or the cufflinks, so immediately after dinner Kingham sent a message down to the servants' quarters, telling Sourav Singh that his masters wanted to see him right away in the Battery.

'His wife watched him go, but with some trepidation. She knew that her husband was guilty of theft, and, afraid of what might happen, she followed him to Kingham's flat with her child in her arms. Servants' wives were not allowed in the Battery building, so she had to wait outside, looking up at the open window. After a while she heard voices raised in anger, and what she thought was a cry of pain from Sourav Singh. This alarmed her so much that she ran as fast as she could back to the servants' quarters, calling out for help. "The masters are hurting my husband," she said.

'A number of the other wives joined her at the Battery. By then it was getting dark, and a light shone out from the window of the flat. The voices were still raised in anger, and they heard at intervals what sounded like protests and cries of pain. Then all of a sudden there was a piercing scream. Lakshmi was distraught. "They're killing him," she sobbed. "The masters are killing Sourav Singh. What can we do?"'

Sir Alan paused again. 'There was nothing they could possibly have done,' he said, 'because at that very instant the unexpected happened. Without any warning, the body of a man fell from the lighted window. It was Sourav Singh. As he hit the ground, Lakshmi screamed and dashed forward. Still clutching her baby, she cradled Singh in her arms and called out his name, but he didn't reply.

'For a moment or two there was utter confusion, then Kingham and Beresford came running from the Battery. Kingham bent down, then he turned to the other man. "Find a car," he said, "we need to get him to a doctor."

'It was all to no avail. Sourav Singh was already beyond recall. He never regained consciousness and died that night in hospital.'

7.

Gregg nodded slowly. 'So Kingham was charged with murder.'

'They were both charged with murder. Beresford too. But not right away. There was more trouble to come.' He peered closely at Gregg in the flickering light. 'Would you like a break now, or d'you want me to carry on right to the end?'

'Carry on, sir, please. I'm still wide awake, and I need to know all you can possibly tell me.'

'Well,' said Sir Alan, 'I knew that the firm was in a difficult position, and I had to tread carefully. It was obvious that charges were going to be brought, and I needed to know all the facts of the case. I called in both the men and spoke to them separately, and they both gave the same account of what had occurred. When Sourav Singh arrived at the Battery, they said, they'd seated him on a chair with his back to the window and began to question him. They showed him the clothes Ram Gopal had recovered, and then asked him what he'd done with the ring and the cufflinks. He said he knew nothing about a ring or a pair of cufflinks. He'd taken the clothes, yes, but only because he'd needed money to pay a debt. He'd intended to bring them back later on, but he'd never touched anything else. They told him he was lying. He'd stolen them and sold them down in the bazaar. No, he hadn't, he'd protested, he'd never even seen them.

'According to what both men told me, Singh, by this time, appeared to be very frightened. He was sweating profusely, twisting on his seat, and seemed to be searching for some way to escape. They told him again that he was nothing but a liar. If he hadn't sold the ring and the links, he must have hidden them somewhere. So where were they? If he didn't tell them now, here and on the spot, they'd take him straight down and hand him over to the police.

'At this, Sourav Singh glanced desperately to left and right, then all of a sudden leapt up from his chair, made a dash for the window and threw himself out.

'That was their story, but, needless to say, it wasn't the one that was noised around in the servants' quarters. Kingham sahib, they said, and Beresford sahib had tortured Singh to make him confess. They'd beaten him so hard that at last they'd killed him, and then, to save their own skins, thrown him out of the window.'

Sir Alan seemed to hesitate, collecting his thoughts. For a moment or two he let the silence lengthen. When at last he spoke again, he said, 'You'll realize, Inspector, that the situation was a very delicate one. I couldn't be seen attempting to influence any of the legal proceedings – that would only have further damaged the firm's reputation – but I had to make sure that, as employees of ours, Kingham and Beresford received fair treatment. There would have to be an inquest, and it seemed to me that, lacking independent witnesses to what had happened that night in the room at the Battery, the verdict would depend on the results of the autopsy on Sourav Singh's body. I therefore decided to wait on events.

'At first they seemed to vindicate my decision. The pathologist's report declared that all the injuries on the body were consistent with a fall from the window of the flat, and there were, moreover, no signs that Singh had been tortured, beaten or physically maltreated in any way. The magistrate therefore returned a verdict of suicide. It was plain, he said, that knowledge of his own guilt and fear of the consequences had so disturbed the balance of Sourav Singh's mind that he'd taken his own life.

'So far, it seemed, so good. Apart from the disciplinary proceedings I'd have to take against both Kingham and Beresford, the case, it appeared, was closed. But it wasn't. Far from it. News of what had happened that sultry night at the Battery had spread far beyond Calcutta. There'd been headlines in the papers all over India, and once the inquest was over, Hindu indignation at what was regarded as a grotesque verdict transformed those headlines into screams of outrage. Hadn't Singh's cries of pain been quite clearly heard coming from the flat? Was this magistrate merely a lackey of the British? Had the company paid him to falsify the evidence?'

Sir Alan sighed again. 'And that, of course,' he said, 'was the point when the Kali took up the case.'

8.

Gregg frowned. 'The Kali?'

'To give it its full title, the Sons of Kali, a fanatical Hindu youth organization, named after the goddess of death and destruction. It was a wayward offshoot of one of the larger Hindu political parties, and some of its aims appeared innocent enough – the preservation, for instance, of Hindu customs and culture, and a return to the pure Hinduism of two thousand years ago – but it was also violently anti-Muslim, and another of its often-declared intentions was to eradicate Islam root and branch. It was believed to have had associations, though these were never proved, with Apte and Godse, the men who were hanged for the murder of Gandhi, and who killed him, you remember, because he was preaching brotherly love and toleration of Muslims.

'The affair at the Battery, with all its potential for explosive publicity, was just the sort of case to attract the attention of the movement's leaders. A young Hindu, as they believed, had been murdered by foreigners, and the killers had got away with the crime scot-free. This could not be allowed to happen. Justice must be done, and be seen to be done.

'So what did they do? Something that threw the whole case once more into turmoil. They directed Lakshmi, Sourav Singh's widow, to bring a private prosecution for murder against Kingham and Beresford.'

He paused.

Gregg waited. 'That must have been distinctly awkward, sir,' he said.

'Yes, it was.'

'What did you do?'

Sir Alan leaned forward and tossed another log on the dwindling fire. 'As a matter of fact, Inspector, I did nothing at all. I'd resolved long before not to interfere in the legal process, and, indeed, it seemed to me that the best thing that could happen for the sake of both men was for all the known facts of the case to come out in open court. Given the pathologist's evidence at the inquest, I found it impossible to believe that any such court could return a guilty verdict against either Kingham or Beresford.'

'So the trial went ahead?'

'Yes, it did. It lasted five days, and on every one of those days members of the Kali packed the public gallery, giving the prosecution vociferous support. But the outcome, of course, was exactly what I'd predicted it would be. The two men were found not guilty and discharged.'

'But that wasn't the end of it?'

'No, it wasn't, not by a long chalk. The leaders of the Kali left the court more outraged than before, vowing that Kingham and Beresford must pay for the wanton murder of an innocent Hindu. In the next few weeks both men received death threats, and it became quite clear that, for the sake of their own safety, we needed to get them out of the country as quickly as possible. We therefore put them on the first available boat and sent them back to England.'

'And that was the last you saw of them?'

'Yes, it was, thankfully in Kingham's case.'

'You heard no more of him?'

'No, and I made no inquiries. Frankly, Inspector, I just didn't care. My concern was for the company. Getting rid of him was purely a cosmetic process, like cutting out a wart. I don't think it made much difference to him anyway. He'd have left of his own accord before completing the course. He was, by that time, an independent spirit, and a wealthy one too. The strain of it all, coming so soon after the death of her husband, had proved too much, even for his mother's indomitable will. Three weeks before the trial she'd suffered a series of strokes and died within a day. He'd inherited everything, including her substantial holdings in the firm. He was free and unrestrained. He could do what he liked, and he'd never made any secret of the fact that it wasn't his prime objective in life to be the manager of a mill, or to spend any longer in India than he had to. What we did merely forestalled the inevitable. He'd have left us even if this trouble hadn't happened. He'd already made arrangements to sell his mother's shares.'

'And he must have been already married by that time.'

'Yes, he was. As soon as he knew we intended to send him back to England, he arranged to marry some girl from Calcutta. I don't know who she was, and I didn't try to find out. All

I know is what I heard: that she took the next boat and followed him home.'

'And you heard nothing more about him until this weekend?'

'Not until you arrived tonight and mentioned his name. I won't say I'd completely forgotten about the man, but I'd thrust him to the back of my memory, and that's where I fervently hoped he'd remain. He'd caused enough trouble in the short time he was with us, and I can't say that Mr Reginald Kingham formed part of my happiest recollections of India.'

9.

'And now,' said Gregg, 'we've brought him back into mind. I must apologize for that. I did contact your London office and spoke to a man called Dauncey, but he said it was against company rules for him to answer any queries about Mr Kingham. He referred me to Calcutta, and since we needed to know the facts of the case urgently, I thought it best to come and see you.'

'Ah, yes,' said Sir Alan, 'company rules. My fault, I'm afraid. At the time of the trouble, to avoid worse publicity, I gave out instructions that no one was to answer any questions from outsiders about either Kingham or Beresford. Any such inquiries were to be passed straight to me. Apparently, though I'm no longer with the firm, my writ still runs. I'm sorry about that. You did right to come to me. I can only hope that what I've told you tonight answers all your questions.'

'All except one, sir, and that, to us, is the most important of all.'

'And what would it be?'

Gregg took his time. When at last he spoke, it was with some hesitation. 'D'you think it possible, sir, that the vengeance of the Kali could have followed Kingham here?'

Sir Alan frowned. 'Are you asking me whether they could possibly have killed him?'

'Yes, sir, I am.'

'Then first I must ask *you* a question, Inspector . . . How did he die?'

'We believe he may have been pushed or thrown from the top of a tower.'

Sir Alan nodded thoughtfully. 'Then I'd say yes, it's possible.'

'You mean, sir, that after more than a year a couple of Hindus could have travelled six thousand miles just to satisfy the fury of the Kali?'

'Indians have long-abiding memories, Inspector. Time and distance mean little enough to them. It was twenty years after the massacre at Amritsar that Sir Michael O'Dwyer was shot by an Indian while attending a London meeting. A year's a mere fleabite, six thousand miles a thing of no consequence in a matter such as this . . . But tell me, why did you say a couple of Hindus? One would have been enough.'

'We've evidence that two coloured men, possibly Indians, were seen around the tower on the day before Kingham's death, and we know he was bound and gagged sometime before he died.'

Sir Alan seemed to ponder the statement. At last he said, 'I can only tell you what I personally feel. I may be right, I may be wrong. It's for you to decide. But from what you've told me and from what I already know, yes, the Kali could well have had a hand in it. You see, Inspector, I've another piece of evidence that you won't know about.'

'You have, sir?'

'Yes. You asked me whether I'd heard anything about Kingham, and I said no, I hadn't, but you never asked me about Beresford.'

'And you've heard something about *him*, sir?'

'Oh yes,' said Sir Alan. 'More than enough to waken some suspicions in my mind. He settled in Eastbourne and took a job with a shipping firm in London. Then, one morning last August just after dawn, he was found dead at the foot of the cliffs at Beachy Head. At the inquest the coroner returned an open verdict. There was nothing to show exactly what had happened. His car was still in the garage at his flat. Suicide seemed unlikely, so who can tell, Inspector? Was he driven to Beachy Head? Was he thrown? Was he pushed? Or did he simply take a walk in the darkness and lose his footing? It's all very strange, and I wish I knew the answer.'

'So do I,' said Gregg, 'and I think my Chief Inspector's bound to feel the same.'

Sir Alan raised his hand. 'How long ago is it since Kingham was murdered?'

'Roughly ten days, sir.'

'Then a word of warning. If these two men have travelled all the way from India, they'll be out of the country by now, and it may be next to impossible to find them. On the other hand, if they're living in England – and the Kali has its adherents here too – you may stand a chance, but you'll have to move fast before the trail grows cold.' He stood up and stretched. 'Wish your Chief Inspector the best of luck from me,' he said. 'I've a feeling he's going to need it.'

VIII

THE PERVERSITY OF LUBBOCK

'You are old, Father William,' the young man said,
  'And your hair has become very white;
And yet you incessantly stand on your head –
  Do you think, at your age, it is right?'
Lewis Carroll: *Alice's Adventures in Wonderland*

1.

The sound of the phone wakened Mike Tench from a first deep sleep. He groped for the receiver, muttered his name and, still struggling with his wits, heard a voice on the line. 'It's Gregg, sir. From Truro.'

Alert in an instant, he switched on the bedside lamp and glanced at the clock. It showed half past two.

'You're in Truro?'

'Yes, sir. I'm back at the station.'

'You've seen Sir Alan Devereux?'

'Yes, sir.'

'What did he have to say?'

'Quite a lot, sir.'

'Just give me the main points. Leave the rest till you're back.'

Gregg paraphrased as best he could. 'That's the gist of it, sir.'

'Then he thought it was possible?'

'That's what he said, but what he implied was a good deal more.'

'Probable rather than possible?'

'In view of what's happened to Beresford, yes.'

'And what's your impression?'

'I think he's right, sir.'

'Then we need to find these two men.'

'I'd say so, sir, yes. If they're still in this country.'

'Right. That's all I need to know. Relax and get some food. You've a long journey back.'

'Don't worry, sir,' said Gregg. 'I'm taking the early train. There's a restaurant car, and once I've had breakfast I'll be dozing for most of the way back to Paddington.'

'See you later on today then.'

'Yes, sir, unless the points freeze solid near Norwich.'

'I don't think they will,' said Tench. 'The forecast's for milder weather.'

He replaced the receiver, set the alarm for half past five and switched off the light. In another five minutes he was soundly asleep.

2.

At half past six he was back in his office, reading through the reports that had landed on his desk the previous evening.

Two in particular caught and held his attention: Nick Vincent's autopsy report on Kingham, and the one from Lester on his team's examination of the tower.

Vincent's, apart from containing all the points that he'd made in the course of his phone call, added that his analysis of the body's stomach contents proved that Kingham had eaten nothing in the twenty-four hours preceding his death, but had consumed the equivalent of two and a half large bottles of whisky, enough to put a normal man out for the duration. The question was what effect had it had upon Kingham, considering the amount that he regularly drank – a question that, at the moment, seemed impossible to answer.

The scene-of-crime team, examining the tower, had found that the top-storey room contained a table and two chairs, presumably left behind when the Home Guard evacuated the place at the end of the war. One of the chairs had been drawn up to the window, and there were multiple scuff marks and footprints in the dust on the floor, but the prints were so numerous and so overlaid that it had been impossible to isolate any single one. The glass in the window had been shattered many years before, but shards still remained in the frame, and from these the team had removed shreds of fabric which, on analysis, had proved to be threads of black wool. Similar threads had also been found adhering to the edges of some of the stairs.

Lester had been careful to draw no conclusions from any of his findings, but since Kingham had been wearing a black woollen sweater when he'd fallen from the tower, it seemed obvious enough that he'd been somehow rolled or dragged up the stairs, dumped on a chair and then toppled across the window frame, the shards of glass tearing threads from his sweater.

That seemed to Tench proof, if not irrevocable proof, that two men had been involved. It was surely impossible, even if Kingham had drunk himself insensible, for one man on his own to have dragged his dead weight up fifty feet of staircase to the topmost room of the tower.

He read through the whole report once again and then shook

his head. No, it had to be two, and if it were two, who else could they be but the two that Zack Case had seen at the tower? As Gregg had said, they had to be found, and found without delay, and he had to prove when he faced the Chief Super at nine o'clock that he'd already taken every possible step to trace and apprehend them.

He reached for the phone, and spoke to the Duty Sergeant. 'Put me through to Detective Constable Lock,' he said. 'You've got his number. It's a flat on the Aylsham road.'

He waited till he heard Lock's voice. 'That you, Desmond?'

'Yes, sir.'

'Are you up?'

'Getting up, sir.'

'Right. Apart from Inspector Gregg, I want all members of the team in here for a briefing at eight o'clock.'

'Eight, sir?'

'Eight. So get on to them all and let them know, will you?'

A pause. 'Right, sir. Will do.'

'Good. That's all.'

He replaced the receiver, and rang the Duty Sergeant again. 'I want a message sent out,' he said, 'to all forces in the county . . .'

The message was a long one. At the end of it he dropped the phone back on its hook.

For the moment he'd done all it was possible to do.

He pushed himself up, and went down to the canteen in search of some breakfast.

3.

At eight o'clock he faced his assembled team, bringing them up to date with the latest developments.

'These two men,' he said, 'are now the prime suspects for the murder of Kingham, and I want them caught. There's a general alert for both of them throughout the county, so you won't be the only ones searching for them, but the more men we can get on the job the better our chances of tracking them down. I want to know not only where they are, but if and when and where they've already been seen. If we can chart their movements it may help us to find them, so any past sightings should be reported immediately. If you see the men, detain them and bring them in for questioning. Desmond Lock will be here for the rest of the day to take any calls and pass them on to me . . . Any questions so far?'

He looked round the room, but no hands were raised.

'Right,' he said. 'To business . . . George and Steve,' – he turned to Rayner and Spurgeon – 'house-to-house in Breckton. I want to know whether they've been seen in the village. Start with the post office and what few shops there are, then see the rector and the landlord of the pub. After that, question everyone you can possibly find. Sue,' – this to Sue Gradwell – 'I've arranged for Jules Winterton to be available to work with you. You'll need him to help, because yours is quite a job. Ask at all the shops in Holt, and then, if you've time, question the shoppers . . . Bob,' – this was Ellison – 'all the places on the coastal road that you can reach. Ask anyone who's around. That's the best you can do . . . Mac,' – he glanced towards McKenzie – 'as many of the likely places in Norwich as you can cover. I should keep to the city centre. That's the most probable area for sightings.'

He broke off and looked round the team once again. 'Now is everything clear? . . . Yes? . . . Then get out on the ground and do the best you can. It's a monotonous job, I know, but you'll not be the only ones doing it today. There'll be hundreds of others all over the county on the lookout for these two men, and it's vital we track them down. There aren't that many coloured men wandering round Norfolk, so someone must have seen them. I want them here to face me before the day's out. If they're not, we're all in danger of being dumped on the sidelines, watching as the Met take over the case.'

4.

At ten to nine, just as he was ready to report to the Chief Super, the telephone rang and he heard a voice say, 'Mike?'

'Speaking.'

'It's Meg.'

Meg, or Margaret Dennison as she was officially known on letterheads and bills, ran the Riverside restaurant in an old converted watermill down by the Wensum. The widow of a fisherman lost in a storm off Cromer, she was Lubbock's only sister, indeed his only surviving relative. Five years his senior, she was a tall, raw-boned woman, her skin had long been roughened by the cutting Norfolk winds, and her tongue could be as sharp as the winds themselves; but when Lubbock's wife had died early in the war from a virulent form of flu, she'd conceived it her duty to see that he was not merely adequately fed, but also, when necessary, adequately sheltered.

In the difficult years that followed, when Norwich was blitzed by the Baedeker bombers and petrol rationing meant that reaching his cottage at Cley was impossible except at weekends, he'd regularly slept from Monday to Friday in Meg's cramped attic beneath the eaves of the mill. And not only that. She'd set aside for his personal use a little back room overlooking the river, where sundry other members of the Norwich CID could attach themselves to him, sit round his table and discuss their latest case, while drinking cup after cup of her seemingly inexhaustible supplies of both coffee and tea.

Now, bereft once more of his cottage at Cley, he was back at the Riverside, sleeping again in the attic below the eaves, while Meg made sure that he was adequately fed.

She still treated him, as she always had, with an affectionate kind of cynicism, was familiar with all his faults and foibles, and – a sisterly privilege – never shirked from giving him, when she felt it was warranted, the very rough edge of her predictably caustic tongue.

She normally needed no assistance in dealing with her brother's often wilful behaviour, and Tench never remembered her ringing him up from the Riverside in all the six years he'd known her. With a sudden spasm of conscience, he realized that he hadn't heard or seen anything of Lubbock since the previous Saturday evening when Kingham's body had been found beside the tower.

'Something wrong, Meg?' he asked.

'It's him,' she said. 'He's upstairs in bed. He's got a thoroughly bad chill, the silly old fool, standing about in the winter without a topcoat. The doctor's told him to stay in bed and keep warm. I've packed him around with hot-water bottles, but he's driving me crazy. He's read the morning paper and wants to know what's going on in this case of yours. I've told him you're perfectly capable of solving it without his interference, but you know what he is. He's been pestering me to ring you up, and threatening if I don't he'll get out of bed, so for God's sake tell me something that'll quieten him down. I haven't got the time to be running up and down at his beck and call.'

'Tell him not to worry, Meg. We've got everything in hand.'

'That won't be enough. You know what he's like. He'll be out of bed in a flash, and ringing you himself.'

'Then tell him that Kingham didn't kill himself, he was murdered, and the whole county's searching for two coloured men. He'll know what I mean.'

'You think that'll do the trick?' She sounded doubtful.

'All we can do is hope, Meg. Keep your fingers crossed.'

'Didn't you once tell me that crossing one's fingers was just another way of making the sign of the cross?'

'That's what my father said, and he was a canon.'

'Then let's hope it works a miracle,' she said. 'We're going to need one.'

5.

The Chief Super leaned back in his chair. 'Mike,' he said, 'I'm not quite sure what's been happening while I've been away, but I need to be brought up to date, and quickly. Have you seen this morning's papers?'

'Yes, sir,' said Tench.

Hastings pulled one towards him. '"Norfolk police baffled by double murder",' he read. '"Desperate plea for witnesses to mysterious deaths of husband and wife . . ."' That's one, and there are half a dozen others, all in similar vein. So are we baffled?'

'No, sir.'

'Desperate?'

'No, sir.'

'Well, the Chief Constable's read them and he thinks we are. He's been blasting my eardrums over the phone at home, and threatening us with all sorts of dire predictions. So you'd better put me wise to the situation before it gets completely out of hand. Start at the beginning and leave nothing out. I don't want him asking me any more questions till I know enough to answer them.'

Tench started with Lubbock's discovery of the dinghy, and, taking infinite pains, led his Chief Super through the case to the point when Gregg had phoned him from Truro station. The narrative took him all but twenty-five minutes.

At the end of it, Hastings studied the notes he'd made. 'These two coloured men,' he said. 'You've no proof that they're Indians?'

'Not as yet, sir, no.'

'And you've only the word of an untrustworthy tramp that they even exist.'

'That's true, sir, yes, but McKenzie and I have grilled him pretty thoroughly and we feel that this time he's telling the truth.'

'Well, let's hope he is. You're relying on him heavily, and on Devereux, a man you've never met.'

'I think Inspector Gregg's opinion's to be trusted, sir.'

Hastings nodded. 'I've no doubt it is, but what of Devereux himself? Isn't it possible that he could be overstating his case just a bit?'

'It's possible, sir, yes, but he should know the score. He's spent long enough in India.'

'That's what worries me.' The Chief Super frowned. 'His mind may be full of India, not freezing, flooded, storm-ridden Norfolk.'

Tench gave a shrug. 'We can only work on the evidence available, sir, and Devereux's judgement puts these two men at the head of the list of suspects for Kingham's murder. We have to act upon that.'

'And you're willing to trust his judgement?'

'I have to be, sir, haven't I? We have to find these men before anything else, and either charge them or eliminate them from the case.'

Hastings seemed to reflect. 'Yes,' he said at last, 'I think you're right. But tell me this, Mike. What if we don't find them?'

'Then we have to assume either that they're already on their way back to India, or that our assumptions about them were wrong.'

'And?'

'We move to the next of our possible suspects.'

'Meredith?'

'Both the Merediths, sir. Both are still in the frame. He threatened to kill Kingham, and he's lied to us more than once, and she's admitted that she drove to Breckton on the day before the storm to kill Mrs Kingham.'

'Then how long d'you propose to go on searching for these coloured men?'

'I'm hoping we'll find them sometime today, sir. If not, we move on.'

'You need to. Make today the limit, then call off the search. Get back to the Merediths. We can't afford to be seen as wasting time on some theory that may or may not be valid. I've got to convince the Chief Constable that we're making some progress.'

'Right, sir.'

'And keep me informed of every step from now on. I don't want to be floundering like I was this morning.'

'No, sir.'

'And I think we should issue a statement to the press. We need to get them off our backs for the moment . . . Don't worry. I'll draft one . . . Get back to the search, and let's hope someone lays hands on these men before the morning's out. Results are what we need . . .'

'By the way,' he added as Tench gathered up his files, 'what's John Lubbock got to say about all this? Don't tell me he hasn't been offering his advice.'

'I haven't seen him since Saturday evening, sir,' said Tench. 'He's in bed with a chill, and the doctor's ordered him to stay there.'

'Then he'd better do as he's told for once,' Hastings said, 'but I doubt if he will. He's never taken a doctor's advice in his life. So, if I were you, I'd keep an ear open for that cherry wood stick

of his tapping up the stairs. If I know John Lubbock, he won't
rest till he's made his opinions known.'

He was right in one sense and wrong in another. Tench heard no
cherry wood stick on the stairs but he wasn't left long in doubt
about his old Chief's opinion. He'd barely got back to his office
before the telephone rang.

It was Meg.

She plunged ahead without any form of greeting.

'I told him what you said,' – her voice was like a klaxon – 'but
all he did was scowl at me. "Waste of time," he said. And now
he's gone out. Given me the slip. I can't keep my eyes on him
all the time, I've a restaurant to run. If he turns up at your place,
don't stand any nonsense. Send him back here. He's not fit to
be out.'

She rang off before he could utter a word, leaving him to
wonder just how he was to turn a sick but very determined
Lubbock away from his door.

6.

If Mike Tench, despite his apparent confidence, had harboured a
secret fear that his quarry had slipped in and out of the country
unobserved by anyone save Zaccheus Case, he was soon to be
disabused of any such notion.

At half past ten that morning, Sue Gradwell, somewhat
wearily, pushed open the door of a small, dingy shop in a side
street at Holt; wearily because, as far as she could reckon, she'd
asked the same question well over a hundred times as she'd
traversed the town, and had met with the same answer on each
occasion. No one had so much as caught a glimpse of two
coloured men, and she'd already formed the impression that
either the residents of Holt were utterly unobservant, or the men
she was seeking had never even set foot in the place.

Nor had she much hope that this particular shop would
provide her at last with a positive answer. Not only was it small
and dingy, it was also nameless. Its window displayed a wide
variety of undistinguished objects, its trade identified merely by

the projecting metal sign that hung above the door, and Sue could conceive of no earthly reason why two coloured men, intent on keeping the lowest possible profile, should ever have decided to pay it a visit.

She was, however, nothing if not thorough. She and Jules Winterton had been told to inquire at every shop in Holt, and that was what she was determined to do.

She pushed open the door and stepped inside.

A quarter of an hour later, the phone in Tench's office began to ring.

He lifted the receiver and heard Lock's voice. 'Sue Gradwell on the line, sir.'

'Put her through, Desmond.'

He waited. The phone clicked. 'Sue Gradwell, sir, from Holt.'

'You've got a sighting?'

'Yes, sir. Friday morning. Three days ago. But it's rather peculiar.'

'How d'you mean, peculiar?'

'Well, sir, they were seen in a pawnshop. Two young coloured men, dressed alike, dark coats and white mufflers. The owner of the shop described them as chocolate-coloured rather than black, both in their late teens, could have been twins.'

Tench frowned. 'Was he sure about their age?'

'Seemed to be, yes, sir.'

'Did they pawn something?'

'No, sir.'

'Redeem something?'

'No, sir.'

'Then what did they buy?'

'Nothing at all, sir. That's the strange thing about it. The shopkeeper said that he didn't think they came to do any kind of business.'

'Then just what *did* they do?'

'They seemed very excited – that was what he said – chattering to one another in their own language. When they spoke to him, their English was reasonably good, but they talked in a kind of sing-song voice. They asked him what the three golden balls outside meant. What sort of a shop was it? He told them he was a pawnbroker. And what was that, they said. He explained as best he could, and they nodded their heads and smiled at one another. But why the three golden balls? He tried to explain that too, but coats-of-arms were a bit beyond them, so he simply told them that of every three articles pawned by customers, two were usually redeemed, but the third never was, and that was the one he sold in his shop. They seemed satisfied with that, nodded and smiled again, thanked him very politely, and just walked out . . . But they were Indians, sir.'

'They were?'

'Oh, yes, sir. The broker was absolutely positive about it. He'd served in India during the war, and he recognized some of the phrases they'd used. They were Indians, he said, but from somewhere in the north. They weren't dark enough to have come from the south.'

7.

Two coloured men, identified as Indians, seen in the area only three days ago.

That was what, above anything, he'd wanted to hear, but Tench was uneasy.

Two coloured men, Indians, seen in Holt, but young, very young for such a murderous assignment, making no attempt to conceal themselves, innocently asking questions that brought themselves to notice. Strange behaviour for men who, only a week before, must have bound and gagged Kingham and thrown him headlong from the top of a tower.

But had they? Were these really the men he was searching for, or were there two pairs of coloured men on the move around Norfolk? That seemed unlikely, but if there were not, then how to explain the actions of these two men at Holt?

He brooded on the matter. There were, of course, possible explanations. What better way for two men intent on murder to proclaim their innocence than by posing as visitors to England, keenly interested in all things English? If they'd worked to a plan, given themselves the time and played their roles with conviction, they could have dealt with Kingham under cover of darkness, returned to their masquerade, and no one would have thought them capable of such a crime.

It was possible, too, that their masters in India could have sent four men to England, to take their revenge on Kingham, two to act as decoys, prepared for a lengthy stay, and two, the real killers, to slip in and out swiftly, without breaking cover.

Or was that perhaps a little too fanciful?

Was he maybe committing a crime himself, doing what others, Lubbock and McKenzie, had warned him not to do: trying to twist the evidence to fit his own theory? Could he possibly be wrong? Were these two men seen in the pawnshop at Holt the same two that Zack Case had seen at the tower, and were they after all just inquisitive tourists? If they were, he was chasing two men who didn't exist, mere phantoms that he himself had created, and all the forces now desperately searching for them were wasting their time.

No. He shook his head forcibly. He had to be right. At this stage he couldn't afford to have doubts. He was on the point of rejecting the idea out of hand, when the phone rang again, shattering his thoughts.

It was Frank Renshaw, the detective inspector from Swaffham.

'These two coloured men, sir,' he said.

'You've seen them?'

'No, sir, but one of our constables thinks he has. A young lad called Yarnold. Last Wednesday it was. He was on patrol by the Butter Cross and the statue of Ceres. They stopped him. Two young chaps in dark coats and white mufflers. Wanted to know who was this lady on top of the dome and what was she doing . . . Well, Yarnold's a good, sound copper, but he's new to the place, and he'd be the last to call himself a classical scholar or, come to think of it, a scholar of any kind at all. But he's nothing if not ingenious. He remembered a picture in a book of bible stories he'd been given as a child, and told them her name was Ruth and she was scattering seed. They seemed to be happy enough with that, and nodded at one another. Were there pictures to be bought, they asked. Well, that was much more up Yarnold's street. He marched them to the nearest stationer's and left them examining racks of postcards . . . D'you think they're the two that you're looking for, sir?'

Tench drew a deep breath. 'Somehow, Frank,' he said, 'I think that's more than likely.'

8.

In the course of the next hour, there were five more calls, from widely disparate parts of the county, all telling the same tale. Whoever these two coloured men were in their dark coats and white mufflers, they had, it seemed, no intention of hiding themselves away. On the contrary, they appeared determined to make their presence known wherever they went.

At half past eleven Inspector Rouse rang from Thetford. Two men answering that description had been seen a week before at Grime's Graves, the neolithic flint mines close by. They were asking why the ground was all humps and hollows. Were they really graves and, if so, who was buried there?

Ten minutes later, Steve Harris rang from Blakeney. Two such men, similarly clothed, had been seen only yesterday examining the old lock-up in the square at Walsingham. They'd been fascinated by it, so much so that they'd made straight for the nearest shop and asked what was this strange little building used for, and what was that basket-like thing on the top? It had taken the shopkeeper some little time, in between serving customers, to explain to them that since the building served three purposes, as a prison cell, water conduit and beacon, it was quite unique, there was no other like it in the whole of England. That, Harris said, had really excited them. Were there pictures they'd asked. Yes, he'd said, and sold them a couple of dog-eared postcards.

Then, just before midday, there'd been two further calls in quick succession. The same two men had been seen at Billingford, near Diss, where they'd persuaded the miller to show them just how a windmill worked, and again on the beach at Eccles, where they'd inquired of an old fisherman was this the place where bells could be heard ringing from underneath the sea?

And just as Tench had rung the canteen for coffee and sandwiches – it was then twenty past twelve – Constable Vernon had called from Burnham Market to say that he'd seen the men outside the Lord Nelson pub at Burnham Thorpe. He was on his bicycle and they'd stopped him, two coloured men, young, in black coats and white mufflers. They'd pointed to the name on the front of the pub, and asked him who was this Lord Nelson and what had he done to make himself so famous?

Tench had a passion for coffee, but its taste that morning was distinctly sour. Everything he'd heard appeared to confirm the one thing he was most reluctant to admit: that these two were nothing but innocent travellers, persistently inquisitive, striving to learn all they could about England. But weren't they perhaps a little too inquisitive, a little too persistent, leaving memory traces wherever they went? Could they possibly be decoys, planted merely to throw him off the scent, while others, the real killers, did their work stealthily and vanished without any traces at all?

He sipped his coffee again. It still tasted sour, but he wasn't yet prepared to admit he'd been wrong. He needed to lay hands on these men and make sure. Then, and only then, face to face with them at last, probing them with the questions he needed to ask – only then could he convince himself one way or the other.

He pushed the coffee aside. It was strange that he'd heard nothing from Rayner and Spurgeon. Had no one seen the men in or around Breckton? If they hadn't, just how significant was that? If they were decoys, Breckton was the very last place in all Norfolk where they'd want to be seen . . .

He glanced at his watch.

It was half past twelve.

It was then that he heard the tap of a stick and the clump of heavy boots on the stairs outside his office.

9.

The door was pushed open, and a haggard, pipeless Lubbock, breathing heavily, sank down on the chair in front of his desk.

'Once again,' he said, 'Mahomet has to come all the way to the mountain.'

Tench frowned at him. 'Mahomet should be in bed,' he said, 'not climbing mountains.'

His old Chief waved a dismissive hand. 'No time to be in bed. This case needs someone to take a firm grip . . . I take it you're searching for Zack's two coloured men.'

Tench was still prepared to stick to his guns. 'Yes,' he said, 'we are.'

'Then answer me one question, laddie.'

'Willingly.'

'Why?'

'Because Kingham didn't commit suicide, he was murdered, and these two men are prime suspects for his death . . . There've been a lot of developments since we last spoke.'

'There must have been,' said Lubbock, 'but you're still completely wrong. Didn't I tell you these men were just casual visitors?'

'They could be, yes, but they could be something more. They might well be decoys in league with the killers.'

'Decoys fiddlesticks!' His old Chief was scathing. 'You're on the wrong track, laddie. All this business is just a waste of time.'

'That's your opinion. Mine's altogether different.'

'It's not merely my opinion, laddie. It's a fact.'

'Then convince me.'

Lubbock showed a flash of exasperation. 'Listen,' he said. 'Every good detective in the course of his career is bound to build up a fund of ill will, but, if he's any sense, he'll build up a bit of goodwill here and there – debts owed to him, that he can call in when he needs a little timely assistance.'

He paused.

'And?' said Tench.

Lubbock took a deep, rasping breath. 'This morning,' he said, 'I decided it was time to call in a debt. If you're searching for something, there's no sense in thrashing around at random. You need to go straight to someone who's likely to know where to find it, and that was what I did. The result? I've brought three men to see you. They're waiting outside. Am I to show them in?'

'Who are they?'

'You'll see,' Lubbock said. He stumped to the door and then

stood aside to admit a grey-haired, middle-aged man, and two others, very much younger and very much alike, wrapped against the cold in dark coats and white mufflers.

'This is Mr Khan,' he said. 'He runs a corner shop in the heart of the city. This' – he turned to Khan – 'is Detective Chief Inspector Tench. Perhaps you'd like to explain things to him.'

Khan gave a little bow. 'These, sir,' he said, 'are my two nephews, Asif and Azim. They are students at the university in Lahore. They are taking a holiday with me in England, and I am hearing from Mr Lubbock that you are wishing to see them.'

Tench looked at them and smiled. 'That's perfectly correct, Mr Khan,' he said. 'Thank you for bringing them here to meet me. Let me assure you right away that they aren't in any trouble.'

'They are good boys, sir. They would not be doing any wrong.'

'I'm quite sure they wouldn't, Mr Khan,' said Tench 'but I'd like to ask them a couple of questions. Which of them is Asif?'

Mr Khan introduced him.

'You've been travelling around a lot, haven't you?' said Tench.

Asif bowed. 'We are trying to see everything we can, sir. It is all very interesting. We are asking many questions.'

Tench nodded. 'And so you should. There's nothing wrong in that, but I think you can help me to solve a little problem. Can you remember where you were on the Thursday afternoon, two days before the storm? That's a week last Thursday, the 29th of January.'

Asif turned to his brother, and Azim drew from his pocket a small red notebook. After flicking through the pages for some little time, Asif nodded. 'In the morning, sir,' he said, 'we are going to a place called Billingford and looking at a windmill, and in the afternoon to Melton to see the hall, but on our journey there we are catching a view of a tall, old building that seems like a windmill fallen to bits. This is very interesting, so we give it a visit. Then we are making our way to Melton.'

'And when you reached this tall, old building, what did you do?'

The two boys chatted briefly to one another, then Asif resumed. 'We are going inside, sir, and looking around. We climb up the steps, but there is nothing inside but chairs and tables, so then we go away.'

'Thank you,' said Tench. 'That's all I need to ask. You've been very helpful.' He turned back to their uncle. 'Thank you once again for coming, Mr Khan. I hope your nephews enjoy the rest of their holiday.'

'I gather,' said Lubbock, once they were alone, 'that those were the men you wanted to see.'

'Yes and no,' said Tench.

'No? Why no?'

'They're Muslims.'

'Of course they're Muslims,' his old Chief said testily. 'They're from Pakistan, aren't they? What did you expect them to be? Latter Day Saints?'

10.

'No. Hindus.'

'Why Hindus in particular?'

'It's a long story,' said Tench, 'and you should be in bed. Meg's worried about you.'

Lubbock gave a grunt. 'How d'you know that?'

'She's rung me up twice, and told me to throw you out.'

'Has she indeed? Well, if she rings again, tell her I'm on duty. Now what's this long story? The sooner you tell me, the sooner you can ring her and say the deed's done: you've stripped off your jacket, rolled up your sleeves and cast me down the stairs.'

'At the moment,' said Tench, 'I simply haven't got the time, so go back to bed.'

His old Chief growled and thumped his stick on the floor. 'You've got to make time, laddie. We need to get this case back on its right course. All it's doing just now is drifting with the current. So get on with it. Tell me.'

Tench told him, as briefly as he possibly could.

'So,' said Lubbock, 'because of some cock-and-bull tale about gangs of Indians, you set the whole county on the trail of two innocent students who were doing nothing more than enjoying a holiday. Well, you were wrong, laddie, weren't you?'

'No more than you when you were so very sure that Kingham had thrown himself from the tower.'

'I was right on the evidence available at the time, and I still think he was the one who killed his wife. Who murdered him is an entirely different matter.'

'Then you've one little problem to solve,' said Tench. 'According to Merrick he wrapped his wife's body in a candlewick bedspread, but the boys in the lab have stripped the Rolls down as far as its frame and they haven't found a trace of any candlewick fibres, so if he didn't use the Rolls how did he get her body down to the boat at Morston?'

'Perhaps he did use the Rolls. Perhaps he spread a sheet in the boot and got rid of it afterwards. Perhaps he hired another car. A man with his money could do almost anything. The possibilities are endless. But whether I'm right or wrong, it seems to me, laddie, you've got to start again from scratch. Forget about the Indians. They just don't exist. Who's next on the suspect list?'

'The Merediths,' said Tench, 'but if I remember rightly, you told me to forget them as well. You said questioning them was a sheer waste of time.'

Lubbock nodded. 'Yes, I did, but that was last Saturday. At that time we'd only one murder to solve. Since then things have changed. Now we have two, and if *I* remember rightly the Merediths had good reason to want both the Kinghams dead, so if I were you . . .'

Tench raised a hand. 'No,' he said, 'don't tell me. I'm the one who's in charge of this case, and for my own peace of mind I need to solve it and solve it on my own. I know what I have to do, and with the Chief Super's help it'll all be done swiftly. Thank you for bringing the boys in to see me – I'm grateful for that – but go back to bed and leave me to sort out the rest for myself.'

Lubbock gave a shrug. 'Well, if that's what you want . . .'

'It is,' said Tench.

'You're throwing me out?'

'I'm throwing you out.'

His old Chief seemed more amused than affronted. 'You know what?' he said. 'I'm feeling better already. I think I'll ask Meg to cook me a good square meal – haddock and egg and a plateful of chips.'

IX

THE TURN OF THE TIDE

As the devil said to Noah, 'It's bound to clear up.'
English proverbial saying

1.

At half past four that same afternoon, Giles Meredith left his office at the Norwick Press and drove home to Blickling.

Some five minutes after he arrived at Green Park, two police cars turned in at the drive and parked outside the house. In the first were Tench, McKenzie and Sue Gradwell; in the second Ellison, Lock, Rayner and Spurgeon.

They gathered outside the door. Tench lifted the knocker and rapped three times. When Meredith appeared, he held up a sheet of paper. 'Mr Meredith,' he said, 'I have here a warrant to search this property, its grounds and outbuildings, and also to impound for forensic examination any vehicles found on the premises. I am, in addition, authorized to remove anything I find which I deem to be suspicious. You and your wife have, of course, the right to be present while we search.'

Meredith took the warrant and studied it, then he stepped to one side. 'Let me place it on record, Chief Inspector,' he said, 'that I resent this intrusion. Search if you must, but I warn you it's likely to prove a fruitless exercise. You'll find nothing here.'

'That, sir,' said Tench, 'remains to be seen.'

He waved his team inside.

2.

The house and outbuildings were extensive, the search slow and methodical, and it was after nine o'clock when Tench and his team withdrew, taking with them two boxes containing the contents of Meredith's desk.

By that time his low-slung Aston Martin and his wife's Morris Minor had been hauled on to low-loaders and driven off to Norwich, where Forensics had instructions to strip them down and subject them to minute examination.

'Well,' McKenzie said as they turned out of the drive, 'he was right, wasn't he? Four solid hours and we haven't found a thing.'

Tench was cautious. 'Not so far, Mac,' he said.

'No gun, no clothes, no candlewick bedspread, not even a speck of dust to connect him with the tower. What else is there to find?'

'Something. There must be. Some clue that proves the link. We haven't finished with him yet, not by a long chalk. We still have to sift through what was in his desk, Forensics have still to examine the cars, and there'll be twenty men doing a sweep of the grounds tomorrow.'

'You mean that something's bound to turn up?'

Tench gritted his teeth. 'Yes, it must.'

McKenzie allowed himself a hollow kind of laugh. 'Wasn't there a chap called Micawber?' he said. 'He went around saying much the same thing, but nothing ever did. It's a forlorn hope, Mike. If there was anything Meredith needed to hide, he's had ten whole days to stow it away somewhere where we'll never find it. It's probably lying at the bottom of a river in the Dordogne, weighted down by a couple of bricks from the cottage he's buying down there.'

'Maybe,' said Tench, 'but murderers always tend to miss something. They make one mistake, and if Meredith murdered one of the Kinghams, then it's up to us to find that one item he's missed that links him to the crime. It's our only hope, Mac, and whether it's forlorn or not we've got to search till we unearth it. So as soon as we get back I'm going to empty both those boxes and go through the papers with a magnifying glass. What you do is up to you. You can snatch a last pint at the Adam and Eve, or you can buckle down and help me. Which is it to be?'

McKenzie gave a sigh. 'That's a bitter choice,' he said, 'in more ways than one, but damn it all, what's a pint when there's a chance of nailing a murder down to that devious bastard? I'll help, of course I will, but if I happen to die of thirst before the dawn breaks, see that I'm duly honoured. I'd like a commemorative plaque on the bar. And don't make it brass. I think I'd prefer one in beaten gold.'

3.

Looking back on the case, Tench always said that Gregg's return from Truro marked the turning point. Not that his report was in any way relevant to the changed situation, but, protesting that he'd slept all the way to Paddington, he insisted on joining them in their search.

Tench cleared his desk-top, emptied out the contents of the first of the boxes, pushing a sheaf of papers across to McKenzie, another to Gregg, and keeping a third for himself. There were receipted bills, letters, contracts connected with the publishing business, packets of old photographs and a host of other documents that defied classification. Tench insisted that every word should be read, and they worked through them slowly with a painstaking thoroughness, dropping them back one by one in the box if they proved to be irrelevant.

At the end of an hour McKenzie dropped his last sheet in the box. 'Nothing,' he said. 'Not a single bloody thing. We're just wasting our time.'

'We've not finished yet,' said Tench. 'There's another box to do.' He turned it out on the desk. 'Get reading, Mac. There's something here somewhere. There has to be, so let's get on and find it.'

McKenzie groaned, stretched, lit a cigarette and drew another sheet towards him.

They ploughed on, all three of them, tossing sheet after sheet into the waiting boxes. Time passed without any positive result, and it was close on midnight when Gregg, who'd been studying a document closely, pushed it across the desk without comment to Tench.

It was a birth certificate dated 25th September 1921, issued in respect of one Richard Giles Meredith, born that day at Willow Farm, Sunningham, in the district of Holt.

Tench read it, and then looked up again at Gregg. 'So,' he said, 'our friend Mr Meredith was born at Sunningham.'

'Looks like it,' said Gregg.

'That's interesting.' Tench turned back to the document. 'A son born to John and Agnes Mary Meredith. Now I wonder if . . .'

He was suddenly interrupted by a sharp exclamation from

McKenzie. He held up a photograph and passed it to Tench. 'That's the tower,' he said. 'Don't tell me it isn't. And that's Meredith there at the end of that group.'

Tench held it to the light. 'You know, Mac,' he said, 'I think this time you've hit the nail on the head. It is Meredith, and the tower, and he's the only one in the group not in uniform. I reckon those are members of the local Home Guard.'

He placed the photograph on top of the birth certificate. 'I think it's time we took another look at Sunningham,' he said.

4.

Shortly before ten o'clock the following morning, Tench pushed open the gate that led to Willow Farm and picked his way up the frozen track that led to the house.

Once there, he paused. The farm stood on its own at the end of the village, and, looking across the bare fields, he could see, half a mile away, the dark shell of Prospect Tower rising against its background of trees. If Meredith had lived here for any length of time, it must have been a sight as familiar to him as the wallpaper in his bedroom. It would have been the first thing he saw when he stepped outside.

Since he could see no bell or knocker, he rapped on the door with his knuckles, and after some moments it was opened by a heavily built, middle-aged man with a ruddy complexion. 'Mr Meredith?' Tench inquired.

'No.' The man shook his head. 'Pickering, Joe Pickering. Merediths up an' left here five year ago.'

'Oh, I see,' said Tench. 'Can you tell me where they went?'

'Aye. Some place down south it were, 'cos of his health.'

He called across his shoulder. 'Maggie, where did Merediths move to? Eastbourne, weren' it?'

'Bournemouth,' came a voice, presumably that of Maggie.

'Bournemouth,' Pickering repeated. 'Got their address some-where. God knows where, though.'

'Never mind, sir,' said Tench. 'Did they have any particular friends in the village?'

The woman who suddenly appeared next to Pickering was

almost as broad as he was. 'Friends?' she said. 'Oh, aye, there were plenty o' them. Can't speak fer him, but Mrs M, she were close wi' ol' Millie Tibbs, her as lives on Main Street, weren' she, Joe?'

'Aye,' said Joe, 'tha's right, Mag.' He turned back to Tench. 'Reckon as she's yer best bet, lad. Go an' see Millie Tibbs.'

Mrs Tibbs, a long-time widow, was, as Tench judged, about seventy years of age, wrinkled, but with hair that was still nut-brown, and eyes that were keen and very much alert.

When he said he was trying to trace some friends called the Merediths that he'd known during the war, she invited him in, sat him down in an armchair and insisted, despite his protests, on making him a cup of tea.

Oh yes, she said, she'd known the Merediths for years. Very close they'd been, she and John and Agnes, and yes, Giles too. Lovely boy he was, and his parents so proud of him. He'd won a scholarship to Gresham's, and then another one to Cambridge. In a way, of course, John had been disappointed. He'd hoped for a son to carry on the farm, and Giles had never shown any aptitude for it. But he wouldn't have stood in the boy's way. He was only too glad to see him doing so well. And he had done well. He'd had to break his time at college to go in the air force, but he'd gone back afterwards and got himself a very good job at the end of it. It meant they'd had to give up the farm, of course, because John had had a bit of a problem with his chest and the doctor said he should go somewhere warmer. He'd had Land Girls to help him during the war, but after that he was left on his own and the farm was too much. They'd sold up five years ago. Gone to live in Bournemouth. She didn't know where Giles was, but yes, she had their address, and she'd write it down for him.

She wrote it in a clear, flowing script on a sheet from a correspondence pad, and held it out to him.

He took it and thanked her.

'I'll write to John and Agnes too,' she said, 'and tell them you called. I'm sure they'll be glad to see you.'

Tench raised a hand. 'No, Mrs Tibbs,' he said. 'Please don't do that. When I do turn up in Bournemouth, I'd much prefer it to be a surprise.'

5.

At the other end of the village, closer to the tower, Gregg and McKenzie, armed with blown-up copies of the group photograph, had been pursuing a different line of inquiry.

Tench drove down and picked them up by the church. Once clear of Sunningham, he pulled in to the side of the road and stopped. 'Any luck?' he asked.

Gregg gave a nod. 'Oh, I think you might very well call it that, sir, yes. Wouldn't you say so, Mac?'

'Isn't there something called serendipity?' McKenzie said.

'Yes.' Tench was quick to confirm the point. 'It's the knack of making happy discoveries by accident.'

'Then that's nearer the mark. Wouldn't you say so, Andy?'

'Undoubtedly,' said Gregg.

Tench looked from one to the other in turn. 'I'm interested,' he said, 'so tell me. What's this happy discovery you've made?'

'Well,' – Gregg produced the photograph – 'we wanted to put a name to this chap here in the middle of the group. The one with the sergeant's stripes. So we went to see the rector.'

'A helpful old boy,' McKenzie interposed. 'Believed everything we said.'

'Told him we were a couple of journalists writing an article on the Sunningham Home Guard,' Gregg continued. 'He accepted it as gospel. Gave us the names of everyone in the group, and wrote them on the back. The sergeant's name, he said, was Kenyon, Abel Kenyon, so we got his address and toddled round to see him. He took one look at the photograph and said, yes, he remembered it being taken. It was back in the summer of 1942. Will Thoday had just got his calling-up papers for the army, and he wanted a souvenir snap to take with him.'

'I asked him which was Will Thoday,' McKenzie said, 'and he pointed to the chap who was standing next to Meredith. So I asked him another question. Why wasn't the chap next to him wearing uniform? Oh, he said, that was young Meredith. He wasn't Home Guard, but he and Will Thoday had been at school together. They were very good pals, and Will had wanted him included in the photograph.'

'And that,' said Gregg, 'led us straight to our serendipitous discovery.'

'Which was?' said Tench.

'That our good friend Mr Meredith was in Sunningham three weeks ago, and he and Thoday climbed up the tower.'

'Did they indeed? Go on. Tell me more.'

'Well, apparently they were close friends at Gresham's. They were both from Sunningham and both farmers' sons, but whereas Meredith went on from there to Cambridge, Thoday went back to help on the farm. He joined the Home Guard, and when Meredith was home on vacation and Thoday was on watch at the top of the tower, he used to go up and sit with him just to pass the time. Both of them got their call-up papers the same week, and that was when they had the photograph taken.

'Meredith joined the RAF and served as a ground crew mechanic at one of the Norfolk bomber bases. Thoday was drafted into the army, and fought his way up the spine of Italy. When the war was over, he married an Italian girl who'd sheltered him from the Germans, and stayed out there.'

'Then a month ago,' McKenzie said, 'his father died, and he came back here briefly to sell off the farm. He'd kept in touch with Meredith, and he rang him up and suggested they meet. Meredith drove over from Blickling, and, just for old times' sake, they climbed up the tower. Thoday's back in Italy, but Kenyon said they both came to see him and told him what they'd done.

'And,' he finished triumphantly, 'if that isn't cause enough to haul in that devious bastard again and put him through the mincer, I don't know what is.'

6.

'It's intriguing,' said Tench, 'but it doesn't exactly prove that he murdered Kingham.'

'It proves that he knew about the tower.'

'That's not the same thing.'

McKenzie exploded. 'It's just another thing he never bothered to mention.'

'Maybe because we never bothered to ask him.'

'He's been hiding the truth from us ever since he first appeared on the scene. He's lied and lied again, and one thing's for sure. If he's intent on hiding what really happened, he must know it's going to put a noose round his neck.'

'Oh, we'll haul him in,' said Tench, 'and I'm quite prepared to put him through the mincing machine, but so far we haven't a single scrap of evidence that links him conclusively to Kingham's murder.'

'Leave me alone with him for just five minutes,' McKenzie said darkly, 'and I'll hand you every bit of evidence you need.'

Tench gave him a look that implied he was far from likely to accede to the suggestion. 'No, Mac,' he said. 'For the moment I think a gentler approach might be more productive. Once we get back, you and Andy can track him down and invite him, very politely, to pay us a visit.'

McKenzie made it clear that he wasn't impressed. 'If we have to invite him,' he said, 'Andy can do it. I wouldn't trust myself to be polite to that scheming rat even if he held my life between the palms of his hands.'

However, as events turned out, Gregg had no chance to display his social skills. Lock, manning the phone in the CID room, had taken a call from the lab. 'Mr Merrick rang, sir,' he said. 'He'd like to see you right away.'

Tench was immediately alert. 'Did he say what he wanted?'

'Yes, sir. Said he'd found something that might be important.'

Merrick had once again set up two microscopes. 'Take a look, sir,' he said.

Tench peered into them. 'Candlewick?' he queried.

'Yes, pink candlewick,' Merrick affirmed.

'Where from?'

'The one on the left is a fibre that was found on Mrs Kingham's body.'

'And the other?'

'We found it trapped in the lock of a car boot.'

'The Aston Martin?'

Merrick shook his head. 'No, sir. The Morris Minor.'

Tench looked first at Gregg and then at McKenzie. 'Now that,' he said, 'is the most serendipitous thing I've heard so far today.'

7.

At half past four that same afternoon, three cars drew up in front of the house at Blickling. In the first was Tench; in the second, Gregg and two uniformed constables drawn from the city force; while the third contained McKenzie and two further constables.

Tench rapped on the door. There was a pause before it opened to reveal Mrs Meredith. She looked down at them with a somewhat weary expression. 'What d'you want now, Chief Inspector?' she said impatiently. 'Haven't you made things difficult enough already?'

Tench made his own response: one that she clearly wasn't expecting. 'Josephine Meredith,' he said, 'I'm arresting you in connection with the death of Valerie Kingham. You do not have to say anything . . .' He gave her the usual caution. 'You'll be taken to Norwich and detained there for questioning.'

'You've no reason to do this, Chief Inspector,' she protested. 'You're making a quite ridiculous mistake.'

Tench ignored her. He turned to McKenzie. 'Take her away, Sergeant,' he ordered curtly.

She gave a little shrug. 'Very well,' she said, 'take me to Norwich, but I'm warning you, Chief Inspector. Unless you can prove your point, I'm quite prepared to bring an action against you for wrongful arrest.'

Then, as two of the constables approached her, she turned on them fiercely. 'Don't you dare lay hands on me,' she said. 'I can walk without any assistance from you.'

Tench watched the car till it disappeared round a bend in the drive, Mrs Meredith in the back, between the two constables. Then, leaving Gregg and the other two in charge of what he knew was an empty house, he followed McKenzie back to Norwich.

Gregg had his instructions.

He'd carry them out.

Politely, of course.

X

LITTLE THINGS

It has long been an axiom of mine that the little things are
infinitely the most important.
Sir Arthur Conan Doyle: *The Adventures of Sherlock Holmes*

1.

She sat face to face with the two detectives, not this time in Tench's office, but across a table in the bleakest of interview rooms. In a corner, also facing her, sat WDC Gradwell, shorthand pad on her knee, ready to record every word of what followed.

'I must remind you,' said Tench, 'that you are now under oath.'

'I'm well aware of that, Chief Inspector.' The words were spoken crisply with a hint of defiance.

'You have, of course, the right to legal representation.'

'I don't need a lawyer. I've nothing to hide.'

'Very well then,' said Tench. 'For the record, ma'am, you are Josephine Meredith?'

'Yes, I am.'

'You live at Green Park, Blickling?'

'Yes, when the police permit me to do so.'

'In a previous interview, Mrs Meredith, you admitted that on the afternoon of Friday, the 30th of January, the day before the storm, you paid a visit to The Woodlands at Breckton, the home of Mr and Mrs Reginald Kingham . . . You don't dispute that?'

'No, why should I? I never dispute the truth.'

'Also, that you drove there in your own car, a gunmetal grey Morris Minor, registration number CL4287.'

'That's right. I did.'

'When you were asked why you went to The Woodlands that afternoon, you said that you went there to kill Mrs Kingham. Is that also correct?'

'Yes, of course it is. What reason would I have to lie?'

'Then tell me again, Mrs Meredith. Why didn't you kill her?'

'For the simple reason, Chief Inspector, that she wasn't there to be killed. The house was locked up. There was nobody in.'

'Were you sure about that?'

'Yes, as sure as I could be.'

Tench leaned back in his chair. 'But that's the whole point, isn't it, Mrs Meredith? You just couldn't be sure. It's most unlikely that Valerie Kingham would have wanted to meet you. If she'd noticed your car, she could easily have hidden away in one of the back rooms, and you'd never have seen her.'

'I suppose so,' – she shrugged – 'but does it really matter?'

'It matters in one sense. It means that the statement you made was possibly inaccurate. It was nothing more than guesswork, and that makes me wonder about the accuracy of other things you said. You see, Mrs Meredith, there are other statements of yours that I find increasingly difficult to believe.'

'Then you must be deluding yourself, Chief Inspector. I can see no reason why you should disbelieve me.'

'Then let me explain.' Tench opened a file that lay on the table. 'You said you intended to kill Mrs Kingham because she was stealing your husband and you couldn't let that happen. "I married him," you said. "He's mine, and no one's ever going to steal what's rightfully mine." You don't deny you said that?'

'No. Why should I? It's true.'

'Yet you made it very clear that, once the storm was over, you didn't go back to The Woodlands.'

'That's right. I didn't.'

'On the Friday afternoon you were fiercely determined to kill Mrs Kingham. You couldn't, because the house was locked up, yet you're telling me you didn't go back once the storm was over? Frankly, Mrs Meredith, I don't believe you.'

'Then I'll repeat it for your benefit, Chief Inspector. Once the storm was over I didn't go back to The Woodlands. Would I lie to you on oath?'

Tench sat back again and pushed the file to McKenzie. 'Perhaps you'd like to explain to Mrs Meredith,' he said. 'She seems to be unaware of certain relevant facts.'

McKenzie, for once, was smooth and disarming. 'Valerie Kingham,' he said, 'as no doubt you already know, was shot dead in the house at Breckton, but her body was found some miles away at Cley. It had been swept there by the storm in a dinghy that its owner had laid up at Morston. It must, therefore, have been moved from Breckton to Morston in some particular vehicle. We have forensic evidence that proves beyond contradiction that during that process it was wrapped in a pink candlewick bedspread, fibres from which were found on the body and also in

the dinghy, though the woman herself was naked when found
. . . You understand that?'

'Naturally, Sergeant.'

'Then can you explain to me, ma'am,' McKenzie said, 'why
similar fibres have been found inside the boot of your car?'

She seemed quite unperturbed. 'Yes,' she replied, 'the
answer's simple enough. It was my car that was used to move
the body to Morston.'

2.

Tench stared at her. 'Are you telling us,' he said, 'that someone stole your car, put the body in the boot and drove it to
Morston?'

'No, that wouldn't be true.'

McKenzie glowered. 'Then just what the devil are you
telling us?'

'That nobody stole the car. I drove it myself.'

'To Morston?'

'Yes.'

'With the body in the boot?'

'That's what I said.'

The two detectives glanced at one another, then Tench leaned
forward. 'That can mean only one thing,' he said. 'You did go
back to The Woodlands.'

'Oh, yes, I went back.'

'Then you've been lying.'

'No.' She shook her head firmly. 'I never lie, Chief Inspector.
You asked me if I went back after the storm. I said no, I didn't,
and that was the truth. I went back that same evening, the Friday
evening. I was still determined to see Valerie Kingham.'

'And you killed her,' McKenzie said.

'Of course I didn't kill her.' She sighed in what appeared to be
sheer exasperation. 'I didn't need to kill her. She was dead when
I got there.'

'And what time was that?'

She thought for a moment. 'It must have been about quarter
past eight.'

'Mrs Meredith,' said Tench, 'I think it's about time you told us exactly what happened that evening. You say you reached The Woodlands around eight fifteen. What did you do?'

'Well, the place was lit up. There were lights streaming out from every room in the house. None of the curtains were drawn, but the rooms I could see into seemed to be empty. I didn't know what to think. The weather wasn't good, it had been blowing hard all day and I was half inclined to turn and drive back to Blickling. Then I thought, why should I? Reg was almost certainly out drinking somewhere, and if Valerie was in, she'd be on her own. I peered through the letter box, but it's one of those that has a double flap, and it was difficult to see anything much at all. So I tried the door very gingerly. It wasn't locked, and when I pushed, a gust of wind from behind me blew it wide open . . .'

She paused. 'And . . .?' prompted Tench.

She looked first at him and then at McKenzie. 'I found myself staring at the muzzle of a gun,' she said.

3.

'He was sitting there – Reg – at the bottom of the stairs, with a gun in his hand levelled straight at me. He looked dishevelled, unshaven, and there was a half-empty bottle of whisky at his elbow. When he saw who I was, he gave a laugh, a horrible, twisted kind of laugh. "Well, well," he said, and his speech was slurred, "if it isn't sweet Josephine! What could be more opportune? The wife who's been betrayed, here to seek her husband. Come in, my dear. Come in and sit down." He patted the stair beside him. "Shut the door behind you, and be very careful. Don't step in the blood."'

She closed her eyes as if she were trying to blot out the memory. When she opened them again, she said, 'It's strange, looking back, but I can't remember being scared. I think at that moment I was simply too shocked to feel any fear. I just stared at him. "What have you done?" I said.

'He laughed again, that same twisted laugh. "What have I done?" Then, without any warning, his mood suddenly changed. "What the devil d'you think I've done, you stupid bitch? Are you so damned thick you haven't seen what's been happening under your very nose? Don't you know your precious hubby's been sticking it up my wife? Don't you know she was three months up the spout with his brat? And you ask me what I've done! You must be not merely stupid, but blind as a bat, you poor, pathetic wretch."'

She closed her eyes again and shook her head very slowly. 'That was what he called me, a poor, pathetic wretch. Well, maybe I was, but' – she looked straight at Tench, and the words she spoke came out in a flood – 'I loved Giles,' she said, 'I'd always loved him. It didn't matter to me what he'd done. He could have had a hundred other women for all that I cared. He was mine, and I was determined he was going to stay mine. That was why Reg's words seemed to me so unjust. They fired me up. Perhaps I should have humoured him, spoken to him gently, but I didn't, I was angry. "You're mad," I said, "mad."

'It was the wrong thing to say. It made him even more angry than I was. He lurched up from the stair, grabbed me roughly by the arm and stuck the gun in my back. "Mad, am I?" he said. "I'll show you whether I'm mad or not! You want to know what I've done. Well, I'll show you what I've done." He jabbed me with the gun and pushed me towards the stairs. "All I've done is what any sane man would have done. No woman's going to play a double game with me and then get away with it."

'I felt the gun in my back all the way up the stairs. Then he kicked open the door of Valerie's bedroom, and pushed me inside. The place was a wreck. It looked just as if a hurricane had swept through it from end to end. He jerked me round to face the bed. "There," he said, "take a look. That's what I've done."

'She was lying there – Valerie – curled like a foetus on top of the pink candlewick bedspread. He grabbed my hand and clamped it on her arm. She was cold as ice, and when I pulled back sharply I could feel that she was stiff.

'She must have been dead for hours.'

215

4.

She bowed her head and covered her face with her hands.

For a moment there was silence: a silence as bleak as the room itself.

Then McKenzie broke the spell. 'You're lying again, aren't you, Mrs Meredith?' he said.

She raised her eyes and stared at him blankly. 'Lying?'

'That's what I said. Lying.'

She tossed her head. 'Of course I'm not. What makes you say that?'

'It's too glib, too facile. You remember every word.'

'Wouldn't you?' she said fiercely. 'I don't often find myself facing a murderer armed with a gun. Of course I remember every single word. They're burnt on my memory.'

'So you say.'

'Yes, I do. It's the truth.'

'Then I'll give you my frank opinion,' McKenzie said. 'It's just about as far from the truth as a tissue of lies. You're a good actress, Mrs Meredith. You've learnt your lines well and you deliver them without any hesitation. But that's the whole trouble. You're not quite good enough to carry conviction. There should be the odd hesitation here and there, but you reel the lines off like reciting a poem you've learnt off by heart. And that's exactly what you have done, isn't it, ma'am? You knew very well that we might find something inside your car, and you cooked up this tale in advance to get you out of a hole. If the words are burnt on your memory, it's simply because you burnt them there. And don't pretend you cooked it up on your own. Your beloved husband, Giles, has something to do with this. He's mixed up in it somewhere.'

'If that's what you believe,' she said, 'you've got more imagination than I have, Sergeant. I'm telling you the truth of what happened that Friday night, and it's nothing to do with Giles. He was miles away, in France.'

'Was he?'

'Yes, he was.'

'All right,' McKenzie said. 'You were standing by the bed, staring at Mrs Kingham's body. I suppose you can remember word for word what you said next.'

216

'Yes, I can. I said nothing at all. I didn't know what his reaction might be.'

'And Kingham?'

She nodded. 'Oh yes, he spoke. He said, "Yes, she's dead. Aren't you going to thank me? You, of all people, must have wanted her dead."'

'And you?'

'I said, "Let me go, Reg. Please let me go," and he laughed like a maniac. "Let you go? Oh, no, my dear, that's not what I have in mind. You and I have a little job to do first. But not just yet, I think. It's a bit too early."'

'There were two chairs in the room. He picked one up and placed it by the bed, then set the other one down by the door. He motioned to the one that was facing the bed. "Sit down," he said, "and make yourself at home."

'He settled himself on the one by the door, and levelled the gun at me. "It's going to be a long night," he said, "so have a little sleep. I'll waken you when it's time."'

5.

McKenzie was ready to interrupt her again, but Tench forestalled him. 'And just how long a night was it, Mrs Meredith?' he asked.

She shuddered. 'It seemed longer than any I'd ever known before. "Have a little sleep," he'd said, but how could I sleep, alone in a room facing Valerie's body and the man who'd killed her armed with a gun? Once I thought he'd nodded off himself. His eyes were closed, and he didn't seem to know I was there at all. I thought if only I could reach the door, I might have a chance to get out of the house. I edged myself slowly off the chair and stood up, but he was awake in a flash, his finger tight on the trigger of the gun. "Sit down," he said, "and don't even think about trying to get away. I've shot one woman, and I'm quite prepared to shoot another. One more makes no odds."

'The minutes dragged by. They turned into hours. I kept glancing at my watch, and willing the hands to turn a bit faster, but of course they never did. Now and then, I think, in spite of myself, I must have dropped off to sleep, but at last I heard him moving and felt the muzzle of the gun pressed against my chest. "Car keys," he said, and when I didn't move he felt in my pocket and took them. I half opened my eyes and watched him. He went to the bed, wrapped Valerie's body in the bedspread and slung it across his shoulder. After that he went out and I heard him lock the door. I waited a moment, then as softly as I could I crossed to the window, but the wall below was sheer and the ground fell away . . . He was gone about five minutes, then I heard the key turn again in the door. I glanced at my watch. It was just after midnight. I closed my eyes and heard him coming towards me. Then the gun was pressed into the back of my neck. "Come on," he said, "wake up. It's time to get going." He led me downstairs and out to the car, opened the driver's door and thrust me inside. He got in beside me and pushed the key into the ignition. "Get driving," he said. "I'll tell you where to go."'

Tench shifted in his chair. 'He forced you to drive at gun-point?'

'Yes.' She gave a nod. 'That's exactly what he did.'

'Where to?'

'Morston,' she said. 'It only took a few minutes. It isn't far from The Woodlands. There's a road branches off in the village to what they call The Quay, but it's really nothing more than a staithe. It's a tarmac road to begin with, but it peters out very soon into merely a track. When we turned off the coastal road, he reached across me and switched off the headlights, and halfway down the track he told me to stop and switched off the rest. Then he took some lengths of cord from the back seat of the car, – he must have brought them from the house – tied my wrists together, lashed them to the steering-wheel and gagged me with what felt like a large silk scarf. After that, he got out and pulled the keys from the ignition. I heard him unlock the boot, then he passed me with the body slung across his shoulder, and disappeared along the track to the staithe.

'I don't know exactly how long he was gone, ten minutes perhaps, then he came back empty-handed, sat down again beside me, untied my hands and the gag, put the keys back in the ignition, stuck the gun in my side and told me to drive.

I asked him where to. "Where the hell d'you think?" he said. "Back to the house."'

McKenzie broke in again. 'Are you telling us,' he said, 'that you were there for something like a quarter of an hour and no one either saw you or heard you?'

She gave him a disparaging glance. 'They wouldn't have done. Use your common sense, Sergeant. That part of the track isn't overlooked. It was well after midnight, pitch dark and blowing hard. The wind was singing in the power lines. The chance of someone seeing or hearing us was remote, to say the least.'

'Go on,' said Tench.

'Well,' – she paused and took a deep breath – 'when we reached The Woodlands, he made me get out, locked up the car and dropped the keys in his pocket. He stuck the gun in my back and nudged me towards the house. "Inside," he said. He didn't lock the front door, but pushed me straight up the stairs and back into the bedroom. I pleaded with him again to let me go, but he scoffed at the idea. "Oh, no, my sweet," he said. "When we leave here, we go together. I don't know where yet, so sit down, keep quiet and just let me think."

'There was nothing I could do, so I simply sat and watched him, hoping that perhaps he might nod off again. He closed his eyes. I couldn't tell whether he was asleep or just thinking. The minutes ticked by, and I began to wonder how much longer this silent kind of torture was going to last. Then all of a sudden it happened. The front door rattled sharply. It was probably no more than a strong gust of wind, but I said out loud, "There's someone at the door." He was alert in an instant and out of the room. I got up and followed him. He was standing at the top of the stairs with the gun pointing down straight at the door. For once he seemed to have forgotten all about me. I was desperate. All I wanted to do was get out of the house and never see the place again. I flung myself forward and pushed him in the back, and he fell head first down the stairs, tumbling over and over. Once he reached the bottom, he lay very still. I didn't know whether I'd killed him or not. I just didn't care. I raced down the stairs and fumbled in his pocket till I found the car keys, scared that any moment he'd come to and grab me. Then I was out of the house, slamming the door behind me.

'I think I drove back to Blickling faster than I'd ever driven before. When I reached home I locked the door and sat down with my back to it. I prayed to God that he was dead, mumbling wild, incoherent prayers. I wanted the Kinghams out of my life for ever.'

6.

There was silence again.

'Is that all?' McKenzie said.

She sighed, a long-drawn-out sigh. 'Isn't it enough?'

'No, it isn't.'

'What more is there to say?'

'A hell of a lot, to my mind. You say you left Kingham for dead inside the house?'

'I had no option.'

'Then can you explain how he came to be bound and gagged and thrown from the top of the Prospect Tower at Sunningham?'

'No, I can't.'

'Remarkable, isn't it? He bound and gagged himself, drove to Sunningham in someone else's car, climbed fifty feet and dived through a window.'

She gave him a withering glance, but it had no effect. 'You say,' he went on, 'that you slammed the door behind you. Are you sure about that?'

'Yes.'

'Then can you explain why, a few days later, the postman found the door open?'

'The wind must have blown it open.'

'But you'd slammed it shut.'

'Then perhaps someone opened it.'

'Someone else? Who?'

She gave a shrug. 'Kingham?'

'Bound hand and foot? That's not very likely . . . When you left the house, all the lights were still burning?'

She nodded. 'Yes, they were.'

'When the postman called, they weren't. I suppose you'll say that Kingham switched them off.'

'Well, he could have done, couldn't he?'

'Before he was trussed up? It's a possibility, yes. I'll grant you that. But the fact remains that someone did truss him up. They opened the door, walked into the house, found him lying unconscious at the foot of the stairs, bound and gagged him and threw him from the top of Prospect Tower . . . So who was it, d'you think?'

She shrugged again. 'I haven't the faintest idea.'

'Could it perhaps have been your devoted Giles?'

She fired up. 'No, it couldn't. Don't be stupid, Sergeant. Giles was in France.'

'Oh, yes, so he was, like you were being held at gunpoint by Kingham. It's a good story, Mrs Meredith, but I don't believe a word of it.'

She flung out her hands in exasperation. 'Then what do you believe, Sergeant?'

'I think Giles was here in England. I think you and he hatched a plot between you to murder both the Kinghams, and that's exactly what you did.'

'That simply isn't true.'

'Isn't it?'

'No, it isn't.'

'Then persuade me otherwise.'

She sighed again. 'I've told you the truth of what happened that night. How can I do any more to persuade you? What can I say?' She turned in appeal to Tench. 'Tell me, Chief Inspector.'

Tench was curt and very much to the point. 'Mrs Meredith,' he said, 'if you'd heard Kingham confess to the murder of his wife, why didn't you tell us when we spoke to you before?'

'I didn't want to be involved.'

'But if what he said was true, you weren't to blame. You had a duty to tell us.'

'You knew how I felt about Valerie Kingham. I was afraid you'd think I'd made it all up.'

'You still maintain that you fled the house and left Kingham unconscious at the bottom of the stairs?'

'Yes, of course I do.'

'And you can't explain how he came to be found at the foot of Prospect Tower?'

221

'No, I can't.'

'You don't know for sure how the door that you slammed was later found open?'

'No.'

'And you don't know for certain who switched off the lights.'

'No, I don't.'

Tench rose to his feet. 'Then at the moment,' he said, 'I can see no point in prolonging this interview. You'll be questioned again later. In the meantime I suggest you consider your position and think very hard about your answers.'

He turned to McKenzie. 'Take her down to the cells, Sergeant,' he said.

7.

Ten minutes later, McKenzie returned. He closed the door behind him. 'Mission accomplished,' he said. 'It'll do her no harm to stew for an hour. After that she'll maybe come to her senses.'

Tench looked doubtful. 'We're getting nowhere, Mac,' he said. 'The tale she tells is quite plausible. It could all have happened just as she says.'

'It could have, but it didn't.'

'We can't prove that it didn't.'

'No, we can't, but we will.' McKenzie wasn't to be deflected from his course by mere negatives. 'That's only part one of the grilling. Part two's still to come, and then, if they're needed, parts three and four. She'll crack in the end. They always do.'

'We need time. We can't hold her for long without charging her, and the first of the inquests is fixed for Wednesday morning. That'll take up time, even if it's only to get an adjournment.'

'We've got time,' McKenzie said, 'but we need to put Meredith himself through the grinder. When's Gregg likely to be bringing him in?'

Tench checked his watch. 'Should be any time now. We know he hired a car, and he's been working all day at his office here in

Norwich. If he left at the usual time, he should have been back at Blickling half an hour ago.'

'Right. So let's think. Let's think about Josephine's plausible tale. I'm not saying that every scrap of it's false. Some of it may be true, but like everything else that she and Giles have told us, it's not the whole truth. It leaves too many facts unexplained . . . I can think of two right away. What happened to Valerie's clothes and the candlewick bedspread?'

'Who knows?' said Tench. 'Probably only God and Mr Reginald Kingham, and since neither of them's likely to communicate with us, the only thing we can do is guess. If Kingham killed his wife on the Friday morning, as we believe he must have done, he had eight or nine hours to get rid of her clothes before Josephine turned up. He could have burned them, buried them, hidden them away in some derelict building. They could be literally anywhere. And added to that, we don't know what she was wearing, so we don't know what to look for. We'll probably never find them . . . As for the bedspread, we know Kingham took it down to the boat at Morston, but he didn't bring it back, because Josephine said he came back empty-handed, and it wasn't in the boat when Lubbock unlashed the tarpaulin cover. So again we have to guess. He probably stuffed it down inside one of the other boats, and it simply got washed away in the storm.'

'Well, fair enough,' McKenzie said, 'but there's another and far more important point. How did the man she says she left for dead at the foot of the stairs come to be bound and gagged and thrown from the top of the Prospect Tower?'

'Well, we know he wasn't dead because Vincent's report made it quite clear that he was killed by the fall.'

'So, after she left, someone opened the door, bound him, gagged him, and dragged him fifty feet up a rickety flight of steps to the top of the tower. And that we can count as an impossibility. No one man could have done it on his own unless he was a giant of superhuman strength. But' – he paused – 'two people, acting together, could have done it, and that brings me back to my original proposition. Giles and Josephine planned this between them. He wasn't in France. He was back here in England. He never slept the night in that tavern at Chaumes-en-Brie. On the Friday morning he left his hotel in Paris, drove to

223

Calais, crossed on the ferry and made his way to Breckton. Like his wife, he's only told us a part of the truth. So, as soon as he gets here, we need to grill him till he sizzles.'

'Oh, we'll grill him,' said Tench, 'but whether we can make him sizzle is a very different matter. Suspicion's one thing, proof's quite another. We've got nothing to connect him to Kingham's murder beyond the fact that he was born and brought up in Sunningham and knows the tower well, and that could apply to thousands of other people who've never seen Kingham in the whole of their lives. We still need some solid piece of evidence to throw at him, Mac.'

As if in answer to his thoughts, the phone on the wall began to ring insistently. He crossed to it, picked up the receiver and listened. 'Well thanks, Ted,' he said. 'Let's hope there's more to come.'

'Merrick?' McKenzie asked.

Tench nodded. 'Yes. Forensics have found some black woollen fibres down behind the back seat of the Morris Minor. They're identical to those from Kingham's sweater.'

'Well, that's a start at least. We can throw those at him.'

Tench was dismissive. 'They mean nothing, Mac. They're not solid evidence. According to Ted, such sweaters are two a penny. You can buy them in shops all over the country. There's nothing to say that those fibres are from the sweater that Kingham was wearing. Someone else may have travelled in the car wearing one. Meredith may even have had one himself. If that's the only evidence we can produce, we may as well forget about charging him with murder. Any counsel worth the name would laugh us out of court. No, Mac, we still need something more.'

'Leave him to me,' McKenzie said, 'and I'll get you something more. We've been far too gentle with our friend Giles Meredith. By the time I've finished with him, he'll be sobbing his socks off and pleading to confess.'

'And we get a confession made under duress? A fat lot of good that's likely to be.'

'Well, please yourself,' – McKenzie gave a shrug – 'but if you want quick results . . .'

'We'll get them,' said Tench, 'and we'll get them without any bare-knuckle fighting. Trust me, Mac. I've a feeling in my bones that someone's going to hand us the one piece of evidence we've been struggling to find.'

8.

There was a knock on the door, then Gregg pushed it open, stepped inside and closed it behind him. 'We've got him,' he said. 'He's here, under guard.'

'Any trouble?'

Gregg gave a grin. 'Well, he wasn't best pleased, but he could hardly make trouble with two hefty coppers ready to grab him.'

'You've cautioned him?'

'Yes.'

'Then bring him in,' said Tench.

To say that Giles Meredith wasn't best pleased was something of an understatement. He glowered at Gregg, and then at Tench and McKenzie. 'I gather,' he said, 'that for some obscure reason I'm under arrest.'

Tench pulled a file towards him. 'The reason, Mr Meredith, is quite a simple one. We need to question you under oath about your involvement in the murder of Reginald Kingham.'

'Which is utterly pointless. I had no involvement.'

'You are, of course, entitled . . .'

Meredith raised a hand. 'And don't ask me if I want a lawyer. I don't. To say that I did would be tantamount to admitting that I'd something to hide. Since I haven't, I'm quite capable of answering your questions without the assistance of some legal hack who knows nothing about the case.'

'Very well then.' Tench nodded. 'For the record, Mr Meredith, you are Giles Meredith of Green Park, Blickling?'

'You know darned well that I am. Get on with the questions.'

'Can you explain why fibres from a candlewick bedspread, identical to those found on Valerie Kingham's body, have been found in the boot of your wife's Morris Minor?'

'No, of course I can't. How can I possibly know everything she does with her car?'

'Then can you tell me how black woollen fibres, similar to those from the sweater discovered on Reginald Kingham's body, were also found in that car?'

'No, I'm not my wife's keeper.'

'You can offer no explanation of either?'

'No, I can't.'

'I can,' McKenzie said. 'On the night before the storm, you used your darling Josephine's car to dispose of both bodies.'

Meredith gave a disparaging laugh. 'That's plainly ridiculous. I've told you where I was on that particular night. I was in France, at the tavern at Chaumes-en-Brie. And in any case, how could I possibly drag a man the size and weight of Kingham to the top of that tower?'

'You had help.'

'Whose help?'

'Your wife's, Mr Meredith. You plotted this double murder between you.'

Meredith laughed again. He was even more disparaging. 'Are you seriously suggesting that I murdered Valerie? I loved her. Why on earth would I do such a thing?'

'She was pregnant.'

'So what?'

'The child was yours, and you knew it was yours. What better way to keep the truth from Josephine than by agreeing to a plot to get rid of both the Kinghams? You knew she wanted Valerie out of your lives, and you'd have given a great deal to see Kingham dead.'

Meredith stared at him. 'That's an insane suggestion.' He turned towards Tench. 'Chief Inspector,' he said. 'I think you should have your sergeant examined. He's out of his mind.'

Tench didn't hesitate. He cut straight to the point. 'You deny all involvement in either of these killings?'

'Yes, I do, most strongly. Unless you can produce some evidence to prove otherwise, you may as well release me here and now, on the spot.'

In the silence that followed, there was a rap on the door. Gregg answered it and then beckoned to Tench. 'It's Lock, sir,' he said quietly. 'He says it's something urgent.'

The Chief Inspector went out and closed the door behind him. 'What is it, Des?' he asked.

Lock wasted no time. 'Inspector Randall's here from Holt, sir. I've put him in your office. He's got a young soldier with him. He says he needs to see you right away.'

'Right,' said Tench. 'Has Winterton managed to get through to that place at Chaumes yet?'

'No sir, still trying. There's a fault on the line, and the phone engineers in France are on a twenty-four-hour strike.'

'They would be,' said Tench.

9.

The soldier was tall, broad and muscular, with keen, deep-set eyes. He wore a sergeant's stripes and the shoulder-tabs of the Royal Engineers. Randall introduced him. 'This is Sergeant Treadgold, sir,' he said. 'He lives at Morston. His father's just died, and he's on compassionate leave from BAOR in Germany. I'll let him tell you the rest of the tale.' He turned to Treadgold. 'This, Sergeant, is Detective Chief Inspector Tench. Perhaps you'd like to tell him what happened.'

The sergeant seemed uncertain how to begin. 'I really should have told you all this long before, sir,' he said, 'but the first night after I got back to Morston was the night of the storm and the house was flooded. We've been staying with my uncle and aunt in Baconsthorpe, and what with that, arranging Dad's funeral and looking after Mum, I didn't open a paper until this morning. It was only when I read about the murders in the *EDP* that I began to connect them with what I'd seen, and since I'm due back from leave on Thursday, I thought I'd better tell the police at Holt.'

Tench nodded. 'There's no need to apologize, Sergeant,' he said. 'It was only natural that your family's troubles should be more important than anything else. Thank you for coming when you're so pressed for time. So what have you got to tell me?'

'Well, sir,' – Treadgold paused as if trying to collect his thoughts – 'I'm not sure just how important it is, but I got the news about Dad on the Thursday before the storm, and left for England early on the Friday morning . . .'

Tench intervened. 'A week last Friday, the 30th of January?'

227

'That's right, sir, yes. But there were all sorts of hold-ups. I missed the ferry at Calais by a matter of minutes, and the train I caught from London was at a standstill for a couple of hours somewhere near Cambridge. Broken points, so they said. Because of that I didn't get to Melton till after one in the morning. I'd missed my connection, and at that time, of course, there wasn't a bus to be seen. Well, the last thing I wanted to do was doss down at the station and wait hours for signs of life. The family's only recently moved to Morston. I was born and brought up in Melton and know the roads between there and the coast well enough. The chances of picking up a lift at that time were pretty bleak. Morston was only seven or eight miles away, and I thought if I kept to the by-roads, and stepped it out along the tarmac, I could be home in less than an hour and a half. So I set off to walk. I planned to take the road to Sunningham past the Prospect Tower, and then through Field Dalling and Langham.'

The sergeant paused. 'Well, sir,' he said, 'I didn't see a car at all till just before I reached the turn-off to Prospect Tower. Then I heard one behind me, so I stepped off the road into the trees at the side. The car was just about to pass me, when another one came from the opposite direction. It was travelling very fast with its lights on full beam. The driver didn't dip them, and I think the man at the wheel of the car that was passing me must have been suddenly blinded, because he pulled to a halt right beside me and waited for the other one to pass. I don't think he saw me, but for just a few seconds, in the beam of the headlights, I saw him quite clearly, and the woman nearer to me in the passenger seat. She was wearing a bobble hat. Bright red it was. Then, as he moved ahead again and turned up the track that led to the tower, I saw the car itself. It was a Morris Minor, sir. The shape's quite distinctive.'

'What time was this, Sergeant?

'Must have been round about two o'clock, sir.'

'You didn't happen to see the number plate?' Tench's voice carried with it all the tension he was feeling.

Treadgold gave a little laugh. 'Oh yes, sir, I did. There was a small light below it that showed it up quite clearly.'

'You remember the number?'

'Yes, sir. It was CL – that's a local number – 4287.'

'You're sure about that?'

'Certain, sir. It was a number I couldn't possibly forget.'

'Why was that?'

'It was the last four digits of my army number, sir, 5954287.' The sergeant drew a pay book from his pocket, and handed it to Tench. 'That's something,' he said, 'that every soldier learns off by heart.'

10.

When Tench returned to the interview room, Gregg and McKenzie were deep in whispered conversation, Sue Gradwell was still sitting primly in the corner, her notepad on her knee, and Meredith was staring at the table in front of him, seemingly determined not to acknowledge his presence in the room.

As he nodded towards them, Gregg and McKenzie broke off their talk and took their places at the table, and Sue Gradwell once more took up her pencil, ready to record in shorthand every word that was spoken.

Tench pulled out his chair and sat down. 'To resume, Mr Meredith,' he said, 'you deny all involvement in the murder of Kingham?'

'Yes, of course I do.' The man spoke wearily. 'How many times do I have to repeat myself, Chief Inspector? I was miles away in France. How could I possibly have anything to do with his murder?'

'Then how does it come about that you and your wife, both in her car, were seen turning up the track to the Prospect Tower at two o'clock on the Saturday morning, the day of the storm?'

Meredith blinked. 'Are you serious, Chief Inspector?'

'Perfectly serious.'

'Then I can only think you've taken leave of your senses. I was never anywhere near the Prospect Tower.'

'You were seen, Mr Meredith.'

'Who by?'

'A very reliable witness.'

'Then your very reliable witness has a strong imagination.

I repeat, I was nowhere near the Prospect Tower. I was sound asleep in the tavern at Chaumes.'

'But our witness says otherwise. You were in your wife's car. She was sitting beside you. You were searching for the turning that led to the tower. You were blinded by the lights of an oncoming car, and stopped right beside him. He saw you quite clearly.'

'Then he must have been mistaken. It was someone else's car.'

'He saw the number plate, Mr Meredith. The number was clearly visible. CL4287. According to your wife, that's the number of her car.'

'Then the driver must have been some friend of hers. It certainly wasn't me.'

'You're suggesting your wife was out driving with another man at two o'clock in the morning?'

'And why not? I don't know what she does when I'm out of the country.'

The questions came now in rapid succession. 'You still say you were in France?'

'Yes, I was at Chaumes. How many more times?'

'You weren't near the Prospect Tower?'

'No, I was not.'

'You weren't driving your wife's car?'

'No.'

'And she wasn't with you?'

'No.'

'You deny you killed Kingham?'

'Yes.'

'You deny you were taking his body to the tower?'

'Yes, I do.'

'You weren't looking for the track that led to the tower?'

'No.'

'You deny that you stopped before reaching the track?'

'Yes.'

'You were blinded by the lights of an oncoming car?'

'Yes.'

'Then you did see the lights.'

'No, I didn't.'

'You said that you did.'

'I meant that I didn't.'

'You were there by the tower.'

'No.'

'You killed Kingham by throwing him down from the top.'

'No.'

'If you saw the lights, you must have done.'

'No.'

'You killed Kingham.'

'No.'

'I repeat, you killed Kingham.'

That was when Meredith suddenly snapped. 'What if I did?' he said savagely. 'The bastard deserved to die. He'd killed the only woman I ever really loved.'

Tench pushed back his chair and stood up. 'Giles Meredith,' he said, 'I'm charging you that sometime on the night of Friday the 30th and Saturday the 31st of January this year, in conjunction with your wife, you wilfully murdered Reginald Kingham. You are not obliged to say anything . . .'

Meredith turned on him. 'Go to hell,' he said.

Epilogue

THE STAR-CROSSED TRIANGLE

Thrice to thine, and thrice to mine,
And thrice again, to make up nine.
Peace! The charm's wound up.
William Shakespeare: *Macbeth*

It was Friday evening, four days later. Meg's little back room at the Riverside was comfortably warm and, looking down through the glass panel set in the floor, Tench could see the old millwheel still turning slowly with the flow of the Wensum.

He sipped his coffee. Lubbock pushed aside his plate and poured himself a second cup of tea. 'So,' he said, 'you charged them both with murder.'

Tench nodded. 'We did.'

'McKenzie was right then. They'd plotted together to get rid of the Kinghams.'

'No.' Tench shook his head. 'Mac, as usual, was only partly right. We were all only partly right.'

'Then what really happened?'

'We still don't know for sure. Not every detail.'

'We never do,' Lubbock said. 'In any murder case there are bound to be loose ends. But you've a pretty shrewd idea?'

'We think so, but that's as far as I'm prepared to go. We grilled them for three whole days, and much of it came out. It wasn't what we'd expected, but there was one vital fact that we hadn't known about. It changed the whole complexion of what happened that Friday night at The Woodlands.'

Lubbock took out his pouch and began to fill his pipe. 'Go on,' he said.

'Well, earlier on, when we'd asked Meredith why he chose to spend the night at the tavern at Chaumes, he'd told us that his plan was to fix a night with Mrs Kingham when they'd escape together to France. He was to work late at the Norwick Press, and once Kingham had left the house on his normal drinking

233

spree, she was to phone him at the office and he'd drive straight to Breckton, pick her up and take her to Chaumes. What he failed to tell us was that the night they'd arranged for this flight into France was that Friday before the storm, the very night when, unbeknown to him, his wife chose to pay her own visit to The Woodlands, and found herself facing Kingham with a pistol in his hand.'

Lubbock raised a couple of bushy grey eyebrows. 'So when Meredith reached the house, he found Valerie dead and Josephine being held at gunpoint.'

'No,' said Tench, 'not exactly. He thought he had everything arranged to perfection, but, as Robbie Burns said, the best-laid schemes of mice and men "gang aft agley", and his went completely haywire. He left Paris on that Friday morning, drove to Calais and crossed on the ferry. He intended to reach his office in Norwich around seven o'clock that evening, when all the staff had left. That meant he'd plenty of time, so he thought. He could take things leisurely. He had a meal in London, and it was about five o'clock, when he was approaching Ipswich, that the lights on his car suddenly failed. He had to tramp into the town, find a garage that was still open, and have the car towed in. The lights proved something of a complicated problem, and it was close on ten o'clock by the time they were fixed.

'He was desperately worried by that time. He'd rung the house at Breckton, but got no reply, so he thought he'd better forget about Norwich and drive straight there. Once again it seemed that the Fates were conspiring against him that night. A fallen tree had blocked the road, and he was forced to make a long and difficult detour. It was nearly one in the morning by the time he reached the drive that led up to The Woodlands. He expected to find the house locked and in darkness, but he had a key to the front door that Valerie had given him, and he felt that if Kingham were sound asleep in his usual drunken stupor, he might still wake Valerie without any noise and spirit her away. So he parked the car among the trees and began to walk towards the house, but when it came into view . . .'

'. . . He found he'd been wrong,' said Lubbock. 'The place was ablaze with light and Josephine's car was standing on the gravel.'

'Exactly,' said Tench.

234

'So what did he do?'

'He said that for a moment he was utterly confounded. He didn't know what to think. Then he knew that he'd have to find out what had happened. He approached the house warily. There was no sign of life in the lighted rooms, so he took out his key and tried to turn it in the lock. It wouldn't turn, and he realized the door was unlocked. He turned the knob and pushed it open, but a sudden gust of wind from behind him tore it out of his grasp, and it swung back and hit the wall. He saw the lighted hall, heard a scuffle from above, and then Kingham came tumbling head first down the stairs, and Josephine flung herself into his arms.'

Lubbock nodded. He struck a match, lit his pipe and sent billows of smoke rolling up to Meg's recently painted ceiling. 'And . . .?' he said.

Tench threw out his hands. 'After that, it's largely a matter of conjecture. That was the point where Meredith clammed up. Even though we grilled him for hour after hour, he refused point blank to say anything more. We got little enough out of Josephine either, but in one unguarded moment she did make a very telling confession. She said that once he knew what had happened to Valerie, he seemed to go raving mad. "The bastard!" he said. "Well, if he's still alive, he's not going to live. I'll make sure of that," and he picked up the gun that was lying by Kingham at the bottom of the stairs, and levelled it at him. "I thought he was going to shoot him," she said, "but he didn't."'

'No,' Lubbock said, 'we know that he didn't, but did she tell you what he did do?'

'No, I think she realized that she'd already blurted out too much, and, like Meredith, she simply refused to say any more. So all we can do is guess.'

Lubbock blew out more smoke. 'My Shakespeare never was up to much,' he said, 'but didn't he mention somewhere a pair of star-crossed lovers?'

'Yes, Romeo and Juliet.'

'Well, Giles was hardly a teenage Romeo, and Josephine was no Juliet, but they were certainly star-crossed, those two, weren't they? The Fates were against them.'

Tench reached for the pot and poured himself more coffee. 'I'd have called it a star-crossed triangle,' he said. 'Josephine loved her husband, don't ask me why. She'd always loved him, and she always would. As she herself said, he could have had a hundred women, it would have made no difference, she'd still have had him back. For his part, he was desperately in love with Valerie Kingham. I don't think there's any doubt about that. If you like to put it another way, it was a case of two conflicting loves working together in harmony for a brief space of time.'

'You mean he needed her help to get rid of Kingham, and she knew if she didn't help him she'd lose her only chance of winning him back?'

'That's right.'

'So they got to work together, bound and gagged Kingham, carried him out to her car, laid him on the back seat, drove to the tower, dragged him up to the top, and threw him out of the window.'

'Yes, but I think there was more to it than that. When she blurted out that bit about him going raving mad, I think she intended to say something more. She was going to say that he turned away from Kingham, levelled the pistol at her and told her that if she didn't help him, then that was the end. She'd never see him again.'

'So for the second time that night she could have found herself threatened at the point of a gun?'

'She could. It's more than possible, but he needn't have bothered to threaten her. She'd have helped him in any case.'

Lubbock laid down his pipe. 'There's just one thing,' he said. 'If Meredith was attempting to fake Kingham's suicide, there were easier ways to do it than by driving to Sunningham and tossing him from the tower.'

'True,' said Tench, 'but I don't think that faking a suicide was ever in his mind. If it had been, he'd have taken both cars, told his wife to drive her own, driven the Rolls himself, and left it parked by the foot of the tower. But I'm pretty sure the idea never entered his thoughts. Once he knew that Kingham had murdered Valerie, the one thing in his mind was the thought of revenge. The man wasn't going to live, he'd make sure of that. He knew the tower well. He'd climbed to the top only a few weeks before. What better way was there to get rid of the bastard than by throwing him from the top? I think, as you said, they dragged him between them up the stairs to the top, and pushed him out of the window, still bound and gagged and probably still unconscious. Then they stripped off the cords, removed the gag, left him lying on the ground, and drove back to Breckton.'

'And after that?'

'We can only guess and guess again. He must have handed the Morris over to Josephine, and told her to drive back to Blickling as fast as she could without getting herself booked. He probably told her to give the car a good clean, inside and out, then lie low and say nothing, forget she'd ever been anywhere near Breckton that night. Then he took his own car and sped back to Dover. He had his own alibi already lined up. As far as anyone knew, he'd been in France since Wednesday. In one respect he must have been lucky, and caught the last ferry across the Channel before the sailings were suspended. Since we haven't found the gun, he probably dropped it overboard in the course of the crossing. If I'd been in his shoes, that's what I'd have done. It's probably lying somewhere on the bed of the Dover Straits . . . Then, once back in France, he drove straight down to Châteauroux, reaching there late on the Saturday night. He stayed in France till the following Thursday, got back about midnight, and then turned up at The Woodlands on the Friday morning when Mac and I were there, and pretended to know nothing about what had happened.'

'But it all went awry. The Fates conspired to thwart him.'

Tench gave a nod. 'Yes, but if they hadn't, he and Josephine might well have got away with it. We were lucky, very lucky indeed. The same Fates that thwarted him conspired with us to reveal in a matter of minutes the one vital piece of evidence we'd been searching for. It was lucky for us that Treadgold was held up, missed his connection and had to walk home to Morston; even luckier that he'd just reached the turn-off to the tower when the Morris overtook him. It was lucky that at that very moment the driver of another car forgot to dip his lights, and Meredith had to stop right at the spot where the sergeant was standing; and it was incredibly lucky that Treadgold happened to be perhaps the one person in the whole of Norfolk who couldn't possibly forget the number of Josephine's car. Oh yes, for a couple of minutes the Fates turned their faces away from

Meredith and smiled upon us, and that was enough. It gave us the one piece of evidence we needed. We had him on the rack, and we could tighten the screws.'

'And he snapped.'

'Yes, at long last he snapped, but we still don't know the whole of the truth.'

'And you never will, laddie.' Lubbock picked up his pipe, tamped the tobacco down with his thumb, and struck another match. 'It's the same,' he said through puffs of rolling smoke, 'with almost every case of murder that I can remember. There are always loose ends, I've told you that before, so forget about them, banish them completely from mind. My career's been littered with a host of loose ends. If I'd worried about them I'd have gone mad long ago. As long as you know enough to prove the killer's guilty, that's all you need to know. The case is over, finished, so close the file.' He paused. 'Let's talk about something else. Ask me about the cottage.'

Tench laughed. He drained the last of his coffee and pushed the cup aside. 'Right,' he said, 'how's the cottage faring?'

'Not well,' said Lubbock, 'and it won't be until the weather gets warmer. It's going to take months for the place to dry out. I'll be lucky to be back there before midsummer.'

'But you're going back?'

'Oh yes, I'm going back, laddie, and when I do there'll be a housewarming such as Cley's never known. The whole team's invited. Bring them all down, and I promise you one thing. If, sometime that day, I stumble across a body, I'll remember I've retired, and say nothing about it till the following morning.'

Tench feigned a mild deafness. 'Did I hear you say "retired"?'

'You know you did, laddie.'

'Then I'll keep my fingers crossed. I've a feeling I'm going to need to.'

Lubbock looked down his nose. 'You need coffee,' he said. 'I'll ask Meg to send in an extra-large pot.'